Anthony Gilbert and The Murder Room

>>> This title is part of The Murder Room, our series dedicated to making available out-of-print or hard-to-find titles by classic crime writers.

Crime fiction has always held up a mirror to society. The Victorians were fascinated by sensational murder and the emerging science of detection; now we are obsessed with the forensic detail of violent death. And no other genre has so captivated and enthralled readers.

Vast troves of classic crime writing have for a long time been unavailable to all but the most dedicated frequenters of second-hand bookshops. The advent of digital publishing means that we are now able to bring you the backlists of a huge range of titles by classic and contemporary crime writers, some of which have been out of print for decades.

From the genteel amateur private eyes of the Golden Age and the femmes fatales of pulp fiction, to the morally ambiguous hard-boiled detectives of mid twentieth-century America and their descendants who walk our twenty-first century streets, The Murder Room has it all. **>>>**

The Murder Room
Where Criminal Minds Meet

themurderroom.com

Anthony Gilbert (1899–1973)

Anthony Gilbert was the pen name of Lucy Beatrice Malleson. Born in London, she spent all her life there, and her affection for the city is clear from the strong sense of character and place in evidence in her work. She published 69 crime novels, 51 of which featured her best known character, Arthur Crook, a vulgar London lawyer totally (and deliberately) unlike the aristocratic detectives, such as Lord Peter Wimsey, who dominated the mystery field at the time. She also wrote more than 25 radio plays, which were broadcast in Great Britain and overseas. Her thriller *The Woman in Red* (1941) was broadcast in the United States by CBS and made into a film in 1945 under the title *My Name is Julia Ross*. She was an early member of the British Detection Club, which, along with Dorothy L. Sayers, she prevented from disintegrating during World War II. Malleson published her autobiography, *Three-a-Penny*, in 1940, and wrote numerous short stories, which were published in several anthologies and in such periodicals as *Ellery Queen's Mystery Magazine* and *The Saint*. The short story 'You Can't Hang Twice' received a Queens award in 1946. She never married, and evidence of her feminism is elegantly expressed in much of her work.

By Anthony Gilbert

Scott Egerton series

Tragedy at Freyne (1927)

The Murder of Mrs
  Davenport (1928)

Death at Four Corners
  (1929)

The Mystery of the Open
  Window (1929)

The Night of the Fog (1930)

The Body on the Beam
  (1932)

The Long Shadow (1932)

The Musical Comedy
  Crime (1933)

An Old Lady Dies (1934)

The Man Who Was Too
  Clever (1935)

**Mr Crook Murder
  Mystery series**

Murder by Experts (1936)

The Man Who Wasn't
  There (1937)

Murder Has No Tongue
  (1937)

Treason in My Breast (1938)

The Bell of Death (1939)

Dear Dead Woman (1940)
  aka *Death Takes a
  Redhead*

The Vanishing Corpse (1941)
  aka *She Vanished in the
  Dawn*

The Woman in Red (1941)
  aka *The Mystery of the
  Woman in Red*

Death in the Blackout (1942)
  aka *The Case of the Tea-
  Cosy's Aunt*

Something Nasty in the
  Woodshed (1942)
  aka *Mystery in the
  Woodshed*

The Mouse Who Wouldn't
  Play Ball (1943)
  aka *30 Days to Live*

He Came by Night (1944)
  aka *Death at the Door*

The Scarlet Button (1944)
  aka *Murder Is Cheap*

A Spy for Mr Crook (1944)

The Black Stage (1945)
  aka *Murder Cheats the
  Bride*

Don't Open the Door (1945)
  aka *Death Lifts the Latch*
Lift Up the Lid (1945)
  aka *The Innocent Bottle*
The Spinster's Secret (1946)
  aka *By Hook or by Crook*
Death in the Wrong Room (1947)
Die in the Dark (1947)
  aka *The Missing Widow*
Death Knocks Three Times (1949)
Murder Comes Home (1950)
A Nice Cup of Tea (1950)
  aka *The Wrong Body*
Lady-Killer (1951)
Miss Pinnegar Disappears (1952)
  aka *A Case for Mr Crook*
Footsteps Behind Me (1953)
  aka *Black Death*
Snake in the Grass (1954)
  aka *Death Won't Wait*
Is She Dead Too? (1955)
  aka *A Question of Murder*
And Death Came Too (1956)
Riddle of a Lady (1956)
Give Death a Name (1957)

Death Against the Clock (1958)
Death Takes a Wife (1959)
  aka *Death Casts a Long Shadow*
Third Crime Lucky (1959)
  aka *Prelude to Murder*
Out for the Kill (1960)
She Shall Die (1961)
  aka *After the Verdict*
Uncertain Death (1961)
No Dust in the Attic (1962)
Ring for a Noose (1963)
The Fingerprint (1964)
Knock, Knock! Who's There? (1964)
  aka *The Voice*
Passenger to Nowhere (1965)
The Looking Glass Murder (1966)
The Visitor (1967)
Night Encounter (1968)
  aka *Murder Anonymous*
Missing from Her Home (1969)
Death Wears a Mask (1970)
  aka *Mr Crook Lifts the Mask*

The Black Stage

Anthony Gilbert

An Orion book

Copyright © Lucy Beatrice Malleson 1945

The right of Lucy Beatrice Malleson to be identified as the author of this work has been asserted in accordance with the Copyright, Designs and Patents Act 1988.

This edition published by
The Orion Publishing Group Ltd
Orion House
5 Upper St Martin's Lane
London WC2H 9EA

An Hachette UK company
A CIP catalogue record for this book is available from the British Library

ISBN 978 1 4719 0984 9

www.orionbooks.co.uk

Affectionately to
Mary Dwane

''Tis the good reader makes the good book.'

Emerson

Oh, comforting – killing night!
Black stage for tragedies and murders fell!

Shakespeare

Chapter 1

ANNE VEREKER got out of her first-class carriage at Little Ebbisham, thanked her fellow-traveller for handing down her rawhide suitcase, her hat-box (to match), and her travelling rug, which was a souvenir from her years of service, and said she didn't want a taxi, because she was expecting to be met.

'I suppose so,' agreed the young man with a sigh. He was fascinated by her youth, beauty, and poise, all of them representing a security he personally had never known. 'Still, I'll just hang around, if I may. If your Rolls should have broken down maybe I could offer you a share of my taxi.'

'How very kind!' murmured Anne, with a smile as brilliant as electric light and about as personal. 'But Alistair's cars never do break down.'

'Oh!' murmured her companion, reflecting that, though they had travelled from London together and he had made her a present of most of his life-story, this was the first hint she had given him of hers. 'I beg your pardon. Your husband, perhaps.'

Anne laughed. 'Oh, Alistair has very high standards,' she said. 'But they mostly belong to about 1910.'

'Old-fashioned?' hazarded the young man. He'd never met a girl quite like this before. She looked, he thought, as though she might have pretty high standards herself, being one of those cream-and-roses, gold-and-blue girls of Edwardian fiction. Steady, courageous, assured, age, say, twenty-five. He wondered what she had been doing during the past five years. He'd been flying himself. Five years was a pretty good record for a risky job like that. On impulse he asked her.

1

'Oh, just jobs,' she told him vaguely, looking along the platform for Alistair, who wasn't generally late – all part of his Edwardian standards of good manners.

'I see,' said the young man, not seeing much beyond the fact that she wasn't disposed to be communicative. Her beauty might not be a remarkable type, but it was striking in degree. He thought that if they'd made a poster of her and put it up in the Middle East, say, over the caption – What we are fighting for – it would have heartened quite a lot of fellows who weren't quite sure what it was, and if it was worth all they were being asked to pay for it. A girl like this was bound to be expensive.

'I'm staying in these parts a while,' he ventured. 'Maybe we'll meet again.'

'I hope so,' she said kindly, but the most imaginative young man couldn't have read much more than politeness into that. 'Oh, don't bother about me. You might lose your taxi. There aren't so many of them nowadays. Alistair's bound to turn up, even if he arrives in a donkey-cart.'

He hated the unknown Alistair, who at that moment he perceived striding towards them. The next moment he amended his thought. Striding wasn't the word for this tall, slightly lounging, curiously correct-looking Englishman who came down the platform as though he owned the station, and walked up to Anne almost, thought the young airman, as though he owned her, too.

'Train's punctual,' he remarked. 'That's unusual these days.'

'And you're not,' agreed Anne. 'That's even more so.'

'It's Aunt Tessa's car,' Alistair explained. 'It can't keep pace with the rapidity of her return to a pre-war standard.' He glanced questioningly at the young man, and Anne, turning to him, said, 'It was kind of you to offer me your taxi, but now that my cousin's here . . . '

She didn't offer to introduce them and Alistair said, 'Can we give you a lift anywhere?'

He wanted to say yes, but instead he told him, no, he guessed he'd take a taxi, because he had seen at the first moment that Anne didn't really belong to his world, and in spite of all the White Papers and good resolutions with which contemporary civilization had been showered for the past five years or so, they still remained at different levels.

Alistair didn't pick up the suitcase and hat-box. He looked round for one of the porters for whom the alighting travellers had been milling for the past five minutes. Little Ebbisham was one of those improbable stations where you changed for a connexion to the big Midland towns. As if by magic a porter presented himself, took up the luggage, and acknowledged Anne's instant recognition. She said she had heard his father had been ill and he said yes, but the old gaffer was coming along fine and would outlive them all.

'What a sweep you are, Anne,' observed Alistair dispassionately, walking with her up the platform. 'Must you put these fellows on the rack just for fun?'

'I didn't do anything,' said Anne. 'He wanted to talk and I let him.'

'One day,' said Alistair, 'one of them will give you a black eye. And it'll serve you jolly well right.'

They came out of the station and found a long, shabby, dark-blue car in the yard.

'Shall I drive?' suggested Anne.

'No, thanks,' said Alistair. 'After your experience of Greek and Italian roads you've probably forgotten our quiet English ways. We still drive on the left here,' he added.

'So I noticed.' She got into the passenger seat while the porter put the luggage into the back, and watched her cousin, a long cool young man, but older somehow than she remembered – long, fine hands, smooth chestnut head, the family nose that was slightly too large for the face but gave them all character at the expense of symmetry, a type she hadn't seen at close quarters for nearly three years. She marvelled that the brutalities of a world war had enabled it to survive.

'How's Aunt Tessa?' she inquired, as they moved off.

'Getting back to pre-1939 standards with the velocity of a V2' he told her. 'This car's an example. It's like one of those

3

mares you used to see advertised. Warranted quiet to ride or drive. Get her up to forty and she'll call it a day.'

'If Aunt Tessa went faster than forty she might not be recognized,' explained Anne. 'They might think she was just one of these common people driving from one place to another simply because she wanted to get there as rapidly as possible. All Aunt Tessa's moves are thought out in advance and they're all spectacular.'

But Alistair said, 'I don't think you do her justice. She doesn't look far enough ahead for that.' For she wasn't one of these clever women, thank God. She just did the obvious thing. He'd met enough clever women during the war to be grateful to her for that.

'I suppose she dresses for dinner in black velvet and diamonds just as she did in Uncle Theo's day,' added Anne without malice.

'It suits her,' Alistair agreed, taking a corner neatly.

Anne leaned back, taking more pleasure than she cared for the moment to show in the lovely tranquil countryside. You'd hardly guess there'd been a world war raging in every corner for years. And what was the good of eating your heart out for something that was out of date, when your only hope was to move with the times, with the person who could move quickest getting there first.

'I'd forgotten fields could be as green as this,' she allowed herself to say. 'I suppose I know what you mean about Aunt Tessa. She has the courage of her convictions. But so had the martyrs, and look where it landed them. Out there I'd almost forgotten this sort of world existed. I expect you found that, too, didn't you?'

But Alistair said, in his cool, unemotional way, 'No, I can't say I forgot.' And he thought that you remembered the place where you were born and had spent your youth as you remembered your own name, and both were worth living for and both worth dying for. But his face revealed nothing of this.

'Who's staying with Aunt Tessa?' Anne wanted to know, wondering if Alistair had changed much or if all the change was in her.

'Oh – chaps.' Alistair was vague again. Then suddenly his interest crystallized.

'There's one dark horse.'

'There always is. He or she?'

'He.'

'Even a world war doesn't seem to have changed Aunt Tessa much. Where did she find him?'

'In a railway train, I gather. She's kinder to her fellow-travellers than you are.'

'What's his name?'

'Bishop – Lewis Bishop.'

'What does Aunt Tessa call him?'

'Mr Bishop, of course.'

'And what's he like?'

Alistair was unsatisfactorily vague. 'One of these tall, dark chaps.'

'Profession?'

'Commercial artist, since you ask me. By Hatton Garden out of Old Jewry.'

'I see.'

'What do you see?'

'I take it he's already admired Aunt Tessa's diamonds.'

'That, I believe, was his opening gambit.'

'Fortunate for him she likes having her things admired.'

'Fortunate? I think it was more than that.'

'You mean, he read her like a book?' She laughed gently.

'Well, he's not a fool.' Alistair took another corner, swerving to avoid a rabbit that was meditating in the middle of the road.

'And of course Aunt Tessa thinks he's wonderful. She would, of course. Everything that belongs to her is wonderful. Her husband, her clothes, her discoveries. It must be very encouraging to know that everything of yours is wonderful because it belongs to you.'

'Very satisfying,' agreed Alistair.

'One of these days,' exclaimed the girl, moved to sudden irrational anger by her companion's unshakable serenity,

'Aunt Tessa's illusions will be rudely shattered. One of her discoveries will cut her throat, and then ... '

'Don't!' exclaimed Alistair, sharply.

She looked at him in surprise. 'After all the bloodshed you've seen in the past five years I shouldn't have expected you to turn pale at a little thing like that.'

Alistair said nothing. He and Anne were sprung from the same stock, their experience up to the time of the war, allowing for the difference in their sex, had been similar, yet at moments like these they seemed to live in different worlds. She appeared genuinely surprised at his instinctive recoil from her idle words. Yet for years he and she had been risking everything, and for him, at least, how much everything was, to preserve from violence the people and the traditions they loved and in which they had been reared. During nearly six years of total war he had striven with all the capacity of a sensitive stubborn nature to conceal his own loathing of the ugliness and ferocity that had made up his life during that time.

'Anyway,' continued Anne, 'I'm by no means sure that anyone has a right to own necklaces worth twelve thousand pounds.'

'Quite a lot of thugs would agree with you,' said Alistair. He stopped the car in front of the tall iron gate that walled in that aristocrat, Mrs Teresa Goodier, from the outer world. Anne had the unusually imaginative idea that it was symbolical. It was more than a gate that divided her from the world that, after years of war, was now anticipating all the rigours of peace.

'How like Aunt Tessa to be able to keep a gardener to look after her nice winter roses, even in a world war,' she commented. 'I wonder they didn't make her grow cabbages here.'

'Aunt Tessa would make even the W.A.E.C. believe these were cabbages, if she gave her mind to it,' was Alistair's sedate reply. And there was admiration in his voice.

'Yes, there are advantages in only being able to see your own point of view,' Anne agreed, and then they came to the front door, which stood a little ajar. A woman appeared in the hall and seeing the pair of them, said, 'Oh, Alistair, you're wanted on the telephone.'

Alistair said, 'Coming, Dutchy,' and disappeared.

The woman, a pleasant, sensible, middle-aged female in pleasant, sensible, middle-aged tweeds, looked at Anne and said in a dry voice, 'So you're back, Anne. I hope everything won't seem too tame after your adventures abroad.'

'Alistair would say we're reaping where we have sowed.'

'Meaning that you've earned the right to come back? Well, you're lucky. A lot of the lads and lasses only came back to blitzed houses and dead businesses. I tell you, it's hard enough sometimes not to cry in a war, but in a peace . . .'

'We've had the European war. This is the civil one,' said Anne unsympathetically. 'A bit more reaping where we've sowed.' She and Dutchy had never got on too well; she had the feeling that she wasn't altogether approved of, and not all the notions she liked to consider democratic could make her realize the gulf that stretches between the woman who has always had to earn her own living and make her own security and the girl who manages to get born in a safe place inside the fold. There was jealousy in Dutchy's attitude, though neither woman appreciated the fact. 'You don't look much changed, Dutchy. Where's Aunt Tessa?'

'Prinking,' said Dutchy, who was a privileged person, having helped to bring up Alistair and Anne, and being now the virtual guardian of the widowed Mrs Goodier, her house-keeper and watching angel. 'The war seems to have suited you, too.' She went off, leaving Anne standing in the hall. The girl lifted her golden brows and looked about her. The place looked much the same as ever, except that there was a photograph on the mantelpiece she didn't remember. It was Hugh, the cousin who had gone to the Mediterranean and hadn't come back. Hugh had always been Anne's special cousin. They said she could do what she liked with him. But she wasn't sure she could have done what she liked with this Hugh. He looked older than any of them, older even than Alistair. Oh well, she shook herself free of disturbing youthful memories, he was going to miss a lot of trouble, sleeping quietly five fathoms deep with what remained of his ship.

'Yes, bad luck, wasn't it?' said a voice behind her, and she turned quickly. Dark eyes looked into hers: dark hair swept back from an olive forehead; long fine hands rested on the newel-post of the staircase people crossed a whole county to see. Anne stared at him, rigid, like Lot's wife turned to a pillar of salt.

'Bit of a change from driving in the Balkans, isn't it?' said the man politely. 'Didn't your cousin tell you I was here?'

'He said a Mr Bishop. That wasn't your name . . .'

'Changed it by deed poll,' said the man called Lewis Bishop, easily. 'No, fact is I enlisted under another name. Nothing illegal about that.'

'Only expedient,' murmured Anne, and saw the fine dark brows draw together.

'No sense being enemies,' he suggested.

Anne sighed. 'I suppose it would have to be you,' she said, wearily.

'I'm not here to do you any harm,' Mr Bishop assured her.

'Or anyone else any good.'

He said in careful tones, 'Remember I once told you I generally got the best of a bargain?'

'I remember. I've no doubt it's true. Are you going to propose a bargain to me?'

'Not a bargain. Just a suggestion. Suppose we forget we ever met one another before. How would that be?'

'I don't know – yet – why you're here.'

'Because Mrs Goodier invited me.'

'Not knowing you're an – adventurer?' Her voice was soft with scorn. In spite of everything he knew about her, she wasn't without courage. He'd always known that.

'I suppose we all want as much as we can get,' he said coolly.

'And you've decided there's something to be got out of Aunt Tessa?'

He came a little nearer. Close to, one saw that he was older than at first appeared. An excellent figure, and tailoring to

8

match, took five years off his age. In fact, he was about forty, and his face had the stamp of multiple experience. In a way, it was admirable that he should have volunteered for the hard job of ambulance driving in central Europe, but Anne was too disillusioned to believe that patriotism was behind the offer.

'Probably convenient for him to be out of the country for a spell,' she reflected. 'And even in what I daresay he would call the cockpit of Europe there might be pickings.'

An old saying slid into her mind. 'Old sins have long shadows.' You'd have thought it would be safe enough at Little Ebbisham, you could put the past behind you, concentrate on the arduous present. But Fate thought otherwise. Fate believed in people paying their just debts, and you could trust Lewis Bishop to see to it that he drew every conceivable ha'p'orth of interest. She remembered a man out there saying, 'It would save a lot of trouble if I didn't get back.' She'd been contemptuous of that attitude then; she was more sympathetic now.

Bishop was speaking again in that smooth unforgettable voice of his.

'Your aunt and I have a lot in common,' he said.

'And you don't see why you shouldn't have even more,' she suggested.

He looked at her sharply, but before he could speak Alistair came back from telephoning. He was whistling softly.

'I find that Miss Vereker has also been in the cockpit of Europe,' observed Bishop smiling. Anne's lips took a slightly contemptuous twist. Alistair didn't appear to notice the pretentious phrase.

'You were driving there, too?' he suggested politely. 'And you didn't meet?'

'It's a large place, Colonel.'

Alistair's head went up. 'Now that I'm out of the Army I've dropped my military title,' he said. 'It was a purely temporary rank in any case.'

'I didn't know you were anything so distinguished as a colonel,' gibed Anne, softly.

She had Alistair on the raw there, she wasn't sure why. 'I was actually a major,' he said. 'I took over from Nigel when he was killed, because I happened to be the senior officer on the spot. That's all.' He seemed anxious to change the subject. He stooped and picked up her baggage. 'I'll take this up. They're still a bit short-handed in the servants' hall.'

Anne looked at Bishop, and said in her most dispassionate voice, 'Well, I shall be seeing you presently, Mr Bishop,' and accompanied her cousin.

'What a dark horse you are, Alistair,' she complained.

'There was nothing to talk about.' He frowned. 'I can't think why Aunt Tessa wanted to ask that fellow here. Granted it's her house, still he is rather a poisonous specimen.'

'I like you when you're honest, Alistair,' said Anne. 'Yes, he's a natural pirate, isn't he?'

'It wouldn't matter if Uncle Theo were still about.'

'If Uncle Theo were still alive Bishop wouldn't be here.'

'That's true. By the way, his brother's turned up, Uncle Theo's, I mean.'

'What, the wastrel James?'

'I hope there isn't more than one. Easy to see why he stayed away in Uncle Theo's lifetime.'

'I suppose he's come blood-sucking, too.'

'At least he has more right than Bishop.'

Anne said, 'Couldn't we marry him off to Dutchy?' and Alistair laughed for the first time.

'You might suggest it to him. He might even show a clean pair of heels if you did.'

'Dutchy would probably put arsenic in my porridge, though. You were always the favourite there.'

Alistair paused on the landing and moved over to the great staircase window. He seemed tired. Anne noticed it for the first time. From here you could see the countryside rolling on to the skyline, dotted with little farms, little fields like coloured handkerchiefs, yellow and brown and green, hedges like the toys you buy for your children, great white clouds billowing through a sky as polished as alabaster.

Here he had grown up, in this place his spirit was rooted,

so that he sometimes thought, if he fell on foreign soil, it was here it would return; here he longed to spend the remainder of his days. He had little in common with his Aunt Tessa's husband, a self-made merchant looking like someone from a stage play at the turn of the century, but Theodore had bought the Manor when it came into the market, and so given it back to Alistair for his youth, and for that he would always be grateful.

He turned back to Anne. She was leaning against the bannisters, watching him.

'Alistair, have you thought what you're going to do now the war's over?'

He couldn't answer that. He had never progressed further than the thought that he would live – that in itself was a miracle, to live without fear of what the day might do to you. And since to him living implied the Manor he had assumed that he would live at the Manor. He had looked after affairs for his aunt during the two years following her husband's death until it was time for him to go to the war, and since then there had been an agent. Not, he reflected a particularly effective agent, but you couldn't pick and choose with Mr Bevin calling men up right and left, and the fellow had done his best. All the same, Alistair wondered how much experience he really had. That was something else that would have to be discussed soon. Forgetting Anne, remembering the little rabbity figure of Mr Bletsoe, Alistair stooped and picked up the bags again.

Anne was watching him thoughtfully. 'He's an anachronism in a post-war world,' she reflected. 'He's thinking back in terms of the nineteen-thirties. He's no more like the sort of man who's going to possess the future than something out of a museum.'

Alistair dumped her bags and took himself off. Anne began to unpack, resolutely turning her mind from the sinister figure of Mr Lewis Bishop. Yet, despite her resolution, memory betrayed her. She remembered every incident of that terrible night nearly two years ago. Lewis remembered it, too, wouldn't scruple to make use of it. In vain she told herself

that the past is dead, that two years had elapsed, that she had
her record during that time, even that Alistair would understand. Because she knew Alistair wouldn't. You can forgive
things in other people that you don't forgive in your own kin.
Because the Bible's right, you don't live to yourself alone any
more than you die to yourself alone and what you do in-
volves your people; and in imagination she saw Alistair's in-
credulous horror if Bishop should broadcast the story of what
happened on that black night in the Balkans.

Even now she couldn't look back without shrinking and
fear and pain; easy to say all the past things are past and over,
the deeds are done and the tears are shed, but some things are
never done with but remain to colour your life to the end of
your days. And although in that turmoil, surrounded by fear
and dismay, her action had seemed the only one possible,
back here in this quiet place it took on an air of unreality, the
proportions of a nightmare. There was a time theory which
declared that what has happened once happens for ever, is
fixed in a point of eternity and can never die or be changed;
she could believe that about herself and Desmond Frere. But
that Bishop, the one man who could destroy her, should be
here on the premises, holding her to silent blackmail, daring
her to speak and ruin his infamous plans, that seemed a male-
volent move on the part of Providence no one could have
foreseen.

'And if I can't make him withdraw in any other way, I
shall have to speak,' she thought dully. 'And yet – how can
I? Isn't it enough that it had to happen? Wasn't that punish-
ment enough for anything I did?' But it seemed that it
wasn't.

Still, her present resolve was to live for the moment. Perhaps Providence even at the eleventh hour would intervene,
though in her heart she didn't believe any of them important
enough to be of much concern to the Powers that be.

Outside her door someone called, 'You there, Anne?' and
without waiting for a reply the speaker opened the door and
came in. 'I heard you were back,' she said. She was a little
creature, of immense vitality and resolution, with dark

straight hair, small features and no pretensions to good looks. She was a cousin of sorts of the late Theodore Goodier and had been living at Four Acres for a number of years, acting as a kind of companion to Tessa.

'Oh hallo, Alicia. So you got back first. What were you doing?'

'Not the kind of thing that gets your picture into the *Tatler*. I saw yours. Miss Anne Vereker who is driving an ambulance in the Balkans. They don't put pictures of land-girls in the shiny weeklies.'

Anne didn't say anything. If Alicia had wanted to go to the Balkans no one would have stopped her; but she'd never meant to go. She had got her foot firmly inside the door of a country house, and even a major war wasn't going to oust her. Being a land-girl she had managed to go on living at home and working for a local farmer. She looked a little bit of a thing to be doing hard work in all weathers, but she was as strong as a pony really, and had the will-power of half a dozen.

'I told Aunt Tessa we ought to put out the red canopy for you,' she went on. 'But she said you wouldn't expect it. I suppose you've landed a wonderful job by this time?'

Anne looked oddly discomfited. 'I hadn't even thought about it.'

'You couldn't settle down to a quiet life like this after all your excitement,' urged Alicia.

'I don't know why everyone should assume that,' said Anne. 'I should think we're just the people who would like a bit of quiet.' Though it didn't appear that she was one of the people who was going to get it, not so long as Lewis Bishop remained on the scene.

She said abruptly, 'How long has Mr Bishop been here?'

'Much too long,' returned Alicia decidedly. 'But you know what Aunt Tessa is. Anyone can take her in. If you ask me, he hasn't got a penny of his own and he's just staying here to see what he can get. I wish Alistair would turn him out.'

'It's not Alistair's house.'

'Uncle Theo always said he meant Alistair to have it. Why you can't imagine anyone else here. It – it wouldn't be right.'

'It will depend on Aunt Tessa, I suppose,' said Anne, who agreed with Alicia but didn't intend to say so.

'Oh, I wouldn't expect you to care,' flamed Alicia. 'You never have cared about the Manor – not the way Alistair does – and I do.'

'It's a beautiful house,' Anne agreed, and Alicia interrupted as fiercely as before, 'I suppose that's all it does mean to you. You don't think of it having a personality, a soul?'

'Which you've discovered?'

'Oh, I know you think the only people who can understand tradition are people who're born on the right side of the iron gates. Did you ever think it's just luck, no virtue of your own, that got you inside the circle, just as it's sheer bad luck that gave me the feeling and not the position? I tell you, I've worked for years to get past that barrier and now I'm past it and I'm going to stay inside.'

Anne looked at her in amazement. 'No one wants to drive you out.'

'Perhaps not. But you couldn't think of me as the mistress of Four Acres, could you?'

'Oh, this is fantastic,' thought Anne. 'Alicia Turner mistress of the house.' And then stopped. Because hadn't she been telling herself for years that the old barriers and distinctions had gone, and A equals B and X equals Y? So where was the objection in picturing Alicia in Aunt Tessa's place?

'You see?' said Alicia, quietly. 'You're outraged. But tell me if you can why I'm not as good as you? No one would think it odd if you and Alistair . . . '

'There's no question of any such thing,' said Anne sharply, 'and I hope you won't go round talking like that. You'd only embarrass Alistair.'

'Oh, I know you don't care for him. But at least you needn't try and put any spokes in my wheel.'

Anne was astounded at the surge of feeling that overwhelmed her. She'd never thought about Alicia much. She had just been there and presumably one day she would marry – but that she would marry Alistair was ridiculous.

She said in a gentler voice, 'I don't want to seem unkind,

Alicia, but – well, I'm certain Alistair has never thought – I mean . . . '

'You mean, you wouldn't like him to think of such a thing. My life is nothing to you. But I tell you I love the Manor, every stick and stone of it. And I love Alistair. I'd do anything to get him. And I shall.'

Anne opened her mouth to reply, hesitated, and closed it again. Because this was Alicia's affair. And Alistair's. She didn't come into it. And the past was too close, with Lewis Bishop at her elbow, for her to try to give anyone else advice. After all, you could never tell with men. And Alistair might have changed more than appeared on the surface.

So all she said was, 'If you want it so much perhaps you'll get it. They say you can get anything you want.' And then, turning away, she added, 'I must go and see Aunt Tessa. She'll think it frightful of me not to have hunted her out as soon as I arrived. But one gets so untidy on a train.'

Aunt Tessa had left her room, having prinked sufficiently and with becoming effect, and was pouring out tea in the drawing-room. It was a charming place, old-fashioned and restful, not a modern note anywhere. It was part of her aunt's genius, reflected Anne, reminding herself that even stupid people can have genius in their own line, to have obliterated all suggestions of a world war already from the room. Even the photographs of men and women in uniform had been relegated to other parts of the house. The chintzes that had been new just before the war had been taken out of cold storage and returned to the big comfortable chairs that stood about on the Aubusson carpet, all the china matched, the silver shone, there was lump sugar in the bowl, and the hostess herself looked cool, ageless, perfectly turned out and delightfully dressed. Anne, in her well-made tweed suit, felt that the older woman had a distinct advantage. Vaguely she thought of the generations of Vereker males who had found satisfaction in leaving the world of sport and business behind them and coming into this restful room. In a world where women ached to be somebodies Tessa Goodier was content to be a woman.

She was a kind silly creature, who had been beautiful as a girl and had contrived to give a good deal of innocent pleasure in her time. When she was young a great marriage had been prophesied for her, but perhaps her very stupidity had prevented that. She had young men all round her, but somehow they all married her contemporaries, and she had been twenty-eight when Theodore Goodier first set eyes on her and told himself that this was the woman for whom he had been looking. He didn't want a clever sensible wife; he had plenty of brains and all the necessary astuteness to make the most of them. He had fulfilled most of the ambitions of a lad born in poor circumstances in Liverpool, and when he came back from abroad he shut the gate on that side of his life, and resolved to marry a lady and settle down to be a country gentleman. He had not, perhaps, altogether succeeded in his latter pretension, but he had married Teresa Vereker with practically no opposition. He was not the match her family had originally foreseen for her, but in the years before the first World War twenty-eight was a good age for a woman to be neither married nor betrothed. Besides, financially the family had fallen on bad days. The estate was in the market, and there seemed every likelihood that some trading cad would snap it up. No one pretended that Theodore was a gentleman, but he was prepared to buy the Manor and keep it as a home for the young Verekers. Besides, the women of the family had the wit to see that Tessa, for the first time, was head over ears in love. When one of her Victorian aunts protested that Theodore had no pedigree that a Vereker could acknowledge, she said, without malice, but perhaps with more subtlety than the rest of them appreciated, that she had been on the market for a good many years without attracting a bid from a gentleman sufficiently wealthy to make the offer worth considering, and she intended to marry Theodore anyway, if it involved an elopement.

'I'll be no party to an elopement,' Theo was supposed to have said. 'I may not be good enough for you,' and that was genuine, 'but I'm good enough for your relations,' and that was equally so.

The family, having accepted him, found they had done well. He had a certain simplicity that forbade his apeing those who were then called his betters, he was shrewd, generous, and devoted to Tessa. Afterwards one of the uncles had said that the cleverest thing a Vereker had done for a generation was getting Theo into the fold. They spoke of the fold as though it were the Kingdom of Heaven.

'It wasn't really anything to do with me,' Tessa said later. 'He swept me off my feet, just wouldn't take "No" for an answer.'

'Did you try saying "No"?' inquired a slightly malicious contemporary, but Tessa scored with the reply, 'He didn't give me a chance.'

Truth to tell, her family were rather relieved by the situation; Theodore Goodier was clearly the type of man who can be depended upon not to fail his wife; and he had only failed her by dying at the age of 72 – he was twenty years her senior – and leaving her once more feeling helpless and bereft.

'I do miss dear Theo so terribly,' she confided to Alistair. 'He always made up my mind for me. I simply don't know how I'm going to depend on myself now he's gone.'

She did not, of course, make the attempt. For so long as he remained in the country she depended on Alistair. When Alistair was, most inconsiderately, sent abroad, she cast hurriedly about for some man to take his place. She never pretended, even to herself, that Mr Bletsoe was an efficient substitute, but he was at all events a man and, apparently, a man in whom the authorities were not disposed to take much interest.

'And it's only till dear Alistair comes back,' she said. Even Mr Bletsoe realized the temporary nature of his employment; as to what he proposed to do after the war, nobody inquired. Nobody except Mr Bletsoe was remotely interested. And even Aunt Tessa knew that everyone has to do with ersatz in every shape in a war.

Looking at her now, Anne experienced a sense of timelessness, and an almost equal sense of injustice that war, that had changed so many lives beyond recognition, should have made

17

so little difference to this pleasant placid lady of fifty-eight who sat pouring out tea with the little fuss and flurry that had been alluring in women when she was a girl. She thought it only good manners to remember everyone's predilections in the matter of sugar and milk, and her conversation matched her appearance.

'The Temperleys are back at Hunton Chase,' she was saying as Anne came in. 'Tim's engaged to be married; Bertie was killed, of course; but Allison's husband has come back. I expect quite soon the countryside will seem quite like itself again.' Then she saw Anne. 'So you're back, too, dear. How very nice. Haven't you gone thinner? Well, that's not surprising. Have you met Mr Bishop? Oh, you have? He was in your part of the world during the war. I wonder if you met? No? Well, I suppose it's a big place. Now, you must forget all about that and settle down.'

'You mean,' said Anne gently, 'get married?'

'I'm sure you and Alistair were both wise to wait till after the war. So many war widows, and such a charge on the Government, Theodore used to say. But now the boys are coming back we must have a dance. I hope you haven't any of these modern ideas about getting married in a coat and skirt. You might as well be married in a registry office. (Like most people, Mrs Goodier confounded registrar with registry). I shall love arranging for a proper wedding. And then we must start finding a husband for you, Alicia.'

'I'm glad you hadn't altogether forgotten me,' said Alicia with an odd smile.

'Of course not, dear. You've been very valuable during the war, but now you must think of yourself. We'll find you and Anne both nice husbands.'

'And may I have a white wedding too?' asked Alicia.

'Of course, dear. Isn't it lovely to think we're all back together again? Except poor Hugh, of course. And he died a hero's death.'

'Of course,' said Alicia thoughtfully, 'Anne may have made plans for herself. All these years . . . '

'Nonsense, dear,' said Aunt Tessa placidly. 'More tea,

Alistair? She can't have met anyone possible in those dreadful Balkans.'

Alistair looked across at Anne. Looking at her face was like looking at a shut door. He marvelled that no one else seemed to see the change in her.

'Oh no, I'm glad you all had the sense to wait,' Tessa continued. 'There's plenty of time now. And so much to do. Not, of course that Mr Bletsoe hasn't done his best. Did you know he was living here now? The Ministry of Health commandeered the cottage for a labourer – so extraordinary, I'm sure Theodore would never have allowed it – and of course there *was* plenty of room. He has dinner with us – and lunch, of course – but he's really quite a nice little man if only he'd do something about his teeth. I expect he'll be thinking of the future, too, now Alistair's home.'

'You know,' said Anne thoughtfully, 'you can't really put the clock back. The world's changed and so have we. Nothing can ever be quite the same.'

'Oh, I don't know, dear,' said Aunt Tessa comfortably. 'When the rest of these horrid restrictions are removed, and we can get some of the rooms done up – and of course the garden wants a lot of attention, but we simply couldn't get the men. You people who've been abroad don't realize how difficult it was to cope . . . '

'No,' said Alistair gently.

Rescue came from an unexpected quarter. 'Miss Vereker's right,' said Bishop, suddenly joining in the conversation. 'We can't go back. We've lived through an era in the past few years. It's progress or die.'

'The whole social structure is different,' agreed Anne, savagely accepting his co-operation.

'I do hope, dear, you haven't come back one of these horrid socialists. We don't get them so much in the country. You mustn't think, because we stayed at home, we didn't see anything of the war. We had one of those horrid rockets at the beginning of the year. I suppose it was meant for London, but Hitler wasn't aiming so well then. It killed Timothy Tompkins. You remember him, Anne?'

19

'One of Aunt Tessa's special cats,' put in Alicia in her small, clear voice.

'How dreadful!' said Anne.

'Yes, dear, but, of course, it was instantaneous. I tried to comfort myself with that thought.'

'If the war's taught us anything it's that we're all equal,' announced Alicia.

'Then, so far as I'm concerned, it's been wasted,' said Bishop unexpectedly. 'Why, wherever you look you can see that's a fallacy. There's no such thing as equality. For instance,' he smiled at his hostess, 'take those diamonds you're going to wear to-night. Now, I could produce an imitation necklace that looks exactly the same, and only an expert, and with the possible exception of your brother-in-law who seems to know something about precious stones, I don't think we have any other experts in the house, only an expert could tell you the difference. Even the weight is the same.'

'Theodore would never let me have imitations made,' Aunt Tessa assured him. 'He said there was no satisfaction in wearing artificial stones. And he wouldn't let me keep them in the bank, either. He said they might just as well be stolen, for all the use they were to me. He was always a gambler.' She gave them all that smile that had made so many young men once think that perhaps they had met their fate. 'He said it was part of a gambler's duty to see that he backed the right horse.'

'He said that about his marriage, I suppose,' reflected Alistair, but he kept the words to himself. He was probably the only person present who appreciated his aunt at this moment. Being here, in this charming room, tranquilly drinking tea and eating home-made scones with home-made jam, was like turning the pages of a photograph album, and coming back to 1910 or 1912, before major wars ravaged what was then known as civilization. Though his common sense made him agree with Anne that the whole world had changed, all his instinct and desire was piled in the other end of the scales.

Mrs Goodier, who didn't care for what she called political

controversy, here interposed vivaciously, 'Your Uncle Theodore's brother James is staying with us. Did you know? Oh, perhaps Alistair told you. He's what's called a rolling stone. Just fancy, this is the first time he's been in England in thirty years. That's why I haven't met him before. He used to write from time to time . . . '

'When he wanted money, I suppose,' reflected Anne, looking quickly at Alistair to see if the same thought was in his mind. But if so it was so far beneath the surface that she couldn't detect it. She wondered what part the rolling stone was going to play in the drama that was now unfolding itself. He and Bishop and Alicia were odd fish to find in this old house.

But events were going to move more quickly than she anticipated.

Chapter 2

ANNE met Theodore Goodier's brother at dinner. James Goodier's idea of tea was something rather stronger than his sister-in-law provided, and, as he would tell you frankly, he wasn't much of a hand in the drawing-room. He was Anne's dinner-partner and lost no time in telling her that he had spent the last ten years sleeping under the stars in Patagonia, where men are men and there ain't no dames. He was a biggish man, stoutly built, with a big curly moustache and hair that curled at the ends; he had a bouncing manner and big hands with hair on the backs, and his eyes were slightly protuberant.

Alistair watched him, fascinated. He was like something out of a Wild Western film.

'Snug little place your auntie's got here,' he boomed. 'They tell me it's quite an estate in old England.'

Tessa, hearing him, leaned forward. 'If you knew the difficulty we've had during the war to get enough men just to keep it from turning into an overgrown meadow, you wouldn't be so scornful, James,' she said. 'I don't know what I should have done without Mr Bletsoe.'

Mr Bletsoe, a rabbity little man with inefficiency written all over him, beamed nervously. Now that Alistair was back he saw his precarious living disappearing fast, and in a pushing post-war world he'd bound to be trodden underfoot. If he could somehow maintain his footing here, he was thinking, looking from face to face, wondering who would make an ally. It was no use relying on Tessa, because she was like a chameleon, changed colour with each new companion. He looked longest, most hopefully, at Alistair, but Alistair didn't seem to notice him.

'All right for you, ma'am,' announced James Goodier, 'though I can't see Theo here. Must have changed a lot since he was a boy. Ah well.' He looked at the forks in front of him, and then at the company to see which was the right one to use. 'Speaking personally, I never had much use for moss.'

'And what are your plans now?' inquired Anne, politely.

'Just come back to the old country to meet my charmin' sister-in-law. You know, Theo was always tellin' me I should make tracks for home, but somehow I never got around to it . . . ' He threw back his big curly head. 'I have heard the cry of the offshore wind, the beat of the offshore rain, I have heard the song, How long? how long? Put off on the trail again. Still, I'm thinkin' it's about time I dropped me anchor and settled down. I must look round and find a nice little woman to make a good husband of me. Eh, Tessa?'

'We shall have a perfect orgy of weddings,' agreed Tessa cheerfully. 'The war weddings have been so depressing, never sure when we were going to hear the bride was a widow.'

'Oh, the pretty girls are safe from me,' said James, with a wink at the disapproving Miss Dutchley, who dined with the family now Theo wasn't there any more. 'A nice sensible woman is my cup of tea.'

Miss Dutchley looked at the tablecloth, and he wondered whether she thought he'd meant anything personal. He hadn't, of course. She was an admirable woman in her way, having integrity, intelligence, and great energy combined

22

with a strong moral sense, all the virtues, Theo would have said, that a man admires in the woman he isn't expected to marry. Miss Dutchley disapproved of James *in toto*. She knew that he had had too much sense to turn up during Theo's lifetime, and after that the war conditions had probably made it impossible for him to come home, but now here he was, ready and eager, in homely phrase, to milk the widow. Miss Dutchley, at least, had no illusions as to James's financial status. She hoped Alistair was as sensible. You might as well expect grapes of thorns as common sense of Tessa.

In the meantime, James was laying himself out to be spectacular and amusing, and he certainly succeeded in the first. In the second, he failed to some degree with everyone except Tessa, whose thoughts were elsewhere. Anne saw him as a sponging vulgarian, and thought you might have expected anyone as foolish as her aunt to wish this kind of curse on the family circle. Mr Bletsoe resented him enormously. He didn't deserve any consideration and yet that solemn young prig, Alistair Vereker, would probably see to it that he went away with his pockets suitably lined, while he himself, after years of service, would be thrown on to the labour market. Alicia thought him a detestable creature, ever since he had pretended to admire a little watch she wore, a birthday present from Mrs Goodier, in order, as she realized, that he might hold her hand and say, 'How about you and me going dancing one of these nights? I bet I could show you places, and after all, we are cousins, aren't we?'

Only Alistair saw through all that surface bluff and brazenness and realized that the fellow was in a blue funk about something. He himself was barely thirty, but already he understood that there was no place in a post-war world for men like James Goodier, men who've got out of the habit of work, who have expensive tastes and whose physical charms are fading. Alistair couldn't see any future for a chap like that. Anyone who got on now had got to have graft plus intelligence, or intelligence plus an ability to work hard, and all James had was graft. As for Lewis Bishop, he didn't know what pity was and to him it was only a matter of days before

James was thrown out on his ear. If you can't be honest, at least you should be skilful, was his doctrine, and James was a born blunderer, without even the finesse to conceal the fact.

James himself had his eyes everywhere. He might be a fool but he had wit enough to see that he had best ingratiate himself with his sister-in-law's family, since she was clearly the sort of woman who likes to have her mind made up for her. He talked to Alistair, when opportunity offered, of his own experiences in the last war, and not until later did he realize that the confidences had been his and the attention Alistair's. He discounted Miss Dutchley (unwisely), holding the obsolete view that the opinion of a middle-aged spinster, in a subservient position, was hardly likely to be regarded as of much account. Bletsoe he also discounted, but he regarded Bishop with unease. His experience had thrown him a good deal among such men, and he didn't for an instant believe that the fellow was there for any reason save that of feathering his own nest. He eyed him reflectively, wondering if he could propose an alliance for their mutual benefit, but presently he discarded the notion. Bishop would accept his help, so far as it benefited himself, and then cast off his ally, and James was humble enough to know that he was no match for that polished scoundrel.

He realized, however, that the man was by no means a negligible factor in this urgent matter of his own future. His position was parlous. Not only was he extremely short of funds for day-to-day expenses, it was imperative that he should, in the near future, raise a substantial sum of money to extricate himself from a very awkward situation. And the only person he could hope to touch was his sister-in-law, Mrs Goodier.

He looked at her sitting so satisfied, so comfortable, free even from the normal anxieties of existence, at the head of the table, magnificent in black velvet, her great diamond necklace catching every particle of light and throwing back the radiance on the air that actually seemed to sparkle more brightly round her chair than anywhere else. And he thought, 'The price of that necklace would keep me for a couple of years,' meaning, the price he could get for it if it came into his possession. He had been in many difficult places in his life, but none so dangerous as his present impasse.

He was not the only restless person present. Anne and Alicia were both disturbed, though for different reasons. Alicia was watching Alistair, endeavouring to attract his attention; Anne was aware of tension in the atmosphere, and she was exercised in her mind as to the reason for Bishop's presence in the house. That he fascinated her aunt was obvious, but to how great an extent not she or any of them realized until dinner was almost at an end. Then, when dessert was placed on the table, according to the old pre-war ritual, Tessa smiled at her male guests, and struggled to her feet.

'There's something I want to say,' she announced, and James Goodier leaned back and clapped his fat hands and shouted 'Speech! Speech!'

'No, it's not exactly a speech,' said Tessa, colouring rather prettily. 'It's just something I want you all to know, and it seems to me that when at last all the family are under this roof it's a very good night to tell you.'

James twirled a complacent moustache. That 'all the family' was good.

'As you know, I was devoted to my dear husband. No one could have been better or kinder than Theo, so perhaps it's not surprising I feel completely lost without him. I'm not one of the clever modern women who know how to look after themselves. When I was a girl women weren't expected to be enterprising and self-supporting. And I suppose I relied on him more than women do rely on men nowadays. At all events, I don't feel I can do without a man to look after me.'

Here James leaned forward to interrupt in his genial bawl, 'I always said it was my good angel tapped me on the shoulder and told me to come back to the old country. I know I'm not the man Theodore was, but no one ever said yet that James Goodier shirked his responsibilities. I'm the man of your family now, my dear Tessa. I've wandered here and there in my time, but now I've come into harbour.

25

You'll have no more need to be anxious about the future. I may say I'm not a man without experience of life, and I've always cherished the Englishman's desire to settle down on me own little plot of ground, and eventually lay my bones there. For what I'm worth, my dear Tessa, here I am, at your service, yours to command.'

Mrs Goodier, arrested in mid-flow of eloquence, turned to survey him kindly.

'My dear James, how very good and self-sacrificing of you, and you know how welcome a guest you will always be. But I didn't mean anything quite like that. I had – other plans in mind.'

She caught Lewis Bishop's eye, and her glance was so grateful and ardent and at the same time so fatuous that three at least of her listeners knew instantly the nature of the folly she contemplated.

'I've been lonely a long time now,' she went on, catching up the thread of her speech, 'and I do feel I need companionship. Not just the companionship of a brother, but something more – closer . . . ' She turned and threw out her hands – hands she'd kept beautifully all through the war – towards Bishop. 'Lewis, you'd better tell them.'

Bishop was already on his feet. 'Mrs Goodier has done me the very great honour of promising to become my wife.'

Anne had the sensation of being knocked unexpectedly off a diving board into deep water. For a minute she felt choked and blind, drowning, desperately fighting the dark. By the time she could recover her senses the flood of congratulation had swept over the engaged pair. Alistair, not a muscle of his face betraying what must have been practically a death-blow to him (for who could imagine Lewis Bishop giving anything away, particularly not a nice fat legacy like Four Acres?) was standing with his glass raised.

'We must drink their health,' he was saying, looking round the table for support.

Alicia beamed back at him. 'Dear Aunt Tessa, what a dark horse you are! Teasing us about getting married and all the time keeping this up your sleeve.'

Alicia was pleased, not seeing the full implications of the announcement. All she realized was that Lewis Bishop would never live in a place like Four Acres. He'd want a flat in what he doubtless would call the hub of the universe, and that, by Alicia's reckoning, left Four Acres free for Alistair. James Goodier made no attempt to conceal his rage and shock. Just when he thought he'd found a nicely-feathered nest for him to drop into that fat smiling cow his brother had married (mixed metaphors never bothered James) must make a present of the whole caboodle to a fellow with crook written all over him. It meant the other side of the front door for James and damn quick, too. James wouldn't make any of Alicia's mistakes. Miss Dutchley's big mouth was shut like a rat-trap. She ought to have seen this, she was telling herself. It was astounding really that Tessa hadn't done it before, but then during the war there had been practically no opportunities. Bletsoe was babbling something about the pleasure it had been to work for Mrs Goodier and the additional pleasure it would be to work for Mrs Lewis Bishop. But there was no body in his speech. He was just a poor little frightened animal, terrified that he was going to be chased into the open and set on by the dogs of want. As for Tessa, she looked the picture of happiness and pride. She might have been a girl again, except that a girl would have been more embarrassed at being the centre of so much speculative attention. Anne was suddenly aware of Alistair's eyes on hers. She sent him an agonized appeal which he disregarded, and she realized that her moment was past, the moment when she might have sprung to her feet and announced the impossibility of this marriage. Afterwards she wondered if the moment had ever existed. For how, with Aunt Tessa beaming and all the table attentive to the smallest word, could you humiliate a lady of close on sixty who had waited all these years and now believed she had found the true romance?

'But Bishop must know he can't go through with this,' she told herself dizzily. She looked down to the table to where he still stood, and saw that he was smiling, debonair, bland, assured. She knew then that he was challenging her to tell the truth if she dared. Nothing short of the truth could prevent this marriage, and the price she would have to pay for the truth was too appalling to contemplate.

'Anne dear,' said Aunt Tessa, and she realized that the women were leaving the room. She coloured as she got to her feet and followed the others to the door. Bishop was standing there, to touch Tessa's hand and smile into her eyes with a radiance that would have intoxicated a far less impressionable woman than Mrs Goodier. Miss Dutchley professed business and went off to her own office. Tessa settled herself comfortably and began to talk about her approaching marriage.

'You aren't thinking of getting married at once, are you?' suggested Anne.

'There's nothing to wait for, and I'm certainly not getting any younger. Besides, all of you will be getting married soon, and that will put my nose completely out of joint.'

'All the best young men have been killed in the war,' said Alicia gloomily.

'You can't expect a husband to fall into your lap. You have to work for them, just as you do for any other sort of living,' countered Mrs Goodier unexpectedly. 'Of course, I know some people have extraordinary luck. I did with your uncle. And now Lewis.' She seemed to fall into a reverie.

'And if there aren't any men left good enough for us we shall just have to earn our own living,' said Anne lightly.

'I don't know what I could do,' murmured Alicia. 'You're different. You can drive and talk languages and – look after yourself.'

'There are business courses,' murmured Anne, knowing that the outspoken Theodore had never intended to allow his sister's daughter to drift. Had he lived she would have learned some useful trade, accountancy or shorthand and typing or something with a commercial value. Theodore had no false pride about independence. Because nowadays getting married was no guarantee that you wouldn't have to work for your daily bread, and not only under your own roof. Women had won a lot of points in the war between the sexes, women fighting to get in and a large proportion of the men still battling to keep them out. But to gain such victories as they had already achieved they had had to abandon their age-old claim to be clothed and housed and fed.

'Oh, Alicia will marry,' said Tessa comfortably. 'You must come and stay with us later on, my dear, and we'll find a nice husband for you. I'm sure Lewis knows some very nice men.' That was to show Alicia that she needn't imagine her aunt's husband intended to provide her with a home. Alicia was twenty-three and responsible for herself. Besides, as politicians were always telling the country, there was going to be work for everyone for a time.

'Where will you be living?' inquired Alicia. 'I can't see Mr Bishop spending the rest of his life in the country.'

'He has a most charming flat in London, he tells me. I must say I love this house, and it was sweet of Theodore to buy it and keep it in the family, and of course it made a wonderful background for Alistair when he was a boy, but I've often thought how much I should appreciate central heating and constant hot water without having to keep a boiler going on and all the trouble we had about coke in the winter when the roads were frozen. Besides, a new life really demands a new environment. One doesn't want to get into a rut,' wound up Tessa, blissfully unconscious of the fact that she had been in a rut for thirty years.

'Then I suppose Alistair will go on living here,' continued Alicia.

Tessa looked vague. 'I really don't know. I believe Lewis has ideas about this house.'

'You mean, letting it?'

'Lewis says we should never find a tenant. It's very picturesque, of course, but people who could afford to rent it would want all sorts of improvements which we can't afford to put in.'

'Did you mean sell then?'

'Not for a private house. But Lewis says we're going to see

29

a great deal of development – industrial development – in the near future, and we're well situated.'

'You wouldn't leave everything to Mr Bishop, though?'

'He's a realist and naturally I shall be guided by him. He says things have changed since the war, we can't hope to go back to the pre-1939 standard. And he says that Theo would agree with him, because he was a realist too, and women always marry the same kind of men, no matter how many husbands they have.'

Anne said dryly, 'I don't think Mr Bishop has much in common with Uncle Theo,' to which Mrs Goodier replied, 'But you don't know Lewis, dear. You only met him to-night.' Anne looked up quickly, thinking, Is this my chance? remembered Alicia's presence, hesitated and decided it might be better to approach Bishop direct. 'And after all,' Aunt Tessa was saying, 'one must be sensible. Look at my dear father, a most cultured man, and so religious. One foot in the library and the other in Heaven. I remember Theo saying, "Didn't anyone ever tell him there was no money in either?" '

'So Four Acres is to become a factory? Is that what you really mean, Aunt Tessa?' Alicia didn't seem able to believe it. 'But he can't. He can't. It isn't his.'

'It isn't yours either,' said Tessa sharply.

'Uncle Theo always said . . . '

'He said that if it was in my possession at the time of my death it should go to Alistair. Of course, if it isn't . . . '

'Have you told Alistair?'

'There's nothing to tell at present. Really, Alicia, you're being very difficult to-night. And Anne looks as glum as possible. I did hope you'd be pleased at my news. At least it leaves you both free. Otherwise, I might have wanted one of you to come and live with me.'

At this juncture the four men came in. As a rule Bletsoe did not come upstairs, but he felt to-night to be exceptional. Besides, he was sick with anxiety for his own future, and thought that he might be able to pick up some information in the course of general talk. Whatever happened, he must enlist

Alistair's sympathy. Neither Bishop nor Goodier would be of the smallest use to him.

It was obvious that James had had rather more than he could carry. He came over to Tessa's chair and began to pay her heavy compliments, that she did not even hear; she had eyes for no one but Lewis Bishop. Alicia contrived to find a place next to Alistair, and under cover of the general conversation she whispered, 'Did you know that after she's married Aunt Tessa's planning to sell Four Acres for factory development?'

Alistair didn't even take it seriously. 'That's absurd.'

'You'll still be saying absurd when the board of sale is up. Can't you realize what Bishop is? He's a pirate.'

'But Aunt Tessa . . . '

'Will do exactly what he tells her. Alistair, can't you stop it? It's yours really.'

'Not during Aunt Tessa's life-time.' For once he made little attempt to conceal his dismay. He did not realize how closely Bishop was watching him. Bishop's trade had brought him in contact with innumerable rich women, some with a right to the wedding rings they wore, others not, but all linked by a similar burning passion for the diamonds and emeralds he was the means of procuring for them. He had never understood this lust for what were only coloured stones, though he appreciated it, since it had done him a lot of good. But in the eyes of the most possessive he had never seen quite the look that now blazed in Alistair's glance, taken for a moment off his guard. Feeling for some inexplicable reason slightly at a disadvantage, he produced a very handsome cigarette case, helped himself to a cigarette, replaced the case and discovered a very fancy lighter in gold and enamel in another pocket.

'That's a ladylike article,' said Goodier waggishly.

Bishop frowned, and Bletsoe, eager to preserve the peace, said in a propitiatory voice, 'It's a queer thing, none of these mechanical contraptions work with me. If I have a lighter it always goes wrong, wrist-watches stop the minute I strap them on, fountain pens that are perfectly reliable with other people leak the instant I unscrew them. In fact, I've given up attempting to use any of them.'

No one but Alistair even pretended to be interested in his troubles. How, inquired those indifferent, faintly contemptuous faces, was it possible to care what happened to anyone so pathetic and so futile? Alistair had a sudden vision of him surrounded by books of matches, wooden penholders, probably with the nibs crossed, large, solid turnip watches bought at the shop in Westminster that sold them before the war for ten shillings and twelve months' guarantee.

'There are chaps like that,' said Alistair vaguely and Bishop said, 'Well, you don't smoke a lot, do you?' in a bored way. 'I buy my cigarettes in boxes of 500, specially made for me.'

'You must be a very heavy smoker,' said Goodier maliciously, commenting on the fact that Bishop never handed his case round. Bishop, who was no fool, realized the implication and frowned, and Tessa, who didn't miss a single change of expression or intonation where he was concerned, broke in hurriedly, 'I don't know why it is but I never did like smoking. It's my belief a lot of women don't, but they think it's smart to pretend they do. I suppose Anne smokes like a chimney . . . ?'

Anne said yes, she supposed she did, you got into the habit, and Alistair gave her his case, which wasn't nearly as ornate as Bishop's. Alicia decided to throw the baby into the fire by saying, 'I wonder what sort of factory will be built here in, say, five years' time,' and Bishop replied, 'That depends on how wide-awake the local council is. The place has infinite possibilities . . . '

'What's wrong with farming, bar the fact that there's less money in it than gadgets made out of dried milk?' murmured Alistair, and a minute later the pair of them were at it hammer and tongs. Arguments flew to and fro like snowflakes in a storm. Bishop was for profit as against romantic tradition, and Alistair asked what about the men whose vocation was on the land? Bishop said that they'd be well-advised to find some other vocation and you couldn't pay the National Debt with fairy-tales.

'Even the Chancellor of the Exchequer can't tell such good fairy-tales as that,' Alistair agreed. 'This cheap food racket . . . '

'You can't expect the housewife to back you up,' argued Bishop.

'Not so long as money remains the great criterion of what we're pleased to call civilization. I'd hoped that the one good thing to come out of the war was the realization that money is no use unless there are goods in the shops to meet it.'

Tessa said, 'I don't see why we need have all this political argument the first night Anne comes home – and my engagement night. It was only an idea and of course I shall talk it all over with Alistair, only I'm sure Lewis is right, we are too apt to lag along the path of tradition and then, of course, other people get in front of us and we don't win the race.'

James Goodier said, 'On my soul, I see why old Theo married you, Tessa. You're content to leave the running of the world to men. Too many managing women about these days and that's a fact. A woman's first job is to please her husband.'

Tessa put in, with the air of one being extremely witty, 'A woman's first job is to get a husband. I've been telling Alicia so.'

But Alicia refused to be drawn. Putting her head close down to Alistair's she whispered, 'He's in earnest, you know, and no trick would be too low for him to play. In fact, I should think he's won all along the line by playing dirty tricks. That's an idea, Alistair.'

'What is?' murmured Alistair, looking at Bishop, who was now talking to Anne, parrying her thrusts, laughing, protesting. Not an easy man to defeat, he thought. You could understand Tessa's infatuation.

'He's probably got a fearfully shady past. If we could stop the marriage somehow – you know what Aunt Tessa is – then she'd probably take everything you said for gospel.'

'We can't do that,' murmured Alistair. 'To begin with, we don't know anything.'

'We might find out. Anyway, I'll never believe a man with a face like that is honest. And he can marry every belle in New York for me, so long as he doesn't marry Aunt Tessa. What a pity he didn't meet Anne first. He might have taken a fancy to her.'

'Why have you got your knife into Anne?' demanded Alistair. 'If you think he's such a rotter . . . '

'I only mean, Anne can look after herself. She's knocked about so much, got hard-boiled. Aunt Tessa is so – so simple. She just believes a thing because somebody tells it to her. No, Alistair, somehow or other we've got to stop the marriage.'

Chapter 3

I T was obvious that, even before the marriage, Lewis Bishop was taking affairs into his own hands. Tessa unhesitatingly left all decisions to him. To the fury of both girls she seemed to have elbowed Alistair out of his original position of adviser and have installed Bishop in his place. One morning, a week after the announcement, Goodier came raging to the young man, fresh from an interview with the interloper.

'Look here, m'boy, a word in your ear,' he said. 'If you hope to salvage anything from this wreck, you'll have to be damn' slippy. That fellow's like an octopus, got his tentacles on everything. 'Pon my soul, I don't know what my brother would have said.'

Spluttering with indignation, he told his story. He was, admittedly, in a bit of a jam. Old Theo, he said confidently, would have seen him through. Old Theo had had hard times himself, he knew that sometimes the luck's all against a fellow. He, James, had come back to put things in front of old Theo.

'But he's been dead for years,' exclaimed Alistair.

'Well, I don't get many posts where I am,' explained James. 'Anyhow, it's still his money, isn't it? I tell you, m'boy, old Theo wouldn't have turned me down cold.'

'And is that what Mrs Goodier has done?'

''Pon my soul, I don't know what's come over the woman. I could find handsomer things than Bishop under a flat stone. I went to her and I said, "Look here, Tessa, I want a word with you. Fact is, I'm in a bit of a jam, and you're my dear brother's wife, widow rather," and what do you think she said? Before I could get any further she hopped up and told me to talk to Bishop about it. "He's made me promise not to have any money dealings with anyone without consulting him," she said. Did you ever hear anything like it? "I don't understand about money," she said. "I have left everything to Theo." Mean to say, if she must have an agent, what's wrong with you?'

'I'm not going to marry her,' said Alistair. 'Did you see Bishop?'

'I'd sooner get blood out of a stone. You'd think the chap was a money-lender – and not even his own money, that's what galls me – not even his own money. "Well, what's it for?" he wanted to know. "Have you got a bill? Where is this chap?" "I'm not going into all my private affairs with you," I said. "I consider I've a right to a bit of what my brother left, and I've no doubt he expected his wife would do the decent thing in an emergency. My brother, Theo," I told him, "would turn in his grave if he could hear you cross-questioning me like this."'

'And the upshot was he turned you down flat? Well, I don't quite know what I can do. If fifty pounds is any use to you . . .'

'My dear boy, that's damn generous. Mind you, it's only a loan. The luck'll turn. It always does. But these times are a bit hard on fellows like me.'

'Will fifty pounds frank you?' asked Alistair, 'that is, if you don't mind my asking.'

'I asked my sister-in-law for a loan – a loan, mark you – of fifteen hundred. Well, what's fifteen hundred to her?'

'If a pound's worth sixpence,' countered Alistair vaguely, 'it's forty times fifteen hundred if you can do that in your head.'

James looked offended. 'Oh well, if that's the way you do arithmetic. Anyway, these women who've never had to earn a living oughtn't to have money to handle. I'm surprised at Theo, really I am. One thing, he'd have done something about it – my bit of trouble, I mean.'

'So he would,' thought Alistair. 'It 'ud have been the other side of the front door for you double-quick.' You soon became able to recognize the professional sponger. Still, Alistair was a fair-minded young man. He knew that even spongers have stomachs that need filling, and there was really no more reason why Theodore Goodier's money should go to fill Lewis Bishop's stomach than James's.

'I wish you'd have a shot at the old lady,' James urged. 'She'd listen to you, I believe.'

Unwillingly Alistair promised, though he wouldn't hold out any hopes of success.

'Tell you another thing,' continued James expansively. 'You want to watch your step. That fellow means to take the coat off your back, if he can. In your place, I wouldn't lie down under it.'

'What would you do?' inquired Alistair, genuinely wanting to know. 'Murder Bishop?'

'Put him out of the way somehow. A fellow like that probably has the sort of past that wouldn't bear investigation. Trouble is she's absolutely under his thumb already. Everything that is hers is virtually his, too.'

'It's all in the marriage service,' murmured Alistair, finding the conversation increasingly distasteful.

'Tough luck on you, though. Understand you were brought up here. Bit of a blow to see your home turned into a factory.'

'Oh, that won't happen,' said Alistair.

James looked at him in a searching way. 'I wouldn't be too sure, old chap. Feller doesn't mean to waste any time. You remember that chap, Charrington, who was over here a day or two ago. Bit hairy in the heel I thought him, but I daresay Bishop wouldn't notice that. Well, the pair of them went round pretty carefully, and I happened to overhear one or two things, and I wouldn't be surprised to hear he'd made an offer.'

'If Bishop's as fly as you suggest he won't accept the first offer.' But Alistair didn't feel nearly so confident as he sounded.

'Not unless there's something in it for him. There are no flies on Bishop, you know. And he don't mean to let the grass grow under his feet. I went along to have a word with Tessa not half an hour ago – well, I told you what happened and if she thinks I'm goin' to have a fellow like Bishop nosing into my affairs she's all wrong – and he came in with some papers, looking like a crooked lawyer. Well, thanks a lot, old boy.' For Alistair had fished his wallet out of his pocket and was writing a cheque. 'Trouble with women like my dear sister-in-law is they don't know what it's like not to be sure where you're goin' to be sleeping next week. And if you take my tip,' he folded up the cheque and nodded to Alistair as though he were doing him a favour by accepting the money, 'you'll make sure you're not caught short, too.'

'The fellow may be a crook,' reflected Alistair as James took himself off, 'but he's not a fool all the time. There may be something in this Charrington yarn. Besides, there's Bletsoe . . . '

Like Mr Mell, he believed there was no time like the present and so he went at once to the room Tessa called her office. It was just like Bishop to strike while the iron was hot and rose-leaves of December the frosts of June would fret before he'd go back on a bargain that held something for him, and you only had to look at him to see that the ladder up which he'd climbed was made up of successful bargains. Anne could have told him something about that.

Tessa's room was comfortably furnished with a sofa and easy chairs, with a writing-table conspicuously in the middle of the room, though Alistair suspected the sofa saw more of her than the table. This morning, however, as he came in he found her seated at the table, a pen in her hand, and Lewis Bishop at her side.

'Oh, am I interrupting a conference?' murmured Alistair, shutting the door obviously with no intention to take himself off.

'Of course not, dear. There's no hurry.' Tessa laid down her pen. 'Was it something special?'

'In a way.'

'Just give us a moment, Vereker,' said Lewis Bishop, 'and you can have a clear field. Just your signature, there, Tessa.'

'Making a new will?' asked Alistair.

'Not yet. Though Lewis says I must as soon as we're married. He says, of course, my position will be different.'

'It certainly will.'

'As for this, I was going to tell you this afternoon. Lewis thought I oughtn't to lose such a chance. Come and tell me what you think.'

Bishop looked sheer murder. Alistair came across and leaned over his aunt's shoulder. For once, he saw, James was right. The document in question gave Charrington an option on the estate and the right to purchase at what appeared to Alistair a most altruistic figure.

'I wouldn't be in too much of a hurry,' Alistair advised. 'It'll take some time to get the place valued – by the way, has that been done? I hadn't heard.'

'I – I really don't know, dear. Lewis was going to look after all that for me, but I told him he should consult you, since you've been in charge, so to speak, for so long. I don't understand about these things myself. Theodore always looked after things, and then there was you.'

'I certainly think it would be more satisfactory to have a valuation, from everyone's point of view. And of course there's the question of the type of factory Mr Bishop's friend is proposing to erect. There are various regulations still in force, and other people living in the neighbourhood have the right to protest. We're not altogether free of controls and shan't be for some time to come. I think you're letting yourself be rushed, Aunt Tessa.'

'This is a magnificent opportunity which may not come again,' snapped Bishop, his suavity for the moment forgotten. 'Charrington's offering a handsome price . . . '

'If he's offering what the land's worth there'll be other chances. No need to jump at the first one. And if he's offering too much – well, Bishop will agree with me. Men won't do that without some ulterior motive. In any case, why not put the whole shoot up for auction, if you feel you must sell?'

'I think that's a very good idea, don't you, Lewis? And it would still give Mr Charrington a chance to buy, and he'd be more sure of his position by then.'

'There can't be any burning hurry,' Alistair argued. 'He'll have to get permission for labour and materials and draw up plans and have them vetted and approved. It all takes time. And you want to give yourself a chance of looking at matters from every angle. You might, after all, find you'd rather keep the place on.'

He picked up the document, folded it and handed it to Lewis. 'To keep till wanted,' he said.

'I'm afraid you don't like the idea of the house being sold?' said Tessa tentatively.

'I still hope the necessity won't arise. It's been in the family for several generations and in any case I think next-of-kin should be given the option. It won't matter to Bishop what happens so long as he gets his price.'

From the look Bishop gave him he realized that his guess had been right. Bishop was more than just Charrington's good friend; he saw Four Acres as a source of profit, perhaps for the rest of his life, and in that moment Alistair resolved that, come what might, he should never have it.

'There's another point I wanted to discuss with you,' he said, and even Bishop wasn't proof against that tone of voice. Looking considerably disgruntled, he took himself off.

'It's Bletsoe,' said Alistair. 'Apparently Bishop's given him notice on your behalf.'

'He said we didn't really need him now, and he wasn't very efficient anyway. Though I'm sure he's done his best,' she added quickly.

'He's not a young man and he won't find it very easy to get anything else in a hurry. By tying him down here during his month's notice you're preventing him from going after other jobs, and from what he said to me he hasn't much in the way of savings.'

'Poor little man!' said Tessa. 'What do you want me to do?'

'Why not give him three months' pay in lieu of notice and tell him to look for something else. If he'd been in the Army he'd have got a gratuity, and he's right when he says no one's going to bother much with fellows of his age with no army service. I shall be here and can take all the worry off your shoulders'

'You know I have every confidence in you, Alistair. I'll tell Lewis.'

Alistair frowned. 'You don't have to ask his permission in a matter like this,' he pointed out.

'As a matter of fact, he thought it would save me trouble if he took over all the business side of things. He'd arranged to sign my cheques – for that sort of thing – not my private ones, of course – because I really have no business head and I get bothered . . . '

'There wasn't any need to do that,' commented Alistair, still frowning.

'I couldn't very well refuse, when he suggested it. He's been acting as a – a sort of manager for me for some time. I'm afraid Mr Bletsoe rather resented it, and Dutchy's being difficult, too. I'm sure I can't think why. I should have thought she'd be glad to have some of the responsibility taken off her shoulders.'

'People aren't as glad as you might think,' Alistair warned her. 'In fact, if you don't mind my being frank . . . '

'Of course not, dear boy.'

'Bishop's getting himself thoroughly disliked. And as you're going to marry him that's rather unfortunate.'

'He says I've been letting things go. He has a very good head, Alistair.'

'Oh, excellent,' said Alistair dryly.

'And he helped me so much. I really think I was getting into rather a muddle, and he came here and he offered to help me with my accounts, and . . . '

'What happened to Brett?' inquired Alistair, interrupting her.

'Mr Brett? The solicitor? Oh, he's there still.'

'He's the chap you should consult.'

'He was rather ill and I didn't like the man who was in his place. I believe Mr Brett's back now, but I can't very well take everything away from Lewis. You do see that? I know, of course, that Alicia's taken a great dislike to him?'

'What's Alicia going to do? She doesn't, I take it, propose to go on living with you when you're married.'

'Oh, dear, Lewis wouldn't like that. He says she ought to be able to earn her own living.'

'So she ought. Is she trained for anything?'

'She did work on the land during the war. But she isn't really very strong. She ought to get married.'

'Has she – if you don't mind my asking – any money of her own?'

'Theo didn't leave her any, but, of course, I've got her down in my will.'

'The one you're going to change?'

'I'm not going to change all of it. Only Lewis says it's usual to make a new will when you marry.'

'You'll get Brett to draw that up, won't you? And wouldn't it be best to give Alicia something for herself now, when she really needs it, so that she can get a training and keep going while she's having it? She may not marry as quickly as you think.'

'Lewis says her tongue's too sharp.' It was Lewis, Lewis all the time. 'But if you think that's a good idea. Alistair, what's wrong with Anne? She seems to have altered so since she went away.'

'Three years where she's been would change anyone. She wants a chance to slack off, though if I know Anne she won't take it.'

'You all need a rest. That's what I told Lewis when he

spoke of selling the house. I think they ought to have a chance of staying there for a time, before we do anything drastic, I told him. He doesn't understand about being tired, though. He has the most wonderful vitality himself. And he says it's dangerous to slack off.'

'Aunt Tessa,' said Alistair abruptly, 'would you let the place to me for twelve months? It'll still be as valuable at the end of that time, whatever Bishop may think. We all need a chance to adapt ourselves to the peace, and industrialists will find themselves in just the same position. If, at the year's end, you still want to sell and I can't find your price, then it's agreed the house comes on the market. What do you say to that?'

'I think it's a very good idea. I'm sure you deserve a rest. I know Lewis will agree.'

Alistair looked troubled. 'You're still the owner of Four Acres, Aunt Tessa,' he pointed out. 'It's for you to say whether you'll lease the house or not.'

Tessa for some reason seemed a little offended. 'Of course, I know that. Didn't you hear me refuse to sign the option? All I meant was that I shall tell Lewis what I've decided, and then we can shelve the matter for another year.'

'And Bletsoe?'

'Yes. I must really think about that. If you think that's fair I'm sure you're right.'

'And you'll tell him yourself?' Alistair persisted.

'Yes. Yes, of course. I have to go driving with Lewis almost immediately, but to-morrow – yes, to-morrow I'll settle everything.'

As he came away he realized he hadn't even mentioned James Goodier.

*

Despite his aunt's promise, Alistair was by no means certain that he would be accepted as tenant of Four Acres, and events proved his doubts to be well-founded. When Tessa and Lewis returned from their drive his aunt went quickly up to her room, but Lewis buttonholed Alistair in the hall.

'Tessa has told me of your suggestion about renting Four Acres, and has asked my advice. I've felt compelled to tell her I thought she would probably miss her market if she did what you want. The value of land in the next months is going to reach its peak, of that I'm convinced. Later, though controls might be lightened, there will be a limit to industrial expansion—I daresay you agree.'

'So far as I have any knowledge on the subject – yes.'

Lewis whistled softly. 'I see. That was your idea. You thought that if she waited so long she might find the house would only go for residential purposes, and that might be your opportunity.'

'You read me like a book,' said Alistair dryly. 'Still, she'd always get a good price, because the man who could afford what the land will be worth twelve months from now will have enough substance to add the necessary improvements. You're a business man, Bishop. You must agree with me there.'

'Ah, but I'm not like your departed uncle. I'm always in favour of taking the bird in the hand.'

Alistair went away, more troubled than before. He didn't like the hold this adventurer had over his aunt. She was a fatuous creature, for all her genuine kindness and charm, and had he been of a more melodramatic temperament he might have wondered how long Lewis Bishop gave the marriage. He did not convey the impression that he was a man who would for long suffer a tedious relationship, and a more imaginative woman would have hesitated at the prospect. There was no hope, however, of making Tessa see sense; she was infatuated, and as blind as any girl in love. Alistair took his troubles into the garden later that night, finding refuge in a covered summerhouse built some years previously for a crippled younger son who was ordered all possible light and air. He had been there for some time when he heard light steps on the path and Alicia came up the three wooden steps.

'You'll catch cold,' said Alistair involuntarily, but she laughed and shook her head.

'Oh no. I'm wearing my moleskin coat. Aunt Tessa gave it

me last Christmas. It was one of hers that she had re-modelled. It really isn't at all a bad fit. Alistair, one day I shall make my husband buy me a mink coat. You don't know what a mink coat means to a woman.'

She was in a strange mood, over-excited and at the same time confiding. He looked at her closely, and she dropped down on the seat next to him and put her hand on his arm.

'How cautious you are, Alistair. As if we didn't all have to know within a few hours. You needn't have come out here to hug your secret to yourself.'

'My secret?'

'Yes. Lewis told you, I suppose. I saw you talking in the hall.'

'You mean about the house? I wouldn't call that a secret exactly.'

'I don't mean the house in particular. I mean – everything.'

'Now I don't understand.'

She looked at him, incredulity giving way to surprise. 'Do you mean you don't know where Lewis took Aunt Tessa this afternoon?'

Alistair half-rose. 'They're not married?'

'No, no. She wouldn't feel properly married by a hole-and-corner ceremony like that. No, he took her to a lawyer, and he's got her to give him control of all he possessions.'

'Did he tell you that?' Even Alistair was startled out of his normal calm.

'Not exactly. But – I heard him talking to Bletsoe in the library. The door was ajar, and he wasn't attempting to lower his voice. I suppose he didn't care if the whole house heard, probably would have been glad if they did. I suppose Bletsoe had gone to him hat in hand, like the fool he is.'

'I hardly think Bletsoe's position is an enviable one,' said Alistair rather frostily.

'He's like any poor relation, he's got to ride a high horse if he doesn't want to be ridden over altogether. Do you think I don't know that Lewis Bishop means to persuade Aunt Tessa to cut me out of her will altogether if he possibly can, and most likely he can do what he pleases, but you don't catch me kowtowing to him. People like that don't have any respect for subservience.'

'What actually did you hear him say to Bletsoe, who, by the way, has got notice to quit? I don't think there's any secret about that.'

'Oh, I suppose Bletsoe was asking for another chance or something and Bishop was enjoying refusing. Anyway I heard something about Aunt Tessa, and Bishop said, 'That won't help you. I've had to take steps to prevent her being preyed on by a horde of vultures.'

'Hardly a complimentary description of ourselves,' agreed Alistair, 'but not quite so final as your first words seemed to suggest.'

'I bet, if you ask, you'll find they went to a lawyer this afternoon. Oh, she may not have signed anything yet, but she's going to any day now. It's just a question of hours. Nothing can stop it.'

Alistair looked at her oddly. 'It's never safe to prophesy,' he said.

'I shouldn't think many people would stand much of a chance against Bishop. Anyhow, Mr Bletsoe was terribly upset. He began to shout. I heard something about murder, and Bishop laughed and laughed. If I were Bishop I'd think twice before I laughed like that.'

'You said that quite seriously,' murmured Alistair.

'I am serious. Don't you remember someone or other saying that some people are born murderees? I don't think I've ever met one before, but I should say Bishop was one of them. Why, the whole house is full of people with motives for wanting him out of the way.'

'Speak for yourself,' suggested Alistair, dryly.

'It's really preposterous how he has gained such a hold over Aunt Tessa. I know what it is. He makes up her mind for her, and she'd love anyone who saved her that amount of trouble. The truth is, Alistair, she's a very lazy woman. She's made a sort of hobby of it. Uncle Theo knew it, but he thought it rather aristocratic of her. In the world where he grew up women had to be busy and bustling and either do the housework or go out and earn a living, and he thought it was a sign of blue blood that she shouldn't even be able to think, much less do a hand's turn for herself. If only you'd come back first . . . '

'I don't quite see how that would have affected the issue.'

'If she'd had you to look after things it would never have occurred to her that Lewis Bishop was essential. Of course, she had Dutchy, but Dutchy's just a little bit governessy and then she's a woman.'Besides, she wouldn't think it honest to pay compliments. She's the kind that believes every idle word will have to be accounted for at the Last Day. No, I'm not really surprised that Aunt Tessa is infatuated with Mr Bishop, but I didn't think he'd be able to throw his spell over Anne.'

'Anne!' Alistair's tone was one of amazement tinged with displeasure. It was absurd to resent Alicia's suggestion of stricture, but he did so most emphatically. He often didn't agree with Anne, and since his return he had recognized the existence of a gulf between them that hadn't been there before the war, but even so he didn't permit Alicia the right to criticize her.

All this Alicia understood perfectly, but she was wiser than Alistair, inasmuch as she did not allow a hint of her feelings to escape her.

'Surely you've noticed? I don't say she's attracted by him exactly, but they have some secret, and it doesn't seem to me decent when Aunt Tessa's going to marry him.'

'I think you're drawing on your imagination,' said Alistair, stiffly.

'Well, if everything's as it should be, why is Anne making secret appointments with Bishop? Oh yes, she is. She's meeting him in the library at half past eleven to-night.'

Alistair conquered a sense of distaste. 'Is that something else you happened to overhear?'

Alicia said candidly, 'I don't pretend to be awfully devoted to Aunt Tessa. She's never put herself out for a moment to make things easier for me, but I do think it's a shame that Anne should try and put a spoke in her wheel.'

'If you mean Anne doesn't care about the marriage, I thought we were of one mind there.'

'You can not like the marriage without making clandestine rendezvous with the prospective bridegroom,' said Alicia scornfully. 'Oh, you can look as county as you like, Alistair, but you know perfectly well she won't tell Aunt Tessa she's meeting her darling Lewis in the library to-night.' And, flushed with indignation, Alicia turned and left him. She went in by the garden door, leaving Alistair a prey to no very pleasant thoughts.

'I ought to have stopped her. She's out to do Anne a mischief if she can, and Anne's like me. We've never thought of Alicia as one of the family, just someone belonging to Uncle Theo.' He wondered for a minute why it should have worked out like this, and decided it was because Alicia didn't belong to the family either by tradition or temperament, and whereas Theodore Goodier had accepted the fact that he'd bought his way into Four Acres Alicia wanted everyone to believe she was there by Divine Right.

'She is a little fool. It's what they call an inferiority complex these days. All the same, if she's right about Anne – it's the devil of a mess, and so far as I can see she hasn't the smallest intention of confiding in anyone. All this feminism,' reflected Alistair, looking like his own grandfather and arguing on precisely similar lines. 'It's not the least likely that Anne can hold her own with a wily chap like that, but she's got the idea that if and when men and women are equal they accept their own responsibilities, and she'd rather come a real cropper than ask for help.'

Alicia's news had made him too restless to stay where he was any longer, and getting up he left the summer-house. He noticed that a vast change had taken place in the weather during the past hour. When he first left the house there had been a moon like a lamp in the sky, and all the valley beyond the garden was like silver. Now the moon was obscured by a sudden flurry of clouds racing across the heavens like a flock of black sheep, the trees had lost their magic, and a great spruce fir stood out against the darkness like a huge sinister toy cut out in black cardboard. He turned, with a sigh, towards the house. Normally, he would have entered by the garden door that was never locked, in spite of Bishop's warnings to Mrs Goodier that if they had a burglary the insurance company would make a lot of trouble about compensation if it were known that the house was not adequately secured. Mrs Goodier, however, said in her vague way that there hadn't been any burglaries while Alistair was away and there certainly wouldn't be any now he was back, a piece of logic no one attempted either to combat or understand. To-night, however, mindful of Alicia's warning and slightly scornful of himself, he made a detour that took him past the library windows. These were what are known as french windows, opening on to the garden, and the long dark velvet curtains were not quite drawn so that he could see a ray of light in the room itself. He noticed also that, despite the cold airs of evening, one of the windows was still unlatched, and he resisted a temptation to enter the room and challenge Bishop outright. An instant's reflection, however, assured him that he could scarcely divulge the source of his information, and in any case the notion of discussing his cousin with a man whom he regarded as an outsider was too distasteful for serious consideration. Yet, so disturbed was he, he could have wished himself some other sort of man and have entered the room unheard by its occupants and concealed himself behind the dark curtains. It would be like being in a secret room, a little black embrasure where no one could see you and where you could see nothing (unless you parted the curtains deliberately and peered through) but where you'd hear everything that went on. He walked round the house and came in by the central door and up to the little room that had been his since childhood. Nothing here had been altered in fifteen years; the place was redolent of his boyhood and he was glad for a moment to slip away from the anxieties and uncertainties of the present time to those days that seemed part of another world, a world his own sons, if he had any, would never know. He recognized the shabby coverings and the scratched surface of the desk with gratitude; and he stayed there for a while, not thinking of anything at all, trying to make his mind a void and realize that he could do nothing about Bishop, nothing about Anne, nothing about Tessa, and understanding that this is the hardest lesson to be learned by man.

All the same, he couldn't help feeling it was a pity that war killed off the flower of the race and left the prospectors, the speculators, the smooth-tongued men whose gospel was expediency, to reshape the world for which so many armies had died. When later he went up to bed he realized that he and his enemy were not the only late-stayers that night. There was a golden pencil of light under the door of Dutchy's sitting-room, and on an impulse he went in to her.

Chapter 4

DUTCHY was sitting at a table, grimly making notes on a little pad.

'Surely you don't work more than twelve hours a day,' Alistair challenged her. He smiled as he spoke, but there was no answering smile on Dutchy's face as her gaze met his.

'I'm making a good account of my stewardship,' she announced. 'I'm expecting to hand over any day now.'

'Hand over? To whom?'

'Whoever happens to be Mr Bishop's choice. He'd hardly tell me.'

Alistair came further into the room and sat on the edge of the table.

'Dutchy, that chap hasn't had the infernal insolence to give you the sack? Why, he's not in a position . . . '

'It's not for any of us to say what position he's in. At the present rate of going, I should say he'd have everything in his hands in the course of about a fortnight.'

'What's happened since this morning? I thought he seemed rather cock-a-hoop.'

'He's persuaded *her* to give him carte-blanche in her affairs.

49

Says she doesn't understand money, which is true. They spent the afternoon at a solicitor's.'

'Drafting the new will?'

'I don't think you're far out.'

'One really has to admire the fellow's thoroughness. He doesn't overlook anything. And he doesn't give a row of pins how much any of us dislike him.'

'Anyhow, I'm sure they've crystallized their plans, because Mrs Goodier said there was no need to replace any of the kitchen utensils – we badly need some saucepans. And then she said I must be tired after all the war years and how about a holiday. It's a long time since I was at school, Alistair, but even now I know how to add two and two.'

'It's tough on you, Dutchy, because if I know anything of the breed he'll see to it that all legacies are scrapped, and you've been the prop and stay of this house for years.'

'He's going to upset a lot of people's plans, including Mr Goodier's and Alicia's. You and Anne at least have something of your own . . . '

'Oh yes – Anne. I meant to ask you. In fact, that's really why I came in. I realize, of course, that three years of war is bound to change anyone, but – do you think there's anything between her and Bishop?'

'Alicia's been talking to you,' said Dutchy shrewdly.

'Well, yes. She's full of some story of secret meetings, which presupposes either infatuation on Anne's part, which I can't believe, or some disreputable connexion in the past. I wouldn't take any notice of it, if it weren't that girls like Alicia so often are right, and if I know anything of Anne she'd never ask for anyone's help . . . '

'Much rather cut her throat and leave it to someone else to clear up the mess.'

'You don't think Alicia invented it, do you?'

'Alicia would never do anything as silly as that. Alicia's got her head screwed on all right. She's what I believe they call on the films a tough baby. Which is why you ought to look out for yourself, Alistair.'

'I?' Alistair looked amazed and utterly mystified.

'Has the war completely addled your wits?' demanded Dutchy, irritably. 'Can't you see that Alicia's like someone tight-rope walking on a fence, and wants to be sure if she does fall off she falls on the right side? In other words, she's the cuckoo in the nest here and she doesn't mean to be pushed out. You can't blame her. She's nothing but a quite inglorious career to look forward to if she fails. That's why I say watch out for yourself. People without a conscience are always dangerous. It gives them so much rope.'

Alistair shrugged his shoulders as though he would shrug the suggestion away.

'Thanks for the warning, Dutchy. To come back to Anne. Have you noticed anything – particular?'

'N-no,' said Dutchy slowly, 'but Anne was never one of those people you could measure with a footrule. Psychologists would probably say it was due to her mother going off when she was a baby and her father marrying that frightful woman and losing all interest in her. But, whereas with most people you can prophesy how they'll behave in a given crisis, with Anne you could never be sure. You might be right 99 times out of 100, but the hundredth she'd do the one thing you hadn't counted on and give everyone a shock.'

'What a lot you know about us, Dutchy.' Alistair pulled out his cigarette-case and handed it across. 'Oh yes, of course you'll have one. Even you must take down your back hair sometimes. So you think Anne's under some obligation to Bishop?'

'He looks to me exactly like a blackmailer,' said Dutchy rashly.

'It all sounds very melodramatic,' murmured Alistair. 'I must say she didn't turn a hair when I told her the fellow was one of Aunt Tessa's guests. But a chap as clever as that must know he needs allies.' Alistair threw away his freshly-lighted cigarette, just like someone on the stage. But he didn't light another. He had just heard a sound that dismayed him, the soft closing of a door on the floor above and the stealthy creak of feet descending the stairs. He glanced at his watch. It wasn't much after eleven, but perhaps Anne wanted to get the interview over and done with. Listening to that furtive descent he felt a bit sick. In her own house, as it were, Anne, who always walked with a clear distinctive tread, shouldn't have to slink like a thief. He fought down the impulse to open the door, face her, compel her to come in and acknowledge the nature of her trouble, but their old intimacy had gone and so far they had nothing to put in its place. The steps went softly past the door, down and down. After a minute or so he heard the faint creak that heralded the opening of the library door, and he thought as he had thought almost every day since his return, 'I must get that oiled'. He looked back at his companion and saw her face was white and drawn.

'I'm keeping you up,' he said in apologetic tones. 'Don't do any more accounts to-night, Dutchy. You'll only add everything up wrong. And something may happen yet. They're not married, after all.'

But Dutchy took the wind out of his sails by saying, 'I'm worried about her, Alistair. She's given her heart to that scoundrel and I know he doesn't care two pins for her. But I don't see, barring murdering him, that there's anything we can do.'

It occurred to Alistair as he left the room that this was the third time he had heard the word murder used in connexion with Lewis Bishop in as many hours.

As he mounted the stairs the thunder pealed, lightning flashed, and he thought, 'Now we're in for a typical storm.' They came rolling across the open country at a terrific pace, with high winds and great bursts of rain, and they caused any amount of superficial damage. Even to-night, as he pressed the switch in his own room, the electric bulb flickered and for a moment he thought the supply had failed. They made their own electricity from a plant in the old coach-house, and he remembered Dutchy telling him there had been difficulty with the Ministry of Fuel and Power during the war to obtain enough petrol. 'They don't understand,' she had said. 'A twelve-year-old engine needs more petrol than a new one, and we can't get a licence for a new one so long as this func-tions at all. It seems stalemate.' Now that things were easier

they hoped to get the new engine installed, but the manu-
facturers had their own difficulties, both with labour and
materials, and they were still assured of 'our best attention'
and that was as far as they had got.

He felt unaccountably tired and wondered if the water was
hot enough for a bath. On his way to the bathroom to investigate, he stopped at Anne's door and rapped, the familiar
tattoo of their schooldays. But no one answered and he wasn't
going to give the house any further ground for gossip by
standing there at this time of night, so he sighed deeply and
went along to the bathroom where the water was hot enough,
though not as hot as he liked it. The hot bath had a soporific
effect on him and he seemed to drop asleep the instant he had
pulled up the blankets. Afterwards he tried to remember if he
had heard footsteps, but thought, on the whole, he had not.

At all events he scarcely seemed to have closed his eyes
when he was aware of someone knocking violently on his
door, and his aunt's voice saying his name. He was too used to
sudden calls after nearly five years of army service not to be
awake and on his feet in a flash, and an instant later he had
opened his door to behold as odd a deputation as he had ever
set eyes on. His aunt, wrapped in a wadded dressing-gown,
with her hair tied up in a green shrimping net, stood outside,
with a revolver in her hand; behind her was Dutchy, in a
dressing-gown of dark-red flannel (or what his masculine
ignorance believed to be flannel) with a be-ribboned lace cap
over her plain grey hair, grasping a formidable poker.

'Something very strange is going on downstairs,' said Mrs
Goodier, who seemed for once thoroughly roused. 'We ought
to get Lewis, but he appears to be asleep, because, though I
knocked at his door, he didn't answer.'

'Perhaps he's part of the upset,' suggested Alistair. 'You
stay up here with Dutchy, Aunt Tessa, and I will go down
and investigate.'

'I think it's burglars,' said Mrs Goodier firmly, flourishing
the revolver in what the more experienced Alistair realized
to be a very dangerous fashion.

'All the more reason for you to stay up here.' He was particularly anxious to avoid an encounter between her and Anne, and a glance at his wrist-watch assured him that it had just struck midnight. So he had been less than half an hour in bed, after all.

He found, however, that his advice was the counsel of perfection. Both women were resolutely following him downstairs. He purposely made a considerable noise to give warning of their approach, though the clamour of the storm overrode almost every other sound.

'What was.it you thought you heard?' he asked, not looking over his shoulder.

'A lot of voices.'

'That doesn't sound like burglars.'

'It doesn't sound like Four Acres either, not at midnight.'

Alistair pushed open the library door, and his amazement was presumably equalled by that of the trio on the further side. Even James Goodier, who instantly established himself as the spokesman, and who liked to boast that he wasn't easily flummoxed, was tongue-tied for a full minute by the sight of the two women. And Alistair had to admit that they exhibited a pretty alarming spectacle.

'What's going on here?' demanded Mrs Goodier, waving her weapon in a fashion that made Goodier exclaim, 'For God's sake, my dear boy, take that thing away from her before she's shot one of us.'

This seemed to Alistair good advice. 'It's all right, Aunt Tessa. It's only the household.'

To his surprise there was no sign of Lewis Bishop. Goodier and Bletsoe stood side by side, the former with his hands thrust deep into his pockets, Bletsoe with his hands pressed against the ledge of the bookcase; a little way off, her face inscrutable, was Anne. All three were fully dressed. It was an odd group to find in the big, dignified room, with its rows and rows of books, its wall of windows concealed by heavy draperies, its solid standing lamps – nothing feminine or frivolous there. But if that was all a first glance revealed, a second told a far more disquieting story. Some of the books had been displaced, and lay about on the ledge of the bookcase and on the seats of the tapestry chairs worn dark and faded with use. And where the books had been they could all now see the panel of the safe that Theodore Goodier had had cunningly inserted among the shelves.

'Burglars aren't readers as a rule,' he said. 'They'll look behind pictures, but not much behind books. And seeing what your diamonds are worth, my dearest Tessa, it's as well to be on the safe side.'

But now it appeared that someone had been at the safe, more, that he (or she) had been interrupted in this operation. Otherwise, although one or even two books might be displaced, half a dozen would not be lying about as they now were.

It was Tessa who spoke first. She didn't seem to have noticed the safe.

'Anne, what on earth's going on here? Are you rehearsing for a private play or something? and must you do it at this hour of the night? You've disturbed everyone. Poor Alistair was asleep.'

'Poor Alistair!' repeated Anne. 'What did you think was happening? Another unheralded declaration of war?'

'Really, Anne, you're most unsympathetic. I don't know what's happened to you since you went away. And surely you went up to bed ages ago.'

'Yes,' agreed Anne in the same expressionless voice, 'and I came down again.'

'But what for?' Tessa began to sound suspicious. 'Surely, if you wanted to talk to James . . . '

'I didn't. I didn't know he was going to be here. Or Mr Bletsoe either.'

James Goodier said ruddily, 'Matter of fact, I was looking for Bishop. Hoped I might have a word with him. Been trying to get him all day, but since he's become such a lady's man . . . When I came in I realized he'd been here and would be coming back.'

'How did you know?' asked Alistair, in genuine curiosity.

'Left his cigarette-case on that little table. Well, you know how he is with cigarettes. I've only once seen him hand them round since I've been here. Too good for the likes of us, I suppose, and you're not going to get me to believe he'd leave a whole caseful on that table all night. No, no, he's just gone out for a breather or something, and I thought I'd wait. Matter of fact,' he went on chattily, 'I could have done with one of them myself, but he's not what I'd call a matey chap, if you'll excuse my saying so, Tessa.'

Anne said, 'Aren't there any in the morning-room?'

'In that carved box? There may be, but if so they were there this time last year. I've tried one of them, thank you. Musty isn't the word.'

'And Mr Bletsoe?' said Dutchy. 'Were you looking for Mr Bishop, too?'

Bletsoe, who was clutching a huge tubular torch, changed colour and said, 'As a matter of fact, I was anxious to finish a little conversation we had this morning. We got inter-rupted, and, as Mr Goodier says, there simply hasn't been an opportunity of – er – button-holing Mr Bishop since. I – er – you know he was having the auditors in, just a formality, of course, but there were one or two points I wanted to go over with him . . . '

Tessa, with a rare flash of venom, said, 'And perhaps Anne wanted to see him, too.'

'Not wanted to,' said Anne carefully, 'but – had to.'

Alistair looked at her in consternation. 'Hold hard!' he muttered.

Tessa stared. 'I don't know what you mean by that, dear.'

'Joke!' said Alistair impatiently. 'Anne, show some sense. Anyway, since Bishop isn't here, how about breaking up the party?'

'Good idea,' remarked Goodier in hearty tones. 'Wonder if I could take this book along with me. Eh, Tessa? Volume of voyages by a chap called Hakluyt, Dutchy or would it be Norwegian? Anyhow, he knows his stuff. Plenty of adventure in those days.'

'Perhaps,' suggested Bletsoe, shaking with nervousness, 'we might replace some of these books.' He began to pick them up with unsteady hands.

'Is that the way they were when you came in?' asked Alistair.

'That's another reason why I thought Bishop 'ud be back any minute,' chimed in Goodier. 'Whose idea was it to put a safe there? Theo, I bet. Trust old Theo. He was one of the chaps born to be lucky.'

'Perhaps there's been an attempt at a burglary,' said Bletsoe, 'and Bishop surprised the intruder and is – er – chasing him now.'

'They must be having a good time in this storm,' was Alistair's grim comment.

'I think somebody ought just to look in the garden and see if anything's going on,' suggested Tessa.

'Rather more to the point to look in the safe and see if the diamonds are still there,' corrected Alistair.

Goodier made a shocked clicking noise with his tongue. 'My dear chap!' he remonstrated. 'Going a bit far, isn't it?'

'I don't imagine anyone took down those books for fun,' was Alistair's crisp retort.

'And I suppose the next thing you'll suggest is that there was a conspiracy on foot to lift the thing?'

'That's absurd. All the same, the Goodier necklace is valuable and there is some mystery about the safe.'

'And about Bishop,' muttered Goodier.

'I can at least solve that,' said a new voice, and Lewis Bishop, suave, unruffled, polished as ever, stepped out from between the long velvet curtains masking the windows and stood looking at the group before him, his hands holding a curtain at either side in what Dutchy and Alistair privately thought a ridiculously theatrical way.

'I'm sorry to make this melodramatic entrance,' continued Bishop, who had the field to himself, since everyone else was too much surprised to speak. 'But the fact is I've been acutely embarrassed for the past twenty minutes.'

'Have you spent that time behind the curtains?' demanded Goodier sharply.

'I thought I heard footsteps, and I concealed myself, and I

57

think it was as well that I did. I was the witness of a rather peculiar little scene.'

Goodier turned to Bletsoe. 'Did we say anything that could incriminate us, Bletsoe?' he inquired. 'Of course, if we'd known we had an audience we might have been more careful, but I was under the impression this was a private house, not a vaudeville stage.'

'You can cut that, Goodier,' said Bishop. 'I've been waiting for an opportunity like this for some time, and now that all the family is here seems as good a time as any.'

His gaze moved from Goodier to Bletsoe, from Bletsoe to Anne, rested there a moment and then moved on to Dutchy. Alistair frowned; it seemed to him that the position was, as war correspondents say, deteriorating. He put his hand into his pocket and felt the solid bulk of the revolver; somehow the knowledge that it was there was reassuring.

'Oh dear,' said Tessa, feeling the tension in the atmosphere, and instinctively looking for a way of escape, 'how very dramatic everyone looks. I'm sure there's a perfectly obvious explanation about the diamonds, I mean. I'm certain they're safe.'

Lewis Bishop smiled at her. 'I think they're all right – now,' he said.

Alistair, not choosing to be ousted by a man he would always consider an outsider, returned to his original suggestion.

'It would make things a great deal more comfortable for everyone if we knew that the diamonds are, in fact, where they should be.' He looked round. 'Do you still keep the key on that ring on a nail in the wall?'

'It was Theo's idea,' said Tessa. 'He had so many keys – men seem to collect them somehow – I'm sure I don't know why. And he said that if a burglar did break in he'd never think of looking in an obvious place.'

'Then, provided it's not been moved, we ought to be able to settle this point at once.' Alistair went over to the wall, took a number of keys, tied together with string, from a nail placed slantwise in the angle of the mantelpiece, and identi-

fied one of them. The tension in the room was now very great.
Someone was breathing heavily, but it wasn't easy to know
who it was. As Alistair moved over to the safe there was
another roll of thunder; the rain hurtled down as though it
were being pumped out of the sky.

'You won't have a chimney-pot left intact by morning at
this rate,' Bishop observed easily, watching Alistair fit the
key into the lock.

'They've managed to weather the storm for a couple of
hundred years,' was Alistair's reply, delivered in the frostiest
of voices. 'I daresay they'll last a while longer.'

Bishop laughed. 'I'm all for collecting antiques myself –
when there's money in them,' he said. 'But it's like any other
hobby. It can be overdone.'

Alistair said nothing. He swung open the door of the safe
and stood looking at the contents.

'That's the case, dear,' said Tessa anxiously. 'That one.
That's it.'

Alistair took out the case she indicated, shook it slightly.

'That's not empty,' he observed, 'all the same . . . '

'Did you think it would be?' demanded Goodier.

'Why not?' asked Bishop softly.

'All the same,' continued Alistair slowly, 'I didn't know
diamonds were as light as that.'

He snapped the catch of the case and held it out for them
all to see.

'And apparently I was right,' he said.

They all crowded a little nearer. On the dark velvet bed,
in place of the glittering stars that should have rested there,
they beheld a meagre string of beads.

'This chap's got his head screwed on all right,' exclaimed
Goodier. 'Looks like the professional touch to me.'

'You, perhaps, would know.' That was Bishop, light and
deadly.

Goodier's colour changed. 'And what does that mean?'

Bishop shrugged slightly. 'Surely that shouldn't be difficult
to understand.' He looked across to Tessa and seemed about
to continue when Alistair observed firmly, 'Aunt Tessa, you

do see this is a very uncomfortable situation. I think it would be best for us all if we agreed to resort to the old solution of turning out our pockets. Personally . . . '

Bletsoe said in an agitated voice, 'Oh surely, Major Vereker, you don't suspect any of us of – of the substitution.'

'There are no signs that it's an outside job and Bishop put the diamonds away – when?'

'About an hour ago when Tessa took them off.'

'Yes,' agreed Tessa, 'and you said the clasp was loose and we would have it seen to when we went up to London at the end of the week.'

'I didn't know you were going up to London at the end of the week,' commented Dutchy, disapprovingly.

'I think, Lewis, we ought to tell them,' fluttered Tessa, who seemed far less put out about the disappearance of the diamonds than anyone else in the room. 'The fact is that Lewis thinks I need a rest from – from anxiety and responsibility, and, as he points out, I haven't really the right to claim Alistair's time, he has his own plans to make, and so we've arranged to get married the day after to-morrow.'

'What a sudden fellow you are,' remarked Goodier. If he was acting, thought Alistair, he certainly knew his stuff. 'Or – not so sudden, perhaps.'

Bishop smiled and Alistair shivered involuntarily. It was that sort of smile.

'My dear Goodier, since you ask for an explanation I'm delighted to furnish one. As I said just now, it's time for a little plain speaking. I really don't want to be rude to anyone who is a guest of Mrs Goodier, far less a relative, but, uncomplimentary though the remark may seem, there's no burking the fact that everyone at present under this roof, with the possible exception of the servants of whom I know very little, are here for their own ends. That applies both to relatives and to employees.' Tessa here tried a hurried disclaimer but was firmly silenced. 'I think it only fair that everyone shall understand the position. When we return from our honeymoon there will be sweeping changes that will affect everyone.' Undeterred by the glances of contempt and loathing that he received from every corner of the room, Bishop continued, 'The situation in which we now find ourselves is, to my mind, proof enough of an intention to take advantage of Mrs Goodier's kindness of heart and well-known lack of practical sense.' The smile he gave Tessa robbed the words of their sting, but everyone else in the room had stiffened. Alistair stared steadily at the wall ahead. 'He's getting at us all,' he thought, 'warning us. But especially Anne and me – and, I suppose, Alicia. He'll see to it we're out of the place by the time he comes back.' He had a feeling he couldn't have described; a man suddenly struck blind might feel that way, or someone finding himself in a strange city where he knew no one.

'It's come,' he thought grimly. 'Well, I expected it, didn't I? And I've knocked about enough in the last five years to realize there are other places in the world besides Four Acres.'

Goodier spoke next, and there was no disguising his feelings. 'You needn't think, Bishop, we don't know why you're doing this. And in justice to my brother's memory I must warn you, Tessa, that I'd take any possible step to prevent your marrying that scoundrel.'

'You'd like to murder me, wouldn't you?' suggested Bishop.

'You wouldn't be worth swinging for.'

'This is all very dangerous,' bleated Mr Bletsoe. 'I mean, people saying things when they're not really responsible . . . '

'People who aren't responsible should be in lunatic asylums,' said Dutchy, hardly.

'I'm afraid, Goodier, in spite of your objections, Tessa and I are going to be married,' said Bishop smoothly, but Alistair felt the heat of his mood under the calm words. 'We shan't ask you to outrage your feelings of loyalty to your dead brother by coming to stay with us . . . '

'Oh dear, James, I don't think you're being at all friendly,' quavered Tessa.

'Friendly? I'd sooner see you married to a black mamba.

61

I'll go further. I'd sooner see you in your coffin, my dear Tessa, than married to this – this . . . '

'Oh, there's no need to waste so much breath,' said a new voice. 'He isn't going to marry Aunt Tessa on Thursday or any other day. He can't. He's married already.'

Most of the room turned instinctively towards the speaker. Anne met their combined gaze with an air at once irrevocable and hopeless. That she had during these past few seconds come to some vital decision Alistair was convinced, though he was as far as ever from understanding the nature of Bishop's hold over her. Still, it must be something abnormally grave to have compelled her silence for so long. He was the only one of them to turn his eyes quickly from her face and to glance at the man most affected by her remark, and what he saw there appalled him. His defences suddenly struck down, Bishop now appeared so overwhelmed with hatred, so consumed by ferocity that even Alistair, who had seen enough to harden him during the war years, was shocked beyond speech. God – and all of them – help Anne if she really were in his power, he thought.

'That won't do, Anne,' Dutchy's voice broke imperatively through the silence. 'You must explain what you've just said.'

'It would be better if the explanations were left to me,' said Bishop sharply.

He turned towards Tessa who, however, drew back a step. 'Lewis, I don't understand. What did Anne mean?'

'The fact is that your niece has, quite by chance, happened on a piece of information that I didn't give you because it had no bearing on our engagement and I wanted to spare you any possible distress. Miss Vereker is right. I have been married before. It was a short-lived and quite disastrous affair, and I put an end to it a considerable time ago.'

He spoke with confidence, but Tessa still withdrew herself. 'Theo didn't believe in divorce,' she said. 'He said marriage was a serious affair.'

'Your first husband, Tessa, was an extremely fortunate man. There could be no conceivable reason why he should want a divorce. You always find that the opponents to legislation intended to relax bonds that have proved intolerable are men and women who themselves need no such relief.'

'All the same,' said Tessa, 'I wish you had told me. Or that Anne hadn't.'

'I don't think we need look far to discover Miss Vereker's motive,' Bishop assured her, an ugly look on his face. 'When she proposed a meeting here to-night . . . ' He paused artistically and for an instant no one spoke. Tessa always took a little longer than the next person to accept the implications of a situation or a speech. Alistair and Dutchy were watching her narrowly. Goodier looked crafty, Bletsoe clearly only concerned with preserving his own skin.

Tessa said, 'Anne proposed – is that why you were here?'

Anne drew a deep breath. 'We had to get the matter settled. It was getting too late.'

'I must say, young lady, I consider you've behaved in a most callous manner to your aunt,' boomed Goodier. 'If you really thought Bishop wasn't free to marry why couldn't you have come out with the truth at once?'

'Because at first I was too flabbergasted – the engagement was announced the same night that I arrived, and I'd only just recognized him . . . '

'You did know him then,' interrupted Tessa.

'Yes.'

'Why didn't you tell us?'

'Because no one except you, Aunt Tessa, and not you if you weren't infatuated, would want to admit they'd ever known him.'

'Take care.' Bishop's eyes were black with warning. 'Let me remind you . . . '

'Don't remind me of anything. I know it all. I know you'll tell them . . . '

'Tell us what?'

Anne put out a hand as though she brushed the words aside. 'That doesn't matter, not at the moment. The fact is that after that first night, ever since, in fact, I've been trying to persuade Mr Bishop to break the engagement himself, without – without telling Aunt Tessa the truth.'

'What is this ridiculous truth you keep talking about? Really, Anne, you are very mysterious to-night.'

'The fact that he has a wife already, and . . . '

'He's divorced her, and though I don't like divorce . . . '

'Ask him to prove it. You'll find he can't. Besides, this wouldn't be the first time he's got engaged to a rich woman and then . . . '

'She's out of her mind,' said Bishop contemptuously, 'and in a minute I'll tell you why.'

Tessa's face had gone a sort of dull purple. 'You never told us you had met Mr Bishop,' she repeated. 'I suppose the fact is you were in love with him . . . ' She looked furiously from one to the other.

Anne spoke before she could school herself to discretion. 'I? In love with – with . . . '

Bishop threw up his head. 'It ill becomes you to adopt that superior attitude,' he exclaimed. 'You're not so – fastidious – as you'd like to have your family believe.'

Alistair, feeling intolerably embarrassed, broke in, 'Is it necessary to have all this publicity? Obviously there's some excellent reason why my cousin didn't speak before, and I agree that it would have saved a great deal of difficulty if Mr Bishop could have been persuaded to break off the engagement without plunging us all into this impossible scene. Surely if those of us involved . . . '

'My dear fellow, we're all involved,' boomed James Goodier, who had no intention of being hounded out of a situation that he was finding melodramatic and entrancing. If what the girl said was true that cooked Tessa's goose all right, and there was a thing called the rebound – after a humiliating show-down like this Tessa might well shy from even the mention of marriage in the future, and that would be the chance for yours truly, reflected James, liking Bishop more than he had ever done hitherto.

'I think it might be better, since the matter has gone so far, for us to continue in full session,' said Bishop. 'My dear Tessa,

I would have spared you this, if I could. I'm afraid it's going to be very unpleasant for everyone, and I had sincerely hoped that the – secret – I share with Miss Vereker could have remained buried.'

'I think it's quite time we did have some explanations,' put in Tessa. 'I want to know why my niece is stealing downstairs like a – like a housemaid at midnight to meet my fiancé. And why you, Lewis, didn't tell me you had known Anne.'

The air of helpless adoration she was wont to wear where Bishop was concerned had vanished; she looked bitter, dangerous even, as she faced the pair.

'I didn't want to make this melodramatic assignation,' said Anne using a phrase that she felt fitted her companion in secrecy. 'In fact, ever since the engagement was announced on my first night I've been trying to persuade Mr Bishop to break it off – somehow – and he said I needn't worry, every-thing would be all right. But how could I not worry, seeing I knew how the land lay? At last he said if I met him to-night he'd discuss the matter fully, and – I had to come, Aunt Tessa – I had to come. Because he's right. He does know something I'd give everything I possess – which isn't much – to – to keep hidden. I thought somehow we might strike a bargain, though I wasn't very hopeful, but I never meant to let the marriage go through.' She looked imploringly at them all, but in face after face, Tessa, Dutchy, Alicia, James, she saw a stony suspicion. No sympathy, no understanding. She didn't dare look at Alistair.

'If you were so concerned for your aunt why didn't you tell the truth straight away and chance the consequences?' Dutchy demanded.

'You wouldn't ask me that if you knew what the truth was,' returned Anne, simply.

Bishop laughed. Anne was sheet-white. That laugh was horrible to hear. He'd never forgive Anne for spoiling his market, Alistair realized. Whatever the facts of the case, he could be trusted to present them in their worst light.

'Miss Vereker's right,' he said. 'Perhaps it would be as well now to tell you what it is.'

'No. Not now. Not here. I'll tell them myself, if I must. But you . . . '

'I think I'd better hear your version,' gibed Bishop. 'You might forget some of the details. And it's a good story, my dear, it's a very good story. Oh, I don't say they could get you for it over here now, but – the war's not been over very long, and there are still words that have an ugly ring in English ears, words like . . . '

'No. You shall not. You shall not.' Anne seemed beside herself. Alistair moved. 'Take it easy, Anne.'

Bishop swept the gathering with his hard pitiless eyes. 'As a matter of fact, there are quite a lot of things I could tell you, Tessa, things it would be – enlightening for you to know. You're being cheated, my dear, on all hands. And what's more, I can prove it. I've held my tongue to date. I don't want to make trouble. But now I think it's time we had a little light on the situation.'

There was a louder burst of thunder, a wild flash of lightning, and, as though nature herself were in ironical mood, every light in the house went out.

Chapter 5

THEY all heard Bishop say 'Damn!' And Dutchy muttered something about getting a light. Bletsoe said in a low voice, 'The torch! I had a torch,' and Goodier exclaimed, 'Then, for God's sake, switch it on.'

'I can't find it,' said Bletsoe. 'Oh – wait a minute.' And then they all heard something metallic fall to the floor. Bletsoe went down like an animal fumbling in the dark.

Alistair said, 'I've got some matches. Hold on!'

Everyone seemed milling around, banging into furniture, some article of which went over, a small chair or a table. Mrs Goodier exclaimed, 'What happened? Lewis, where are you? Have you gone away?' And then, 'Alistair, give me your hand. I don't like the dark. I don't understand about

Lewis and Anne. They've both been deceiving me. Oh dear, why did Theo have to die and leave me to look after myself?'

Dutchy touched her arm in passing. 'It's all right. I'm going to get a lamp. And don't worry. If Anne's told the truth it's as well you should know it before it's too late.'

'I don't believe her,' said Tessa defiantly. 'Lewis would have told me. Anyway, we're going to be married. Anne's jealous. I knew that. And she isn't honest. Honest women don't slink down the stairs at this hour of the night to meet other people's fiancés. If it were all above-board why couldn't she have told the truth?'

'Because, my dear Tessa, it's not all above-board.' Lewis seemed to have regained his control. 'Vereker, have you found those matches you spoke of?'

'I've got them,' said Alistair. He struck one and held it over his head. It flared smokily, throwing strange shadows on the faces of those standing within its range, then went out. Alistair struck another, but the fragile stick snapped in two and the head was lost.

'That's the last,' said Alistair irritably. 'Bletsoe, what's wrong with your torch?'

'I – c-can't find it,' stammered the miserable Bletsoe.

Mrs Goodier let out a scream. 'What is it?' asked Bishop.

'Someone touched me – deliberately – tried to pull me off my feet.'

'I'm – I'm sorry, Mrs Goodier. I was feeling for the torch.'

'Dutchy will be back in a minute,' Alistair assured them. He moved and someone else moved at the same time. A sudden flash of lightning showed him Bishop standing outlined against the dark window-curtains that he had parted a little when he emerged from his hiding-place. He thought disgustedly he looked theatrical even now, a sort of Demon King. . . .

A new sound shattered the silence, the unmistakable sound of a shot. Someone brushed against him, he didn't know who; the wind rose, a woman shrieked; the french window that no one had troubled to latch swung violently and somewhere further off came the tinkle of glass.

'One of the windows gone,' thought Alistair. 'Bishop may be more right than I realized. The whole place may be about our ears before morning.'

The rain came down steadily. Like a radio set, thought Alistair, feeling slightly light-headed, nothing stops it, not even a shot. And he surprised himself by saying aloud, 'Was that a shot or . . . ?'

'It's not likely anyone's bursting a motor-cycle tyre on your front drive in this weather,' returned Goodier.

Dutchy's voice sounded from the hall. 'I'm coming. I couldn't find the matches in the dark. What happened then? It – it sounded like a shot.'

Tessa said, 'I hadn't got the revolver, had I, Alistair? Had I, Lewis? Lewis!' No one spoke. 'Lewis, where are you? Hold my hand. I'm frightened.'

Still no one spoke. 'What's happened to you?' Tessa demanded. 'Why don't you speak? Why . . . ? Alistair, it wasn't Lewis, was it? I mean, the shot – and something falling.'

'I'm afraid there's been an accident,' said Alistair steadily. 'Dutchy's coming along now with a lamp. Then we can see what's happened.'

Dutchy came nearer, carrying a lamp in unsteady hands so that it threw a long wavering shadow in front of her. Alistair turned and took it from her, setting it on a small table beside him.

'Take care, dear,' said Tessa. 'It's very near the curtains. We – we don't want a fire . . . '

'That's all right, Aunt Tessa. Now then.' He turned but the words he was going to speak remained unuttered. It was as though his tongue was momentarily paralysed. It was Dutchy who broke that silence.

'Anne!' she said, 'in Heaven's name, what's that you've got in your hand?'

They all turned like feeding cattle. Anne was standing by something dark and dreadful that lay sprawled on the carpet, something with a great hole in its head, lying in what looked like a pool of blood. In her hand was the revolver, and she looked down at the body as if she didn't know what it was. Alistair leaned forward and took the weapon from her.

'You shouldn't have touched that,' he told her sharply. 'I suppose you found it on the floor when you were feeling for the torch.'

'I suppose so,' said Anne, vaguely. 'Alistair, whose is that?'

'I always told Mrs Goodier it was dangerous to keep it loaded.' Like someone taking her turn in a game Dutchy took the revolver from Alistair, and dropped it on the ledge of the bookcase. Alistair moved so that he stood between his aunt and the thing that had once been a man.

'Dutchy, take her away,' he ordered.

'It's Lewis,' said Tessa. 'I know it's Lewis. No, Dutchy, leave go of my arm . . .'

'I'm going to get a doctor, Aunt Tessa. There's been an accident and Bishop's been hurt. It's no good your staying because he's not conscious. When the doctor's been I'll tell you what he says.'

'Is he badly hurt?' whispered Tessa. 'No, Dutchy, I won't go till I have an answer. Alistair, is he badly hurt?'

'I'm afraid he may be,' replied Alistair quietly.

'If ever I saw a chap as dead as mutton it's Bishop,' contributed Goodier loudly.

Tessa stiffened. 'Is that true, Alistair? No, don't try and deceive me. There's been enough of that for one evening, and I don't forgive deception easily. Is he dead?'

'I think he may be. It was pretty close range.'

'Hadn't you better get the doctor?' said Anne in the same vague voice.

'I'll get him at once, though I'm afraid it won't be much good. That's right, Aunt Tessa. You go with Dutchy. There's nothing you can do now.'

'No,' agreed Tessa. 'Nothing any more.'

He wondered if the shock of the frightful thing had rocked her balance. She was going now with Dutchy as docilely as a child. And now trouble arose from a fresh quarter. Bletsoe was leaning against the bookcase, rocking himself to and fro and whimpering, 'Cover it up. In God's name, cover it up.'

'All right. Now, Anne, step back. What is it?'

Anne looked down at her feet in some surprise. 'It's blood,' she said. 'I must have been standing in it.'

The soles of her shoes were sticky and she left dark prints on the carpet as she moved away from the human wreckage. And indeed blood was everywhere – on the curtains beside which he had been standing, on the carpet, on a nearby chair . . . It wasn't altogether surprising Bletsoe felt sick.

'He's right,' he muttered. 'A handkerchief . . . '

'He always kept one the size of a towel in his side-pocket,' offered Goodier. He bent gingerly over the body.

'Look out for the blood,' Alistair warned him.

'Might as well tell me to pick a needle out of a nettle-patch and look out for the stings. Well, someone hated our friend pretty drastically.'

Nobody present liked Goodier, but they all had to admit to a sense of gratitude to him for doing a job from which even the hardened Alistair shrank.

'Got it?' muttered Alistair. 'Anne, you'd better get out of this. Go across to the morning-room. We're all coming in a moment. What is it, man? Isn't the handkerchief there?'

'Oh yes,' said Goodier, pulling it out and dropping it over that faceless horror. 'But – I didn't expect to find this here, too.' He straightened himself and stepped carefully back from the pool of blood. 'Look here.' He held out his hand and they all saw what looked like a rain of stars nestled in his palm. 'The double-crossing fox!' continued Goodier simply. He didn't suffer from the finer feelings and had no sense of impropriety in speaking thus of a dead man whose body at that moment lay at his feet. 'No wonder he wasn't anxious to get on with the search.'

Bletsoe suddenly turned away and put his head between his hands. 'D-don't talk like that,' he said. 'The ch-chap's dead, isn't he? Well then, l-leave him alone. He can't do us any more harm.'

But Goodier, refusing to be misled by Anglo-Saxon sentimentality, observed in the same matter-of-fact tone, 'Easy to see you've never been mixed up in a murder. Oh, my dear chap, of course it is. Guns don't get up and fire themselves. His troubles may be over, but, you take it from me, ours are only just beginning.' He turned and caught Bletsoe's arm in a not unfriendly gesture. 'Come on,' he said. 'Let's get out of this. Vereker's going to call the doctor . . . '

'And the police?' whispered Mr Bletsoe.

'Yes,' said Goodier in the same matter-of-fact tone, 'and the police.'

'You – don't seem to mind,' hazarded Mr Bletsoe, looking with wonder and awe at his massive companion.

'Mind?' repeated Goodier. 'My dear chap, the life of a rolling stone teaches you one thing – always expect the unexpected. All the same, it's damn funny really. I came here, just between you and me, to avoid meeting the police, and here they are, or will be in about five minutes, clamouring on my doorstep.'

*

Alistair, far more disturbed apparently than any of his guests, was aware, as he lifted the telephone receiver from its rest, of a stealthy sound on the stairs above him. He paused and called:

'Who's there?'

'Alistair.' There was a quick soft sound of feet and Alicia rounded the head of the staircase. 'For Heaven's sake, what's going on? Has someone been murdered or what?'

'Sh! Be careful what you say.' Alistair's voice was sharp.

Alicia came to a halt on the third step. 'What does that mean? Not . . . ? But, Alistair, it was only a joke.'

'Not to Bishop it isn't. Nor to the chap who shot him.'

'Shot? Bishop?' Her voice was no higher than a whisper. 'Then it was that. I heard it, but I didn't believe it. I mean, things like that don't happen to oneself . . . '

'They have to happen to someone,' countered Alistair grimly, 'and really considering the turmoil and underground movements that have been going on here it's surprising we haven't had a murder before.'

71

'Murder! Oh no, Alistair.' Alicia caught up her pretty quilted dressing-gown and ran down the stairs. 'Why, no one would be such a fool. It would be too dangerous.'

'Murder's always dangerous, but it gets committed fairly frequently just the same. Personally,' he added in an academic voice that alarmed Alicia more than any emotional display would have done, 'I'd have said murder in this household and in the circumstances in which it did, in fact, take place, would be a bit safer than most.'

Alicia was staring at him, her eyes wide with horror. 'Alistair, you don't know what you're saying. Thank goodness, there's only me to hear. Why, anyone – any stranger – might think you didn't think it mattered that someone's been shot.'

Alistair turned back to the telephone, suddenly aware that the operator had ceased saying, 'Number please?' some time ago.

'It's going to matter to the chap who did it. I said that before, didn't I ? As for Bishop, he was out to ruin us all, and this way he won't be able to ruin more than one of us.'

Alicia ran down the last two or three steps and caught his arm. 'Alistair, do drop that inhuman attitude. Tell me what's happened? All I know is that I heard a noise and then voices and people moving about and I wondered what on earth was up. I thought for a minute one of the old chimneys had come down, and that was the crash I'd heard, and then I heard Dutchy talking to Aunt Tessa, and I opened the window and leaned out. Did you know it was raining?'

'I did. Oh, operator, get me 74 will you? Yes. Thank you. Of course I knew.'

'I didn't. I suppose I'd been to sleep. I leaned out and was half drowned.' She pulled a handkerchief out of her pocket and began to rub her hair. 'I'd have put on a bathing-cap if I'd known. Where are the rest?'

'In the morning-room. Alicia, you'd better keep out of this. You can't tell them anything . . . '

Alicia said slowly, 'That'll be for the police to decide. Oh, I know I can't tell them anything about the actual shooting, but they'll want to see everyone in the house, asking about motive, etc.'

'They're going to have their work cut out if they're going to separate one particular motive from another. Yes, all right, I'm holding on.' That was to the operator. 'You wouldn't think anyone would have the nerve to call a doctor out on a night like this, would you? For anything short of murder, that is. As to motive – what was I saying? Oh yes, they won't be able to see the wood for the trees. Bishop had it in for all of us. I was to sell on commission and you could learn shorthand . . . '

'And Anne?'

But Alistair didn't answer. He had got his connexion at last. 'Doctor Tuke? Alistair Vereker here. I say, there's been an accident. Pretty serious, I'm afraid. A man's been shot. Yes, that's what I said. No, I said an accident. Bishop. You know the fellow? Well, I should think so. I mean, half his head's been blown away. Alicia, for God's sake, either join the others or go back to your room. There's enough nightmare quality to this affair without making it worse. No, I was speaking to Miss Turner. Yes, most of them. Oh yes, I was going to do that. Oh – I see. No, I hadn't realized. Well, in a way that saves time, doesn't it? No, no one there now. Right. I'll lock the door and give the police the key when they arrive.'

He stood there a minute longer, listening, then said, 'Goodbye', and hung up. When he turned Alicia was still standing at his elbow. She looked utterly remote from the scene of horror and blood in the library. Without any real claim to good looks she paid great attention to her appearance, and now, faintly perfumed, wearing her usual light apricot powder, her lips a dull rose, little pearl rings in her ears, she seemed to insist on the ordinary normal life from which during these past hours the rest of them seemed to have been utterly divorced.

'I don't want to bother you, Alistair,' she whispered. 'Just tell me one more thing. Whose revolver was it?'

'Oh – I suppose it had once been Uncle Theo's.'

73

'But who brought it out to-night?'

'Aunt Tessa. She suspected burglars.'

'If Aunt Tessa was holding it of course it would go off. I'm surprised it didn't kill two or three other people.'

'She wasn't holding it. I had it.'

'*You* had it?'

'At least, I'd put it on the table beside me when I was feeling for the matches.'

'But – who saw you do that?'

'No one, I should think, since we were all in the dark.'

'Still, they might hear it.'

'If they were near enough the table they could, but there was so much row, everyone treading on everyone else's toes . . . '

'There must have been one minute . . . '

'When I held up the lighted match – yes. But they'd have to have acted like lightning, the shot came almost immediately afterwards.'

'Who was nearest to it?'

'Bishop himself, I should think. He was standing right up against the curtains, sneering at the lot of us.'

'Put a bullet in the back of his head just at the moment when we all most wanted him out of the way? And with Aunt Tessa's diamonds in his pocket?'

'Aunt Tessa's diamonds?'

'Yes. Oh, I forgot. You didn't know about that. The diamonds were missing from the safe, and we were just going to suggest turning out our pockets in the good old way, when Bishop created a diversion. And after he was shot we found he had the diamonds.'

Alicia turned paler, or so it seemed to her companion. 'Alistair! I don't like that.'

'Well, no one likes it, but . . . '

'You don't see what I mean. Was Anne there?'

'I've told you. We were all there, except you.'

'And she had an appointment to meet him in the library at half past eleven. Does anyone know?'

'Yes. She told them. But – for Heaven's sake, Alicia, stop

74

being melodramatic. You can't imagine Anne knew anything about the diamonds.'

'It isn't what you or I believe about Anne that matters, Alistair. It's what the police think. They're coming, aren't they?'

'I forgot to ring them.' He took up the receiver again.

'Then, don't you see, we must be sure what we're going to tell them, before they arrive.'

'Speaking for myself,' returned Alistair tonelessly, 'I'm going to tell the truth. Anything else would be too dangerous and difficult.'

'You're going to tell the police that Anne had a rendezvous with Bishop, unknown to Aunt Tessa, that subsequently Bishop was shot, and Aunt Tessa's diamonds were found in his pocket. Alistair, I don't understand that.'

'It's not our job to understand it. As for Anne having a rendezvous, that's for her to tell the police, not for us.'

'I'm sorry for Anne,' said Alicia. 'Having to tell them everything.'

'What do you mean by everything?'

'The hold Bishop had over her. He had, of course.'

'I don't see that she's bound to tell them that.' He greeted Dutchy's arrival on the scene with a sigh of relief. 'How's Aunt Tessa?'

'I'm not sure. Calmer in a way than I should have expected. Asked if you'd do anything necessary about the diamonds.'

'The diamonds? Why, I'd forgotten. She doesn't know they were found in Bishop's pocket.'

Dutchy folded her lips tight. 'So that was his game? Of course she'd never suspect him. I suppose she'll have to know.'

'I'm afraid so. The police'll be here any minute.'

'Then Alicia had better go back to bed,' said Dutchy. 'She's lucky enough to be out of this.'

'That's what I've told her,' agreed Alistair, 'but she seems to think her evidence may be of value.'

'She hasn't got any evidence. Not unless she was hiding behind the curtains.'

'I may be a poor relation,' said Alicia fiercely, 'but I'm not an imbecile. And I've enough sense to realize that this is a horrible position for Anne.'

'You don't know anything about Anne and Mr Bishop, do you?' asked Dutchy sternly. .

'Only what ought to have been obvious to everyone – that she had met him before.'

'And what do you make of that?'

'I'm wondering what the police may make of it. Suppose she knows something that might prevent the marriage and she's blackmailing him?'

'Did you say you weren't an imbecile?' asked Alistair.

'Naturally you'd stand by her. That's one of the things one likes so much about you, Alistair. I believe even if you knew that Anne had done it – and what a chance when the lights suddenly snapped off in that dramatic way, with the thunder rolling and the lightning flashing and the rain coming down in floods – and no one could swear to anything in the dark – even if you knew she'd done it you wouldn't give her away, would you?'

'It won't arise,' said Alistair, shortly. 'I know no more than anyone else what happened in that room after the lights went out. And here's someone – presumably Dr Tuke. Dutchy, if you wouldn't mind going in with the others. What about the servants?'

'They sleep in the further wing. They wouldn't hear a shot on a night like this with a storm roaming round the house like a giant in iron boots.'

'I never knew you were a poet, Dutchy,' murmured Alicia.

'There's a lot you don't know. Come on, now. That's the doctor's ring and Alistair doesn't want all the family littering about while he's explaining. Can't you ever take a hint?'

'Oh all right, I'm coming. All the same, Dutchy, there's something very fishy here. I mean, it doesn't make sense him being shot now when Anne's spoilt his market. It ought to have been earlier. I don't understand.'

The rest of the party were waiting uncomfortably enough in the morning-room. Goodier had suggested they might wait in their own rooms, but he had been outvoted. Alistair put his head in at the door to say the doctor had arrived and the police were on the way. Would they please all stay where they were for the present? 'And, Dutchy,' he added, 'I think you ought to warn Aunt Tessa that she may be wanted.'

'She's not fit to see anyone,' said Dutchy flatly.

'Tuke will probably ask to see her, and it'll rest with him when and if she sees the police. Anyhow, she ought to be told. It's been a frightful shock and we don't want anything else on our hands to-night.' He took his cigarette case out of his pocket and snapped it open.

'Damn! I forgot . . . Has anyone . . . ?'

Mr Bletsoe, eager to be helpful, jumped up and ran towards the circular table in the window where a rather decorative box of foreign workmanship always stood.

'Don't give him one of those unless you want to poison him,' exclaimed Goodier. 'They're about five years old.'

'No, it's all right,' said Bletsoe at once. 'The box has just been refilled.'

'With Bishop's own cigarettes, b'Gad! Where did you find them, Bletsoe? He's careful enough as a rule.'

Alistair hesitated, not much caring for the idea of smoking a dead man's cigarettes, and Anne, taking her hand from her pocket, said, 'Have one of mine. Keep the case if you like. I don't want it.'

Alistair took the case and went out. Dutchy and he met in the doorway and Dutchy said in earnest tones, 'Just you remember, Alistair, least said soonest mended. The police aren't like ordinary people, they read ridiculous meanings into the simplest word.'

Alicia watched them, with knitted brows. Did Dutchy know anything? Had she been able to see anything in the dark? Or was it just a general warning? She had that form of loyalty so often found in women that expresses itself in terms of personal affection. She would put her duty as a citizen far below her obligations as a friend.

'For Alistair – or Anne,' she thought. 'But for me? Oh well, it doesn't matter.'

77

The two went out of the room and the others looked at one another uncomfortably. No one said much until the police arrived, when the tension increased notably.

'Will they bring their own doctor?' wondered Alicia, but Anne said, 'Dr Tuke is the police surgeon, isn't he?' and Bletsoe said, 'Yes, Miss Vereker, I hadn't thought of that, but I believe you're right. I believe he is.'

Someone came out of the library and went upstairs. That, presumably, was Tuke going to see Tessa. The door of the morning-room opened and Alistair came in.

'Better be ready,' he told them. 'They'll want to see us all in a minute.'

'Will they see us all together?' asked Alicia, but Alistair said he shouldn't think so, he didn't know much about it.

Then came a heavier foot in the hall and the door opened. A police sergeant came in.

'Everyone here?' he asked.

'Except Mrs Goodier and Miss Dutchley. Dr Tuke's with them.'

'It's about the diamonds,' explained the sergeant.

'I gave them to you,' said Alistair, quickly.

'I don't mean that lot,' the sergeant explained. 'I mean the real necklace. That one's just a fake. Lucky we've got Inspector Heath on the job. If it had been just me I wouldn't have known.'

There was, as the papers say, sensation. For an instant no one spoke, then a minor babel broke out, and ejaculations of: Ridiculous! Impossible! and Fantastic! were heard. If they were actors they were doing it very well. You couldn't have told which if any of them had known the truth.

'This case gets sillier and sillier,' said Alicia frankly. 'I mean, I could understand it if they'd been the real diamonds in Lewis Bishop's pocket. After all, he was planning to get everything Aunt Tessa had, so why not take one instalment in advance. And I don't suppose Aunt Tessa would ever know the difference, and if she did find out the last person she'd suspect would be her darling Lewis.'

'All the same, it still doesn't make sense,' objected Goodier.

'If the stones found in Bishop's pocket were fakes, where are the real ones?'

'In the black market, I should think,' said Alicia.

'What do you know about the black market?' demanded the sergeant.

'If there's a black market in food and a black market in clothing coupons, I should think there'd be a black market in jewels.'

'And you'd be right,' said Goodier. 'Money's changing hands on an unprecedented scale. I've been in the jewel trade most of my life and I've never seen anything like it. What bothers me is why we didn't find the fake ones in the safe?'

The sergeant said repressively, 'That's all right, sir. You can leave that to us.'

'If Alistair had gone on with his suggestion that everyone should turn out their pockets Bishop would have looked pretty silly,' murmured Alicia when the sergeant had departed again with a warning that they'd be wanted for questioning any minute now, but Goodier said, 'Oh, I don't know. He's a resourceful chap. He'd have told us all that he'd surprised a burglar and managed to get the stones back and that's why he was behind the curtain.'

'Only he didn't tell us that,' said Bletsoe, wretchedly.

'Because he didn't have to,' said Goodier.

All this time Anne said nothing. You could no more tell what was going on in her mind than you could guess the contents of a locked box. Bletsoe found it disconcerting, and wished the police would go ahead and get things over. He had never been quite so frightened in his life.

Anne was the first member of the party to be summoned, and after she had been questioned she didn't rejoin the others. The sergeant came back and called for Alicia, leaving Bletsoe and Goodier together. Bletsoe looked as miserable as any human being can. His companion rallied him.

'Don't lose your nerve whatever you do,' he said. 'All you have to do is answer their questions simply, and if they're difficult say you don't remember.'

'They might think they could make me remember,' whispered Bletsoe.

'Don't be bounced into saying anything. Nobody can make you remember. I remember being in a police court once – one of the jury that time – and the counsel for the prosecution was trying to bully a witness into making some admission, and the poor chap kept saying he didn't remember. "But you must remember, Mr Smith," said the counsel for the prosecution, and the judge leaned over and said, "How can he, Mr Robinson, when he has just told you he doesn't? A man's memory doesn't work at lightning speed like that." '

'I don't remember,' repeated Bletsoe, fascinated. 'Though what it is I don't remember ... '

'Don't remember anything it's more convenient to forget,' said Goodier, promptly, and then it was Bletsoe's turn, and Goodier was left quite alone. He was surprised to find he wasn't quite cool. After all, he'd nothing to be afraid of, not a scrap of proof . . . even the police, who could perform stranger miracles than Aaron turning a bunch of rods into a pack of serpents, had nothing on him now. He hadn't Alistair's scruples about smoking a dead man's cigarettes, and he went across to the fancy box and helped himself first to a cigarette to keep him calm while he was waiting and then to a handful more to replenish his case. He hadn't made much out of his visit here, nothing like what he'd hoped. He might as well take anything that offered, even at the eleventh hour . . . He practically emptied the box, then remembered that they'd all seen it nearly full not half an hour ago, and replaced a double layer of cigarettes. After all, he'd got something . . . The room seemed very hot, and Bletsoe seemed to be taking a very long time. He crossed to the window, opened it and looked out. The rain was still coming down steadily. The headlamps of the official car and the doctor's little Austin 8 shone through the darkness. Someone was moving in the drive, an additional member of the Police Force, he supposed, put there as sentry to make sure no one tried to make a bolt for it. He shut the window and leaned against the frame. One hand loosened his collar and tie. What the devil was Bletsoe blabbing about in there? There was a chap you could never trust, but you had to gentle him. It was the same with horses, as Kipling knew. Some you must gentle and some you must lunge, etc. He thought and thought and suddenly he heard the police coming across the hall to fetch him, too, to examination, and only just had time to look in a glass and make certain of his collar and tie.

He didn't have much difficulty, after all, just answered their questions in a straightforward manner and, having more knowledge of police ways than the others, didn't offer any suggestions or theories of his own. The police went off presently, saying the inquest would be opened next day. Alistair would do the formal identification. That was probably all they'd do till after the funeral, as the police intended to ask for a remand.

'What does that mean?' inquired Dutchy, who had her hands full with Tessa and didn't want any more trouble.

'It means they suspect one of us,' returned Alistair heavily. 'But they haven't got enough evidence – proof, rather – to bring a charge. At least, that's how I read it. I think they'll ask for a remand, if that's the right word, in order to continue investigations before they take any definite action.'

'While the rest of us wriggle on hooks like worms, I suppose,' said Dutchy huffily.

'Oh, I don't think you need do much wriggling, Dutchy.'

'And when they do make up their minds,' wound up his companion with the unfairness people in trouble are apt to show towards the police, 'there's nothing to say they won't make them up all wrong. I've got a kettle on,' she continued with no change of tone. 'I'll bring you a cup of tea.'

'Don't bother,' said Alistair vaguely, but she said, 'Oh, I can't do nothing, and who's going to sleep after this?'

The answer was apparently no one. Dutchy went round with her cups of tea, first Alistair, then Tessa, who pushed it on one side, then Anne. She found the girl sitting in front of her dressing-table, staring into the mirror and seeing only Hell knew what ghosts.

'Wake up, Anne,' said Dutchy sharply. 'Get this inside you. You'll feel better then.'

Anne took the cup. 'You shouldn't have bothered,' she said.

'What you want's some sleep,' said Dutchy.

'Oh no,' said Anne quickly. What was the good of sleep unless some magician could guarantee that it would be dreamless? When Dutchy had gone she suddenly put her head in her hands. A braver woman, she thought, wouldn't have let things come to this. If she had spoken at the start Lewis Bishop wouldn't have had to die, and though it was difficult to regret his death, it was harder still not to regret the manner of it.

Dutchy meanwhile went along to Alicia's room and found her also sitting in front of her glass, smearing cream on her face.

'Look at that, Dutchy,' she exclaimed, taking the tea. 'The storm's smashed my window.'

'We heard one go,' agreed Dutchy.

'I suppose,' said Alicia dryly, 'it would have to be mine. Dutchy, how's Alistair?'

'How do you expect him to be?' demanded Dutchy. 'Having hysterics? What did you say to the police?'

Alicia got up from the stool, took a little towel from a drawer and began to wipe down the moleskin coat which lay on a chair close by.

'The rain's come in and wet my coat,' she said with elaborate naturalness. 'Why, Dutchy, what could I tell them? I just answered their questions. That's all.'

Dutchy looked at her suspiciously. 'Didn't tell them who you thought had done it, I suppose?'

'I've no idea. Except, of course, one can guess.'

'And probably guess wrong,' snapped Dutchy. 'Anyhow, you can leave all that to the police. It's what we pay them for.'

Alistair proved right in his supposition. Once the first stage was past the necessary arrangements for Bishop's funeral could be made. He didn't appear to have any relations, at all

82

events none attended the funeral, and there was no legal representation. Alistair, conquering a natural repugnance, asked Anne if she could throw any light on his apparently friendless position, but she shook her head.

'It was like the famous bird in the lighted tent,' she told her cousin. 'He came flying in from darkness and back to darkness. If only he'd stayed there for good and all,' she added desperately.

Alistair hesitated. 'I don't want to harry you,' he said, 'but Aunt Tessa's in a pretty bad taking over this. I don't mean just Bishop's death, but the circumstances . . . She doesn't know about the diamonds,' he added.

'So far as I'm concerned they don't come into it,' said Anne. 'What you mean is it would be a help if you knew why I was consenting to meet Bishop by stealth at night in Aunt Tessa's house. I didn't tell you before, I didn't tell anyone. I did honestly hope that when Bishop saw me again he wouldn't push his plans. The police are lying very low at the moment, but I suppose there's no doubt they'll trace his record.'

'So he had one?'

'Oh yes. He'd been married, more than once, always to rich women, and I know he'd served at least one term for bigamy.'

'Are you suggesting that he was like the famous George Joseph Smith?'

'The Brides in the Bath? No, I don't go as far as that. I don't say he ever committed murder. He'd be too careful.' She drew a deep breath. 'As a matter of fact, that was what he had against me.'

For a moment there was a deadly silence between them.

'You mean,' said Alistair stupidly, 'this had happened before? That is to say,' he caught himself up, 'this isn't the first time you've been involved.'

'That was quick,' said Anne. 'The differences in the situations are twofold. Last time no one knew a murder had been committed – except Mr Bishop – and last time I had shot the man – and I didn't shoot *him*.'

The second pronoun obviously referred to the now decently

interred Mr Bishop. Alistair didn't speak for a moment. Then he said, 'This happened abroad? And why? Was he a – traitor?'

'And my lover.'

'You, Anne? Ah, I believe I begin to understand.'

'You wouldn't ever find it very easy to understand a thing like that, would you? And now that I'm right away from it it's easy to say it was shabby and cheap. But out there, when you measured your life by hours, your standards seemed to change. He was waiting for his divorce to come through, and patience was something you had no time for. People over here have no notion what conditions in Central Europe were like after the Army of Liberation began to spread everywhere. The worst they ever knew was fly-bombs and rockets and having to take Iceland cod instead of lemon sole. But out there we had starvation and disease, and murder for bread was a thing that happened every day. If it hadn't been for what the Allied Powers did to maintain order it would have been a perpetual massacre. And so it seemed enough just to love and be loved. I couldn't think about the future. We could only measure it in hours any way.'

'I know,' said Alistair.

'My job, part of it, was driving the C.-in-C. And I soon learned how to divide myself up into two quite different people. During the day I was a unit, a woman in khaki, part of the Army. I didn't even think of Desmond if I could help it. But when duty was over, when I could relax, then I became Anne Vereker, a person with a name and an individuality. It was like coming out of an endless desert into an English garden. Does that sound fantastic to you?'

'No,' said Alistair, 'I know how it is. When I stopped work I came back in spirit to Four Acres.'

'Because that's your love. General Martindale was very worried because he swore there was a leakage of information and he couldn't trace it. He swore if he could identify the traitor he'd shoot him with his own hands. And – of course you've guessed?'

'This chap was the traitor?'

'Yes. He gave himself away quite by chance late one evening when we were together. Just a word or so muttered carelessly, so carelessly that for a minute I didn't appreciate what he'd said. And then I was stunned, so stunned I hadn't the sense to be diplomatic. I just said, "But if you know that, why, that means . . . " and then he realized.'

'And you shot him – in self-defence?'

'Oh no. Alistair, I've often wondered how women could endure to stay with unfaithful husbands, drunkards, men who wouldn't work for a home. It was amazing to me, that attitude, completely lacking in pride as well as commonsense. But I understand now. I could never pass judgement again. Because even when I knew the truth – and what Desmond had done was worse than being unfaithful, worse than being drunk or losing a job – I didn't hate or despise him. I felt what the Victorians called broken-hearted. I couldn't change all in a minute. Because whatever he'd done he was still the same person he had always been. That's what's so difficult to accept. And nobody's only a drunkard or only a traitor. And so I could go on loving what was left.'

Alistair's hand closed thin and hard over hers. 'Go on, Anne.'

'When he saw that I knew what he'd done he didn't seem to mind as I'd have expected. He said, "Are you really going to spread that story?" and I said, "Don't you see, Desmond, I must?" He said, "It isn't going to sound very pretty, my dear. Or don't you realize what everybody's going to believe?" He meant that I'd made use of my confidential position with General Martindale and brought him the information to sell to the enemy. They could hunt for a year, he said, and they wouldn't find the real source of leakage. He asked me if I was quite sure what I meant to do, and I said "Of course." We were in his office and he opened the drawer of a desk, just like someone in a crime film, and took out a revolver. "Suppose this went off," he said. "The General would be desolate to lose such a valuable assistant. And his subordinates would wonder what on earth you were doing here. Don't you think perhaps that might be a better explanation?" '

'And you said?'

' "Since we're having an orgy of truth there's no sense trying to keep anything back. Tell them we're going to be married." And then he began to laugh. I didn't understand right away. But presently he told me. There wasn't any question of getting married. He'd told his wife – about me – and she agreed to forgive him. He showed me the letter.'

'And then?' prompted Alistair.

'Then I shot him.'

'Without another word?'

'Oh, we talked a little more. He said I hadn't an atom of proof and I saw he was right. He said for my own sake I'd better keep my mouth shut, unless I wanted to be ruined, and if I started talking about him, he'd tell everybody it was just jealousy because he'd – because he'd thrown me over. He said everyone would believe it, and I think he was right. When people were guessing who it could possibly be, selling our own men down the river, no one once suggested him. And I still didn't know the true source of his information. If I went home he'd still go on, unsuspected, getting more powerful perhaps. And even if I spoke I wouldn't be believed, and if I were, even if I were, I couldn't see Desmond executed as a spy in front of his own men and know it was I who had done that to him. And so, it didn't seem to me I had any choice. I took up his revolver and shot him. I'd learned to shoot; everybody out there had to, men and women alike. Of course, it was point-blank range . . . '

'But – didn't anyone hear the sound of the shot?'

'There were patrols out and aircraft going by overhead. An odd shot didn't mean much. But you were right. I didn't get away with it.'

'Bishop knew?'

'Yes. He's like a sort of human hyena always on the prowl for refuse. I think he'd known about me and Desmond for some time, and kept the information to himself till he saw a chance of making use of it. When he heard the shot he knocked and called out "Has anything happened?" and came in. I was still holding the revolver. It was smoking. He stood staring, then he said, "I wondered how long it would be before you did that." Not shocked, not horrified, not even surprised as far as I could see. I couldn't say it was an accident, I couldn't tell him the truth. Bishop came and took the gun out of my hand and rubbed the butt clean with a handkerchief. Then he pressed Desmond's fingers on it and dropped it on the ground, and said, "You don't want to be found here, do you? Everything'll come out, if you are." I said. "I shot him," and he said. "Don't tell me. I don't want to be an accessory after the fact. And even in a war murder is murder." '

'Did he know the story?'

'That Desmond was a traitor? I didn't tell him, and I don't think he was in the plot. I don't think he ever took risks like that. He liked money but he liked to be safe, too. But from what he said in the library I think perhaps he did know. Afterwards I thought if I'd kept my head I'd have gone to the authorities and told them there'd been an accident, I'd picked up his gun . . . '

Alistair shook his head impatiently. 'That wouldn't have cut any ice. What was the verdict?'

'They brought in accident, though one or two people didn't agree. Still, they gave him the benefit of the doubt. And even so,' she wound up defiantly, 'it was better it should be that way.'

'I'm afraid that wouldn't be the official viewpoint. If Bishop was threatening to tell – but what on earth would be gained by that now? He'd be asked at once why he didn't speak at the time.'

'It wasn't that,' murmured Anne, and suddenly Alistair saw the whole picture. She'd loved this fellow, she'd taken risks for him, abandoned the standards in which she'd been reared, discovered he was a traitor and shot him. It was a terrible chapter to have lived through, and no wonder she looked changed. His grip tightened. 'Poor Anne!'

Anne said, 'They tell you history repeats itself, don't they? But one doesn't believe it, until it happens. Just imagine, twice in a lifetime . . . '

He said, 'You didn't say anything to the police?'

'I didn't give them any details.'

'Don't. Not till you've seen a lawyer. I don't know how much you have to tell. But to a jury that would sound fatal.'

'A jury! You think it's coming to that?'

'I don't know, Anne. No one can tell. But one has to be prepared. It might be any of us, and Desmond's story doesn't come into this, not unless you're the person they pitch on.'

'As I may be.'

'Any of us. It's a good field. We're like a pack of hounds running so close you could cover us with a tablecloth.'

Chapter 6.

I

BILL PARSONS, glancing at the front page of the most scurrilous of the morning papers, looked up to observe to Arthur Crook, 'See who they've taken in the Bishop Case?'

Crook, without bothering to look up, replied, 'They most likely took a pin and shoved it in at random. They might have collected any of 'em on the stories they told.'

'Well, if they did, the pin marked the Vereker girl. Anyhow, she's the one they're holding.'

Crook crumpled up the paper he was reading and threw it on the floor. 'Trust the police to do the obvious thing,' he said. 'I suppose they're bankin' on the fact that when the lights came on she was holdin' the little gun in her fist. Now, to my mind, that argues she didn't do it. Because there must have been time for anyone quick-witted enough to have pounced on the gun and killed the fellow to have chucked it away again before the Abigail brought in a lamp. What's her version?'

'The same as before. That she was feeling on the floor for the torch Bletsoe dropped and picked up the gun instead and was so surprised she just hung on to it.'

Crook nodded. 'Before the police started taking courses

in psychology that 'ud have sounded a perfectly reasonable answer,' he said. 'I'd be ready to believe it and I daresay so would you. But not the authorities. They'd rather think she staged things so she could be arrested.'

'I suppose she's as likely as anyone else,'. hazarded Bill carelessly. It wasn't their case.

'Better hang wrong fler than no fler,' quoted Crook, who sometimes surprised people by proving that even he could read. 'She don't tell what her maiden secret was, I suppose? And at that,' he added slitting open a large blue envelope scented with musk, 'I don't mind betting it'll be a lot cleaner than any of the *Record's* readers will believe.'

'I've a hunch I've met this chap Bishop,' said Bill, who had been a leading light in the world of men who are interested in jewels, particularly on the windy side of the law, before a police bullet put an end to his private enterprise.

'I daresay he was calling himself Archdeacon then,' agreed Crook. 'Well, 'tain't our pigeon. When's this fellow, Clarke, coming along to tell me how he couldn't have stolen the notes that were found in his flat?'

'He said about ten. And it could be our pigeon yet.'

'That toney lot?' Crook sounded derisive. 'They don't even know Arthur Crook's born.'

But here, for once, he was wrong.

Mr Clarke had still not arrived when Bill came in, shoved the door to, leaned against it, and said, 'Chap to see you. Vereker's the name.'

'Haven't I heard that . . . ? Lord, Bill, it's not that chap.'

'Come up from Four Acres. Said he was told you might be interested and willing to help.'

'The old family lawyer having washed his hands of same. It could be, Bill, it could be. These respectable wallahs don't like murder, not when there's a scandal in the background, and they're too addlepated or too righteous to know how to get their client off. Tradition's their middle name, and tradition can do a.lot, but it can't blindfold justice, not the way common chaps like you and me can. Shove him in, Bill, shove him in.'

Bill went out and brought back a tall, reserved-looking fellow with an obstinate jaw and a full intention of living up to what Crook called the blue-blooded code.

'Mr Crook?' said the new-comer, and if he was surprised to see the tubby figure in its bright brown suiting, with a brown billycock tilted on the back of a head that looked too large for its body, you'd not have guessed. 'I was recommended to come to you . . . '

'Friend of yours?' suggested Crook heartily, indicating a chair.

'Not precisely. As a matter of fact, it was someone who my cousin – Miss Vereker – met on the train travelling north. This man – he had been in the R.A.F. – stopped me in the street and told me that you specialized in difficult cases, and . . . '

'I get you,' said Crook. 'By the way, seen the young lady since she was arrested?'

'As representing the family, the police gave me permission, in order to make the necessary arrangements for the defence.'

'Well,' Crook assured him, 'you've come to the right man. Only one thing to be done, of course.'

'Yes?' said Alistair. Crook didn't much like that stupendous calm. It boded danger, and there was danger enough threatening his client as it was.

'Find the chap who really did it.'

'And you think you can do it?'

'It's what you're going to pay me for. I'll want to see all the witnesses, of course. And I'll get Aubrey Bruce. He's our best man. If anyone can persuade a jury black's white he's the chap to do it.'

Alistair said stiffly, 'I don't know whether I've made myself clear. I believe my cousin to be innocent.'

'Very nice,' agreed Crook. 'But you do see, don't you, it don't cut much ice with the great B.P. as represented by twelve good men and true in the jury box? What you're havin' me for is to show she couldn't have done it, and the only way of doin' that is to show that someone else did. Of course,' he added honestly, 'there are times when that can't be done, mostly because your client is unofficially guilty. Then you have to be satisfied with a Not Proven verdict, but I don't call that satisfactory myself, and I doubt if the young lady would either. It means that for the rest of your life you're pointed out as one of the lucky ones who got away with it.'

'There are plenty of facts to work on,' said Alistair. 'It's just a matter of arranging them in the right order.'

Crook's little bright eyes widened in amazed delight. He thrust a great hand across the table.

'Have a cigar,' he said. 'We usually get to Lesson Three or Four before I can start tryin' to make my clients understand that. Remember Mark Twain, wasn't it? Give me the facts and I will arrange them as suits me best. Words to that effect. Mind you, I'm no miracle-worker. Just one foot after another, one foot after another till you get to the top of the mountain. That's me. If ever I get into the Landed Gentry I'm goin' to have that for my crest – a bowler hat and that motto right round it. Now let's get down to brass tacks.'

'What exactly do you want to know?' inquired Alistair, slightly breathless at the speed of his companion's attack.

'Everything,' returned Crook, comprehensively. 'Everything you saw or remember, everything anybody said or did, never mind if it don't seem important to you – it's the little things that matter, don't you see? The morning's yours and it's still young. But, mind you,' he added warningly, 'this is a professional's job and I don't want any amateurs butting in. And if you don't like my choice of murderer any more than you like the one the police have fixed on, it'll be too late to ask me to throw up the case. I'm like that dog you see in the shop windows with a Union Jack on its back and a cigar in its mouth – I hold on till death – and not my death or the young lady's.'
                                              *

After Alistair had gone Crook called Bill into conference.

'That's a nice chap, Bill,' he said thoughtfully. 'Mark you, he belongs to the age of the Dodo, but there was something to be said for Dodos. Swears his cousin's innocent. Hasn't an idea who did it, of course. And he could be right at that.'

'Got enough sense to realize justice may not see eye to eye with him?'

'Enough sense to know she may have done it. There's a history of something remarkably like murder a year or so back, but I'll know more about that when I've seen the lady herself. Of course, the police will wallow in that yarn. If she put a bullet through a chap's head one year why not the next? As a matter of fact, that seems to me hopeful. If you've shot one chap through the head and seen what he looks like it's long odds against your shooting another. And from what he tells me I should have said she was the sort of independent young woman to put one bullet in Bishop and the next in herself. So much more comfortable than linin' up for the little covered shed.'

'D'you suppose he's gone prancing back to tell her she can't have done it even if she thinks she has, now you've taken the case on?'

'I wouldn't say he was the prancing sort, Bill. I can just see that chap in a white wig and satin unmentionables. No, our trouble's goin' to be the girl. That's where these modern women make the mistake. Too damned independent. They can kick as much as they like but men are still the chaps who cook the world's pudding. Women may add some of the kickshaws, a spot of flavouring here, a dab of angelica there,' carolled Crook becoming positively lyrical as his imagination soared, 'but if you took the bits and pieces away the pudding wouldn't taste very different. I sometimes think,' and now his voice was positively dreamy, 'it must have been wonderful to have had a job like this at a time when women didn't want to stand on their No. 6 feet, but just swooned about on day beds and sociables – so much less interfering.'

But Bill only said that swooning on a sociable wasn't his idea of comfort. He was like one of those flash lighters that are all looks and no flint. You could literally work your fingers to the bone without getting an answering flash from him.

Crook told him so.

II

The murder had taken place on a Tuesday. The police arrested Anne Vereker on Friday, Alistair came to town to see Crook the following Tuesday and on Wednesday morning Crook started his investigations. He went first of all to the prison to see his client and when he'd verified some of her story he decided to call it a day. Thursday he'd start tracking down some of the other witnesses. But before Thursday dawned something else had happened which threw fresh light on the tragic affair.

Act Two, Scene One, of the drama was set for nine o'clock on Wednesday night, scene the Embankment near the Houses of Parliament. It was one of those wild cloudy nights well-known to the British in winter, with racing clouds flying through a dark sky, and a haggard moon perpetually overwhelmed by their ferocity. As Big Ben struck nine, the sound loading the air, thought the man hiding in the shadows, with awful portent, the moon disappeared altogether, and as though he had been waiting for a sign, as people have done all down the ages, the watcher crouching by the railings with the river on one side and Westminster Underground Station on the other, took a timid step forward and hesitated on the kerb. He knew, of course, that Crook had taken over the case, and he had taken the trouble to make some inquiries and realized that Crook was that dangerous creature, the man with a professional conscience. There was no stone too deeply embedded for Crook to leave it unturned, and his nerves were so strong that nothing he found there would dismay him. Ever since that night in the library when some unseen hand fired a fatal shot and took a human life, the poor wretch had forgotten what it was to move without fear at his elbow to whisper threats in to his ear, fear at his pillow to disturb his sleep, fear waiting on the step as he opened his door to accompany him throughout the day. At any instant he expected a hand to descend on his shoulder. He had feared Lewis Bishop living, but not as he now feared Lewis Bishop dead.

He was racked by the thought that his movements were being checked, that he was being followed at every turn. He would stop suddenly in a crowd, expecting someone to speak, to halt him. He heard voices where no voices rang, and footsteps that existed only in his fevered imagination. He knew that Crook would never be satisfied until he had set Anne Vereker free, and he knew, too, that he wouldn't care if the whole of the rest of the household was strung up so long as he attained that end.

He had meant to cross to the Station and put through a telephone call from one of the boxes there, but as he stepped off the kerb it seemed to him that the place was full of people, among whom was the one detailed to watch his movements, and he made a sudden swerve that almost threw him under the wheels of a passing lorry. Oblivious to the driver's fury he ducked away and down on to the Embankment where he found a solitary telephone box almost in the black shadow of the bridge. He shut himself inside, cast a fearful glance over his shoulder, realized that the darkness might conceal a horde of devils unperceived by him, and proceeded to dial a number. When he heard a hearty voice speak he replied in a whisper, scarcely audible inside the box itself.

'Over to you,' said the voice, and he muttered, 'Is – is that Mr Crook, Mr Arthur Crook?' He was like some insect darting out its tongue for a fraction of a second to secure its prey.

'Press Button A.' suggested the voice with unimpaired cheerfulness.

'Yes – yes, of course. Stupid of me.' He pressed the button and heard the coins fall.

'Now then, let's have it,' said the voice.

'Mr Crook?'

'That's right.'

'It's – I'm afraid it's a bit late to be telephoning, but – er – the fact is . . . '

'Don't trouble to explain,' said Crook smoothly. 'I've heard 'em all. Matter of fact, the P.M.G.'s thinking of putting on a special charge for calls after dark, there are so many on this line.'

The anonymous caller began a creepy little laugh, then checked it as though that, too, might be heard. 'The fact is, I – I wanted to see you. It's urgent. And very secret.'

'They're all that,' said Crook, in a kind voice. 'Did you say a name?'

'Oh. Smith. Mr Smith.'

'If that's the way you want it,' agreed Crook. 'When did you think of looking in?'

'I thought – I suppose, of course, it's too late to-night.'

'Wait a little longer and it'll be morning and then you'll be able to suppose it's too early. I'll expect you in ten minutes. By the way, where are you speaking from?'

'I – I'm in a telephone booth at Westminster. On – on the Embankment. My telephone's out of order. That is, I'm staying at an hotel and . . . '

'I didn't suppose you were in a place of your own,' said Crook placidly. 'Otherwise, why Button A?'

'Oh? No. You're right, of course. I – I suppose you get used to thinking of everything.'

'All that matters is for me to think of it before the police do.'

'Yes. As a matter of course, it's – it's about the Goodier-Bishop case I wanted to consult you.'

'Ah!' For an instant he had jerked Crook out of his casual pose. 'Come right up. Going to tell me who did it?'

'No. No. Only – I know it wasn't Miss Vereker, whatever the police may believe.'

'Well, I could have told you that,' expostulated Crook. 'No sense paying for a taxi round here if you haven't got more than that to tell me.'

'I have. I have. Oh, I don't mean I know who did it, but I do know it couldn't have been her. I suppose you think I ought to have told the police right out, instead of bothering you, but I didn't think . . . '

'No bother,' Crook assured him. 'Little jobs like this are my bread-and-butter, remember. Besides, I like to come in on the ground floor before the flatties have put their great feet over everything. Be seeing you.'

The man in the telephone booth hung up the receiver very gently, even trying by some complicated manipulation of his fingers to silence the discreet tinkle of the telephone bell. He stood for a moment longer in the box, then jerked abruptly round and opened the door. He took two steps forward, stopped and looked round again. The night seemed darker than ever. The moon was still obscured. He knew a pang of resentment because of that. What was the moon in the sky for except to light the night? If you'd mentioned tides to him he'd have turned away in childish exasperation. He stood where he was, trembling with indecision, reminding himself that it still wasn't too late to draw back. Crook only knew him as a voice – for who was Mr Smith among the thousands of Smiths in the Metropolis alone? It was dangerous, look at it whichever way you liked, to come into the open. The pseudo Mr Smith hesitated. Better perhaps to let events take their course. Everyone said British justice was paramount, and if a girl hadn't committed a murder she couldn't be hanged for it. All the same, he shivered. He couldn't forget the horror of the previous week, the day they'd come for her and taken her away, the look in Alistair's eyes, the feeling as though Death had just alighted at the door and stood on the porch with folded wings.

'I'll have to go,' he told himself desperately. 'I've gone too far to retreat now. I told him Smith, but he's not a fool. He may guess who I am, and then if I don't come he'll think I'm implicated.'

He wheeled round, and it seemed to him that something under the shadow of the bridge wheeled with him. For a second he was transfixed with horror, then moved quickly towards some place where a street lamp might provide a little illumination. It was ridiculous to have put this booth in so dark a corner. There was an odd sound that he did not at first identify as the beating of his own heart. Then, with sudden resolve, he stood a step forward – and another; but as he did so his earlier suspicions were confirmed. Something in the darkness had turned with him, the shadows jerked, and, as he stopped, icy with fright, the hand he had feared ever since the night of Lewis Bishop's death, fell firmly on his shoulder.

'Why, if it isn't Mr Bletsoe,' boomed a genial voice. 'Queer place to find a fellow on a night like this.'

Mr Bletsoe had to wait a minute before he could control his voice. Then he said huskily, 'Telephone – had to telephone. Mine's out of order, the one at my hotel, I mean.'

'They do go wrong without warning, don't they?' agreed Mr Goodier. 'It's funny about yours. I rang through to your hotel a little while ago, and it seemed all right then.'

'Haven't got an instrument in my room,' explained Bletsoe hurriedly. 'Don't put them in the small rooms on the top floor. What was it you wanted?'

'Just wanted to make sure you weren't getting into mischief.'

Bletsoe thought he detected the sound of an approaching taxi and made a quick dart forward. Instantly the hand on his shoulder tightened like a vice.

'No hurry. You've got a minute for an old friend, surely.'

'It's a taxi,' said Mr Bletsoe wildly, trying to shake himself free.

'What if it is?' The other sounded truculent, dangerous even. 'You don't want it.'

'But I do. It's important. I – I have an appointment.'

'Oh? Just made it perhaps?'

'I – you've no right to try and detain me like this.'

'Funny sort of appointment if you couldn't make it from your hotel. Quite one of the lads, aren't you?' The grip relaxed a little as the taxi went out of sight and earshot. Mr Bletsoe drew a long breath that was almost a sob.

'I wanted that taxi,' he said.

'No, you didn't. You don't want any taxi. You just want a bus to take you back to wherever you're staying. Don't you? Don't you now?'

'I – I wanted that taxi.'

'Who were you going to see?'

'Just – just a friend. It's no affair of yours,' added Mr Bletsoe, plucking up a little courage.

'That's what I want to be sure of. It wasn't the police, by any chance?'

'No. Of course not. I – I've seen enough of the police to last me a lifetime.'

'Nor Mr Crook perhaps?'

Mr Bletsoe gulped, 'That's my affair.'

'And mine. Don't you realize, you fool, we're all in this together? What were you going to tell Mr Crook?'

'That – that she didn't do it. I know she didn't do it.'

'So does he. But can you prove it?'

'I – well, yes, in a way.'

'There's only one way and that is by confessing to the crime yourself. Is that what you were going to do?'

'Of course not.' Bletsoe sounded indignant. 'How could I? I didn't shoot Bishop. I wouldn't know how to handle a gun. But Miss Vereker didn't either – shoot him, I mean.'

'Funny you've only just thought about it. Or is this something you told the police and they wouldn't listen.'

'No. I didn't tell them. I hadn't thought – I mean . . . '

'I know what you mean. You mean you've only just thought up a story. Well, what is it? Remember, Crook's like a human rhinoceros, tears through anything at all flimsy. Your story'll have to be cast-iron to get by him.'

'It is cast-iron. I'll tell you what it is. When the lights went out Miss Vereker was standing by me.'

'Well?'

'I – I don't like the dark. I never did, even as a child. I hated the blackout, it frightened me more than any of the raids. When I was a boy . . . '

'Never mind about your being a boy. That's too far off to matter. What happened?'

'When the lights went out I put out my hand just to – to reassure myself I wasn't alone, and I caught her wrist. I held it . . . Why, what are you laughing at?'

For the big man had put back his head and was roaring away in a low bass chuckle that nearly drove Mr Bletsoe demented.

'You poor sap!' exclaimed Goodier, when the paroxysm

had passed. 'Is that what you're going to tell them? Well, you can forget all about it. Because it wasn't Miss Vereker's wrist you were holding – it was mine.'

'But . . . I don't believe it. Why didn't you say anything about it before?'

'Think I wanted to give the police anything else to laugh at? Two grown men standing in the dark, holding hands. Besides, no one would have believed us.'

'Why not?'

'Too obvious. Because if we were holding one another then neither of us could have been the killer.'

'Well,' said Mr Bletsoe in a whisper, 'we weren't. At least, I wasn't.'

'They're only too ready to believe we're plotting together in any case,' continued Goodier inexorably. 'We were the first on the scene, remember.'

'I remember.'

'Do you?' said Goodier. 'I don't know why you should sound so mysterious about it. There's nothing special to remember – is there?'

'N-no, of course not,' said Bletsoe, but there was no conviction in his voice.

'Then you do see you haven't really got any reason to go and talk to Mr Crook, have you? And Crook's a dangerous man. All he cares about is getting this girl off. Justice is a word he couldn't even spell. If you go round to Crook he'll disembowel you, and how is that going to help you? Besides, why didn't Miss Vereker mention that you were holding her wrist?'

'I thought she might not have remembered – but if it was your wrist I was holding . . . Though I don't really believe you . . . '

'Well, perhaps I don't either,' conceded his companion. 'But you see what a silly story it is. You could never prove it, never. And if you take my tip you'll lie low. Being marked down for murder's no fun, and you wouldn't get Crook to defend you. Your best tip is to keep out of the limelight. Directly you move they'll all be on to you. That's what they're waiting for. Ever seen a cat after a mouse? Besides, just you go on remembering a little longer, and you'll see how good my advice is.'

'I don't understand you.'

'Oh yes, you do.' He laughed again, a great bawling sound that went rolling across the dark water and startled the gulls who were perched, like a white fringe, on the edge of a barge rocking mildly with the tide. They rose up in a white cloud, hesitated and settled again. 'Listen. Bishop was getting someone in to audit the accounts, wasn't he?'

'Well?' Bletsoe's voice was suddenly sharp. 'Why not?'

'Not very convenient, was it?'

'I don't understand.'

'Don't go on saying you don't understand, or I shall think you're completely bughouse. Still, let me refresh your memory? You haven't forgotten Miss Trentham?'

The silence that followed that question was as black as the night about them. Out of it presently came the merest whisper of sound that was Bletsoe's voice. 'Did you say – Miss Trentham?'

'Yes. Your last employer, wasn't she? Don't they say history repeats itself? There was some trouble about accounts there, wasn't there?'

'She – never made any accusation,' flashed from Bletsoe's white lips.

'But she thought, in the circumstances, it might be as well if you packed your grip. No hard words, but – well, she felt a bit safer with you off the premises.'

'I don't know how you know so much about my affairs . . . '

'Make it my business, my dear fellow. As soon as this thing broke I thought it would be best for you and me to hang together – no pun intended. And since Bishop was getting the auditors in – it occurred to me there might be a spot of bother you'd be glad to avoid.'

'There's nothing I couldn't explain.'

'Trouble is chaps like Bishop generally prefer their own explanations. Besides, you've just admitted you don't know anything. You don't, do you?'

'I – of course I don't.'

'That's what I thought. All the same, Crook's a persuasive chap. It would be a pity to open your mouth too wide, wouldn't it? I mean things once said, if they aren't true, leave an impression not always easy to wipe out, and so – well, I'm sure we understand one another,' he wound up, softly. 'You didn't tell this chap anything on the phone, did you?'

'No. He didn't give me the chance.'

'Wise fellow. And, you know, the police don't pull in a young lady like that in her auntie's house, not without some good reason.'

'I – suppose not. All right. I – I think I'll be getting back.'

'Good idea. Hallo, isn't that another taxi? Now, you sound a bit tuckered up, why not stand yourself a nice drive home? You were going to take a cab anyway. Taxi!'

The vehicle drew nearer, halted at the kerb. 'In you go,' said Goodier jovially.

Bletsoe, unaccustomed to taxis, infinitely preferring a bus where the fare was fixed and there was no vexed question of tipping, was nevertheless sufficiently anxious to be rid of his companion to turn eagerly towards the waiting cab.

'Where's he to go?' inquired Goodier.

'Oh – Hunterscombe House, Marlowe Street. It's a sort of hotel. I'm just staying there for a few days.'

'Here,' said the driver suspiciously, 'you sure your friend's all right?'

''Course he's all right,' said Goodier. 'Aren't you, old man? Got a bit of a cold, that's all.'

'I don't want any gentleman being ill in my cab,' said the driver. He looked a morose sort of man.

'He's not going to be ill. Wants to go back to a hot toddy and a nice fire, that's what he wants. Well, so long, old man. I'll ring up some time.'

He stood watching the little red light until the cab disappeared. He wished he knew what Bletsoe, that poor little worm, had in mind. He was such a fool he'd risk his skin without knowing what he was doing. Suddenly he remembered that Crook would be waiting for his visitor, and if he didn't arrive was perfectly capable of descending on the Hunterscombe Hotel and digging his quarry out. Terriers had nothing on Crook when he was on a case.

Goodier turned back towards the telephone box, and found Crook's number and made the connexion.

'And now,' he thought, 'what the devil do we do next?'

The trouble with a jam like this is that you can never be sure what the other fellows are doing, and they can cook your goose completely by taking some unanticipated action which throws all your careful planning utterly out of gear.

Chapter 7

MR CROOK, having jauntily hung up his receiver, turned to his companion and observed, 'There, praise the pigs, was the missing link. Now all we have to pray for is that he don't get bowled over by a taxi or a big bad drunk on his way round.'

Aubrey Bruce, K.C., to whom consultations with Crook at this hour of night were no novelty, said in his cool voice, 'Kind of him to walk into your net, isn't it?'

'Ever heard of self-preservation?' inquired Mr Crook. 'He ain't coming here because he wants to save Miss Vereker. You and me are going to do that. He's coming because he wants to make sure we don't put him in her place.'

'What a cynic you are, Crook!' objected Bruce, following his usual conversational occupation of drawing fishes on the blotting-paper. 'What's he like?'

'He says his name's Smith.'

'That's helpful. Who is he really?'

'If he shows up, we'll both know. Drawin' a bow at a venture I should say it began with a B.'

Bruce began to draw a little pale fish with a head too big for its body and a tail too feeble to act as an efficient rudder. Crook watched him with some disapproval.

'One of these days,' he warned him, 'you'll commit a

crime yourself, just to show how it's done, and you'll give me the job of proving you couldn't have done it because you weren't there. And then you'll give yourself away by leavin' a picture of the victim as a sturgeon or a lemon sole or something on the underside of the mantelpiece, and all the fat'll be in the fire. And I'll lose my reputation, which, as ladies in more innocent days used to say about their honour, is more to me than life.'

Bruce laughed. 'You'll end up in Parliament yet, Crook,' he prophesied.

'Only as a corpse. Though I daresay I wouldn't be particularly noticeable at that. But seriously, Bruce, it's a bad habit. You ought to break yourself of it. Anything's bad that stamps a man.'

'And how about your brown billycock? That must be known from Land's End to John o' Groats.'

'That's different,' said Crook, as Bruce had known he would. 'All I have to do is leave the billycock at home and buy something at Henry Heath, and I'm immediately mistaken for a country gentleman. No one would ever guess.'

Bruce thought that uncommonly likely, but all he said was, 'It's to be hoped this chap will give us a line. It's not a very promising case to date, particularly knowing what we do about the girl's past history. It won't come into court, of course . . . '

'But every lady who's had her hat tilted over her eyes fighting for a seat will know it was something too shocking for decent women like herself to know about. Matter of fact, there's no reason why her story shouldn't be true. The guilty generally think up somethin' much more elaborate.'

'Pity so many people handled the weapon,' suggested Bruce. 'No chance of identifying any particular finger-prints . . . '

'And that might have been a mixed blessing. Too many of them anyway. That's the trouble with this case,' he added, producing a fresh supply of cigars. 'Too much altogether. It's like one of those pictures you see. There are too many people with a motive for putting this chap, Bishop, out of the way. Of course, in the pictures it's done to make it harder – for the audience, I mean. What I like is a case where there ain't too many chaps in focus. Then you can pick out a likely one and build up a case. But who am I expected to choose here? It could have been practically any of 'em.'

'Hardly young Vereker,' suggested Bruce. 'Even if he was capable of shooting a man in the dark in what he still regarded as his own house, he wouldn't let his cousin be tried for murder.'

Crook groaned. 'You toney chaps!' he said. 'Take it from me, Bruce, even if one fellow's been to Eton and the other to the elementary school, there's not much to choose between 'em when it comes to getting hanged. They're both pretty keen to see someone else do the dangling.'

Bruce felt, as he'd sometimes done before, as if he'd banged his head against a stone wall. However, he knew from experience it was no use trying to argue the point with a man as sure of himself as Crook invariably was.

'Mind you,' Crook continued, 'I'm with you. I don't think Vereker did do it. It's not easy for an amateur to strike matches and shoot off a gun at the same time. But all the rest of 'em could be in it. And even he had enough motive for six murders, and he could have done it, Bruce, he could have done it. That type – you'd have thought a second world war would have stamped it out, but no! up it pops out of the wreckage. He wouldn't think so much of putting Bishop out as some of the others. I've noticed fellows like that think a house and history matters much more than an individual, and you can't altogether blame him.'

'No?' murmured Bruce, ironically.

'Well, a grateful Government's been payin' him for years to go round jabbin' a knife in all and sundry – so long as it wasn't an ally – and that kind of thing becomes a habit. It does really. When I came back from France at the end of '18 the first time a chap got in my way I looked round for my pig-stickin' iron. Still, you say a chap that was at Eton doesn't act that way and you should know. There's Suspect No. 1, washed out. No. 2's the girl, and she can't have done it

because you and me are frankin' her, and speaking for myself
I don't like stringing along with the police anyway.'

'Then, of course, she's out. How about the housekeeper?'

'Well?' said Crook, 'why not? She's goin' to find herself
out of a job and maybe short of a legacy, once the knot's tied.
And she's no chicken.'

'And they've got her finger-prints on the weapon,' en-
couraged Bruce.

'And at least three witnesses to swear they saw her take
the gun away from young Vereker – what's eating us, Bruce?
Of course she didn't do it. She wasn't in the room.'

Bruce smiled. 'I didn't think you'd let a little thing like
that stop you.'

'I have known it happen,' Crook admitted. 'You don't
have to be on the spot. Then there's Mrs Goodier herself. It's
amazin' what lengths a deceived woman will go to, and the
older they are the harder they take it. What 'ud happen if
you had a deceived nonagenarian I hate to think. And don't
tell me she didn't believe there was some hanky-panky going
on between her best-beloved and that girl. She's a woman of
her generation and she knows that chaps and dames don't
meet at half past eleven in sleeping houses, by stealth, except
for one reason, and a whole Bench of Bishops plus the Presid-
ent of the Law Courts couldn't tell her different.'

'If you're right,' meditated Bruce, 'why didn't she shoot
the girl?'

'Because if she had it 'ud be as clear as mud who was the
guilty party. No one else in the room had any motive. The
girl had done all the damage she could, and this might be
killin' two birds with one stone.'

'Meaning that things have worked out the way she anticipated? You may have something there, Crook, though
you're going to have your work cut out to prove it.'

'You're telling me,' said Crook. 'Trouble is the lady has a
slow brain. By the time she got round to thinking there was a
gun in the room and that people can be killed with guns the
sun would have risen on the new day – leastways, that's how
I read the dame. Still, hate's a great educator, and I daresay

you're right. There's nothing 'ud please Mrs G. more than to see the girl swing for a murder she hadn't committed.'

'The morality of women is something that fills a legal man with awe,' said Bruce, putting his pencil down. He spoke as if he meant precisely what he said.

'Don't tell me,' begged Crook.

'If Mrs Goodier did kill Bishop she'd be quite capable of arguing that, since her niece had committed something worse than murder she'd be perfectly justified in holding her tongue.'

'And if it wasn't that that young chap had had the sense to tell Vereker to contact me, she might have held it to the day of doom and after,' Crook agreed. 'And before long she'd have persuaded herself that the girl was as guilty as if she'd pressed the trigger.'

'That leaves the two most likely suspects, Bletsoe and Goodier. I wonder what exactly they were doing in the library that night.'

'Ah well, maybe that's what Bletsoe's coming to tell us,' suggested Crook, optimistically.

'He ought to be here any minute now, unless he had trouble with a taxi.'

'If he comes.' Crook sounded a bit grim. 'I wouldn't care to be in his shoes if he has got anything to tell. In fact, in his place I'd go straight from here into a nursing home with four policemen round my bed, two at the foot and two at the head, one to watch and one to pray and two to keep the wolf away.'

As he finished speaking the telephone started to ring. Crook put out his hand.

'You do have a lot of night callers,' murmured Bruce gently.

'I don't think this one's a caller. I think this is a chap changing his mind.'

He took off the receiver, listened for an instant, then hung up again.

'Bletsoe not coming?' asked Bruce, when it seemed clear that Crook was not disposed to talk.

'No,' agreed Crook. 'Not to-night anyway.'

'Lost his courage, I suppose. Or got halfway here and decided it was too risky.'

'That's a funny thing,' said Crook, and now he was merely meditative, not annoyed or disheartened as you might have expected. 'You see, I'm pretty sure the chap who rang up just now isn't the chap who telephoned before.'

Bruce digested that for a minute. 'Meaning he's being followed?'

'It could be.'

'And the follower's dissuaded him?'

Crook got up. He looked positively agitated. He put out his hand and grabbed his shapeless mackintosh from a hook in the wall. 'I don't like this, Bruce, I don't like it one little bit. Why didn't Bletsoe ring up himself the second time? And where is this telephone booth on the Embankment?'

'I suppose you mean we're going to look for it,' suggested Bruce impatiently.

'Just to make sure there isn't anyone inside who shouldn't be there,' explained Crook.

His meaning was perfectly clear. Bruce had a picture of the pair of them opening the door of the booth and something slumping out into their arms. A Corpse by Candlelight, he reflected, pulling on a coat that made Crook's look more disreputable than ever. Crook didn't waste words, and this gravity impressed his companion. He knew there was fear in the lawyer's mind. They found a taxi and asked the driver if he knew where there was a telephone box on the Embankment, and the driver said he didn't, but if there was one they'd find it, and they cruised along until Crook said they might as well get out here and walk. After that they tried every telephone booth they came to, but though there was a hulking great lout gesticulating and shaking his fist in one, and a girl with a long yellow bob and a picture black velvet hat was doing her stuff in another – just as though we'd got television already, said Crook scornfully – they found no sign of Mr Bletsoe or anyone like him. Nor were there any bodies scattered about the fairway, though Crook, who was con-

ANTHONY GILBERT

scientiousness incarnate when he was on a case, inspected
the occupants of all the benches, saying it was an old trick to
lay a stiff out, particularly in winter, and hope the doctor
who examined him would be so blind drunk he'd think he'd
succumbed to exposure. But there was no one on the benches
remotely like Mr Bletsoe – or the wolf, come to that, though
they didn't yet know what shape the aforesaid wolf might
assume.

'There's still the river,' said Crook, when he had exhausted
every other possibility.

'You weren't thinking of dragging that to-night?' objected
Bruce politely.

'Mustn't do the police out of a job,' returned Crook in
gloomy tones. 'They get a quid a corpse, you know, and if we
drag 'em out they keep half anyway and it's supposed to be
noblesse oblige to let 'em keep the other half. Putting temptation in the way of the Force, I call it,' he added with some
warmth. 'See some old misery leaning over the edge, all he
wants is a shove from a leg of mutton fist to go under, and
there's money for jam for P.C. Smith, Brown, and Robinson.'

'He might get him out alive,' objected Bruce.

'He'd be a damn fool if he did. He'd only get a medal, and
don't tell me anyone's goin' to give you a quid for the sort of
medal they issue at the Home Office. Ah well, call it a day.
I'll dig the little chap out in the morning – Mahomet and the
Mountain, you know.'

But, as it happened, the morning was too late.

Chapter 8

In a small room at the end of the corridor on the top floor
of Hunterscombe House, a second-class hotel of the boarding-
house type in Marlowe Street, WC1, a doomed man sat
crouched in a chair feverishly working a typewriter. He was
not a very skilled operator and he made a good many mistakes, but he persevered, perpetually encouraging his poor

efforts with the thought that once this was done, mistakes weren't going to matter any more. For this night would spell the end of everything for poor, ineffectual Henry Bletsoe. Death wasn't a nice thought, particularly the type of death involved here, but at this stage it was the only solution. He kept reminding himself of that as he typed the last will and testament. He found a certain poor sort of humour in the phrase.

'This,' he typed laboriously, 'is the last will and testament of me, Henry Bletsoe, late of Four Acres, Martinshire, and now of Hunterscombe House, London.' (He didn't know much about law but he supposed that was all right.) It was a wretched story, this life of a man who had never really achieved anything for which he had set out, a tale of poor beginnings, mediocre attainment, mistakes that had proved too costly to be met, chances taken and stakes lost, fear and a feeble grasping after a security that had played cat and mouse with him, only to elude him at the last. When the sorry tale was told and the clods had rattled down on to the coffin – would they bring it in suicide while of unsound mind or would he even be refused the sanctuary of consecrated ground? he thought most likely the latter – it would be as though he had never existed, except that Anne Vereker would be free and the rest of the party safe from the suspicion of murder. He worked slowly, with long pauses, because he had to put all the relevant facts into their right order and he couldn't do the job twice, he had neither the nerve nor the time. It was hard enough as it was with a dead man, so to speak, at your elbow. He'd got to be careful, because really every word was important. He'd made so many messes in his life. This mustn't be yet one more to add to the list. No sense Henry Bletsoe dying if his death didn't achieve its object.

He came back to the typewriter. 'This is the last will and testament of me, Henry Bletsoe. I never meant to make it, not like this, but I've no choice now. I thought I could go through with it, but I can't. I didn't mean it to work out this way.' He stopped, staring at what he had written. He had meant this last echo of a lost life to have a fine romantic

109

flavour, so that people would say there must have been something there if someone had dug deep enough. Twopence
coloured, that had been his intention, though his experience
had nearly all been penny plain, damnably so. 'Before I go
on I have a confession to make.' (It didn't really matter how
bald it was) 'I killed Lewis Bishop. Yes, I killed him, and in
any civilized country I'd be regarded as a public benefactor.
He's the sort of man who's a murderer a hundred times over,
but the law can't touch him. There wasn't one life in that
room that night he wouldn't have taken if he could, just as
surely as if he deliberately put poison in their food. Such men
shouldn't be allowed to live. I hadn't meant to kill him, all
the same. I didn't think I'd have had the pluck.' He meant
to elaborate that, but a glance at the watch on his wrist
warned him that time was drawing short. Someone might
come in, something might spoil everything, and now he had
embarked on the job he had got to finish it. To-morrow
would be too late. 'But the chance came suddenly when the
lights went out, and I realized that he meant to crush me as
surely as you put your shoe on some insignificant insect that
crawls a little too near you. I'd better start at the beginning.
That means the diamonds. You see, I needed money, I
needed it desperately. It's infamous that because of one mistake a man has to go on paying and paying all his life.' (He
hesitated; better not say any more; keep it vague, uncertain.
There'd be questions asked as it was.) 'Well, there it was.
I needed money. Mrs Goodier might have lent it me, but not
Bishop. He had a piece of ice where his heart should be.
When I mooted the point, what happened? He gave me the
sack. After all I'd done during the war, he told me I could get
out, when I'd finished working out my notice. You'd think
rich people could afford to be a bit kind, and what had they
ever done for their money? But there's not enough money in
the world to help a chap who's down and out. It was the same
when I was with Miss Trentham. She was fair, oh yes, but a
penny over the bargain and it 'ud be, "I don't understand
this account, Mr Bletsoe. It seems to me . . . " Mrs Goodier
wasn't so precise. I could pull the wool over her eyes a bit.

110

When Bishop came, though, I knew we were heading for trouble. At first I didn't care. I thought he was just a visitor. But he stayed on, began to have a finger in every pie. Suppose I had juggled the accounts a little? What were a few pounds more or less to Theodore Goodier's widow! And she never suggested paying me more. Then Vereker came home. I hoped that would mean the end of Bishop, but it was too late. He'd dug himself in by then. She was infatuated.

'Bishop didn't lose any time. He got me the sack and said before I went he'd get the accounts checked. That made me desperate. You see, it didn't give me enough time to put things straight. And all the time I was being hammered for money. I couldn't even sleep at night for hearing voices. People say money doesn't matter. That isn't true. The only time it doesn't matter is when you've got plenty. Anyhow, there it was. I had to have money. I couldn't get it from anyone in that house. They say a man who's worth while has friends who will see him through bad times. The man who said that had never had a bad time. It's in bad times your friends go abroad or get married – anything that makes it impossible for them to help you. Well, here I was, needing money, having to get it from somewhere, faced with unemployment, and there in the safe were the diamonds. I knew they were worth a packet and I thought it was worth taking a chance. I could say next morning I'd had a letter or a telephone call asking me to go to town for an interview. Even Bishop couldn't refuse that, and I could take the diamonds with me. Anyway it seemed worth risking.

'I suppose I should have known it would be a failure. That that would be the one night that half the household would be awake and listening. It seemed all right at first. I got the safe open and the diamonds out, working by torchlight, and then without warning the door opened – I hadn't even heard footsteps – and Goodier came in. I don't know what I thought – offering him a share, perhaps – pretending I was putting them away – anything. But I didn't get a chance. He's too downy a bird for me. "You everlasting fool," he said, "put those things back. Do you want to do ten years?" I tried to say that Mrs Goodier had sent me down to get them, but it wasn't any use. We were still arguing when Miss Vereker came in. I didn't see at first what had happened to the dia- monds, but Goodier snatched them out of my hand, and told Miss Vereker we were waiting to see Bishop. Of course, she saw the safe at once, and I knew she didn't believe a word we said. I asked her if she knew where Bishop was and she said no, but if we were waiting for him, so would she. I didn't know then it was a rendezvous. She didn't talk any more, just leaned against the book-case. I wanted to put back the books that concealed the safe – I'd already put the key back because the safe closed automatically – but when I started to move she said no. Whoever had removed the books would probably like to replace them. Goodier said perhaps there had been a thief, and Bishop had surprised him and was on his track, and she said, yes, perhaps, but I don't think she believed it. Anyway, she didn't seem to care. After that I somehow wasn't surprised when the rest of the family turned up. I suppose we'd been making more noise than we realized. In about five minutes everything began to happen at once. I had an appalling shock when Major Vereker suggested we should all empty our pockets. I don't know what we'd have done, but Bishop saved the situation for the moment. But only for the moment. As soon as he said he'd been behind the curtains all the time I knew it was him or me. What I didn't under- stand was how I could possibly win. Then the lights went out, and I thought of strangling him, only he was twice my size, so that was no good; then Major Vereker lighted his match and held it over his head and in the flash I saw the revolver where he'd put it down on the little table by the curtains. Everybody was moving about and it seemed to me there was a one-in-a-thousand chance. No one could swear to anything in the dark. As for finger-prints, several people had handled it already, and if I threw the thing on the floor after firing it the odds were someone would pick it up to examine it and obliterate my finger-prints. Anyway, it seemed to me worth the risk.

'I dropped my torch deliberately to give me an excuse to

move about, and with everyone muttering and colliding it wasn't difficult to grab the weapon and fire it at point-blank range – there was a streak of light from the windows and I could hardly miss – and then drop the gun and drop back on the floor. I grabbed Mrs Goodier by the ankle so she should know I was down there. Then, I thought, they wouldn't suspect me.' Was there anything else, any detail he'd left out? He might as well make the whole position clear, since no one was going to be able to ask any supplementary questions once the confession was found. Time was rushing on, it was time to make an end. He was feeling a bit reckless. Everything was so nearly over. 'They say British justice doesn't err. It erred this time, though I daresay Arthur Crook will put it right. But if he does it'll only be by picking the real killer, and I can't stand the suspense. Anyway, how could I let her hang? It's not as though I'd anything really to live for. I'm like a man chasing his hat all his life and never quite catching up with it.

'I see now that Goodier was right. If I'd told my story I'd never have been believed, and it would only have meant putting off the evil day. This is best really. I can see that now.'

It seemed to him rather a drop from the lofty ending he had originally conceived, but he couldn't make any alterations, there wasn't time. He didn't even stop to re-read what he'd written. There might be an interruption and that was the one thing he couldn't face. For some minutes now he'd heard restless movements next door and once he thought he'd heard someone knocking on the wall. He supposed that the would-be sleeper in the next room objected to a typewriter being driven at eleven o'clock at night.

'It's all right,' he found himself muttering. 'I've finished now.'

Taking a pen from his pocket he was shocked to find that his hand was shaking. He glanced at the last sentence on the sheet he had just peeled out of the machine and signed it – Henry Bletsoe. Careful crossing of the T, neat little line under the second half of the signature – all men had their idiosyncrasies. He took up a bit of blotting paper and laid it carefully over the bright blue signature. He put the sheets together –

no time to correct typing errors and the sense must be clear enough even to a moron – folded them, thrust them into a long cheap envelope lying on the table and stuck it up. To The Coroner – that was how it had to be addressed, though he supposed it was really the police who would open it – he didn't know for sure. There was a packet of Victory sign labels, produced for the benefit of a war-time charity, lying on the table – this sort of charitable economy was produced for people like Mr Bletsoe – and he ripped one out and wound it into the machine. But as he began to type the words – and only three of them – something happened that stiffened him with horror, so that for the moment he was even past trembling.

Someone was knocking at the door. Whoever it was knocked a second time. He called out, in a trembling unrecognizable voice, 'Who – who's that?'

'I say,' said someone, 'are you going to type much longer? It's gone eleven, you know.'

'N-no. Not another word.' He was half-choked with relief. and he called out again, 'S-sorry you've been disturbed.'

'That's all right,' said the voice. 'I know work has to be done, but – well, after eleven's a bit thick.'

Feet went along the passage and the nearest door was heard to close.

'No, Henry Bletsoe,' said the man staring at the confession he'd just signed, 'no time to lose. Quick, before your nerve goes.'

He stuck the label on the envelope, didn't stop to cover the typewriter; might make a row and bring that chap back. His eyes turned, fascinated with horror towards a corner of the room. Here in the ceiling someone had caused a hook to be placed, why no one knew, unless it was that a cautious fate had foreseen the hour when ineffectual little Henry Bletsoe would dangle there. He threw one final glance round. You'd say that hook wouldn't take the weight of a body, but you'd be wrong. He opened the window wide, turned out the fire and went slowly, slowly over to the corner, carrying a chair with him.

*

It was, perhaps, a minute later that Miss Mittens, who had a room directly under Mr Bletsoe's, heard a sudden sharp crash, such as might be made by a chair overturning, as she explained later. Mr Hunter and others thought it would have been more convincing if she had suggested the chair before knowing it couldn't have been anything else. Miss Mittens was one of those disappointed women, called by the heartless 'elderly girls', in whom hope, though drooping, is never utterly defeated. She had believed as a girl that life would be delightful, gay, adventurous, and romantic. She had cherished dreams of youthful love, had seen herself, when these failed to materialize, as the charming not quite so young companion of an intelligent man – say, a Member of Parliament – and when even this hope was proved vain, she thought she might mother some ineffectual little creature who needed kindness and confidence. She had marked out Mr Bletsoe on sight. Such a poor little creature, who obviously needed someone on whom to lean.

When she heard the sound overhead she jumped to her feet, telling herself perhaps he had fainted. She hesitated a moment, recalling the lateness of the hour and the fact that she was somewhat loosely wrapped in a home-made hostess gown. Surely it would not be outraging the proprieties to run upstairs and at all events knock on his door and make certain he was all right. He was a bachelor, you could see at a glance, the sort of man who's never had a woman to look after him. Hurriedly she began to pull on a more sedate dress. Feet sounded on the stairs and she hesitated again. She didn't realize the difference those few seconds were going to make. What mainly concerned her was the thought of what people might say if they saw her, a spinster, going uninvited, after eleven o'clock at night, to a strange man's room. Since she came to live in hotels she had been shocked at the state of people's minds, and though one must not shrink from doing one's duty one need not go out looking for martyrdom, which generally turned out to be a most unbecoming state of affairs.

What with one thing and another probably as much as

five minutes elapsed between Miss Mittens hearing the sound of the falling chair, as it subsequently proved to be, and her stealthy, half-fearing, half-entranced ascent of the stairs. The lighting here was poor and it was improbable that she would be recognized even if her form were seen gliding (so she liked to think) towards the top floor. Her breath was coming rather fast, and she paused to be sure she had full control of her voice before she whispered his name. Even at this moment she remembered Mr Rush in the room next door, Mr Rush who was a civil servant and therefore a person of great enterprise. It was Miss Mittens' experience that people with enterprise can find plenty of opportunities for exploiting it, without having any extra ones handed them on a silver salver with parsley round the edge. Besides, he was a natural F-F. F-F had been the name in her family for Fault-Finder. If Mr Rush had ever had a wife, thought Miss Mittens, saying a little louder, 'Mr Bletsoe, Mr Bletsoe, are you sure you're all right,' she would have left him long ago, either for Heaven or some more congenial companion.

When Mr Bletsoe did not answer she ventured to rap on the door, very softly at first, then somewhat louder, at the same time repeating his name. And still there was no response.

'Dear me!' thought Miss Mittens, 'perhaps I should call Mr Hunter.'

But she had the spinster's natural shyness of men and their equally natural aversion from the thought of causing trouble – the impoverished spinster, that is. She knew that if you have no wedding ring and no money you practically have no right to be alive. So, having listened very carefully for the sound of movement within the room and the sound of footsteps without, she turned the handle and opened the door a crack, and, no thunderbolt falling and no voice cursing her from Heaven, she dared to put her head round the door. The light was full on or naturally she would have gone away, modestly assuming that Mr Bletsoe was in bed and had, perhaps, having a nightmare, thrown over a table.

She was mouthing an apology as her head came round the door, but it was never spoken. Instead she forgot all about disturbing the difficult Mr Rush or the diffident Mr Bletsoe, and the whole hotel was aroused, shocked and in some cases enraged, in others titillated, by the sound of one piercing shriek following another, descending from the top floor. Up the stairs came pounding feet, preceded by voices wanting to know what on earth – the hell – in Heaven's name – was wrong, and was it murder or what?

Mr Hunter, the proprietor of Hunterscombe House, was furious at the development. Nothing got a hotel a worse name than a suicide, particularly when the suicide was connected with a murder trial that has not yet taken place. Suicides meant police on the premises and quite a lot of people, with unexceptional connexions, don't care much about the police. And to have the police calling at their hotel late in the evening, asking questions and making notes, and then sending for an ambulance and using words like 'strangulation' and 'mortuary' was gall and wormwood to Mr Hunter. If only Miss Mittens hadn't been so officious nothing would have been discovered till next day, when half the residents would have departed to their work, and he might have got rid of all signs of the tiresome little hypochondriac before their return. Men had no right to come into other men's houses for the purpose of taking their lives. If they were tired of them, what was wrong with the river? Then (as Crook had observed to Aubrey Bruce) someone profited, if only the police to the tune of a pound a body, whereas this way nobody profited, and the hotel definitely lost some of its reputation, and it hadn't very much to lose at the best of times.

He, of course, came up with all the rest to find Miss Mittens having hysterics, several ladies standing by, futilely slapping her hands or beseeching her to sit up, there's a dear, while two men had contrived to cut down the grisly little burden from its hook, and were trying to induce some sign of life therein. But, of course, entirely without success.

'Not that I'm surprised,' said one gloomy gentleman to another. 'Can't think what they put these hooks here for. Temptation to the feeble-minded, that's what they are.'

Mr Hunter swallowed his rage for the time being, sent one

of the waiters to fetch a doctor, and addressed himself to Miss Mittens. He made it quite clear that he thought it a bit fishy that she should be up in a male visitor's room at this hour. She was still trying to explain when the police arrived and took over from him.

She explained that she didn't really know Mr Bletsoe, he'd only been at the hotel for a few days, but she'd noticed him because she could see he had something on his mind. No, he'd never talked to her, she hadn't liked to intrude upon his grief, whatever it might be, but somehow he'd been on her mind (You know how it is, and the officer said patiently and with truth, yes, he knew) and when she heard the bang she thought perhaps there'd been an accident, and anyway there couldn't be any harm just coming to make sure.

'Good thing you did come. Otherwise no one would have known about it till morning.'

Miss Mittens said with a deep watery sigh, 'I'm afraid it didn't help him much.'

'Well, that's not your fault. Did you see him earlier to-night?'

'As a matter of fact, I saw him come in. I happened to be on the stairs. The front door's open till about eleven so as to save the servants, and he happened to pass me. I said "Good-evening", but I don't think he heard. I suppose he was thinking then what he was going to do.' She looked as though she was going to relapse into hysterics once more.

It was obvious to him that she didn't really know anything, and he passed on to Mr Rush. Mr Rush assumed a certain importance in that he was the last person who had actually spoken to Mr Bletsoe.

'I knocked on his door just after eleven to ask if he intended to go on typing much longer. He'd been pretty restless most of the evening. I heard the door open and shut once or twice, and bumping sounds as though he were repacking his bag. I wondered if he was in some sort of trouble and was planning a moonshiny getaway. And then the typing started. That would be, I suppose, somewhere around ten o'clock. I knew he had a typewriter, because I'd seen it on the table one day

118

when his door was open, but he didn't use it much as a rule. Writing for jobs, I daresay.' He tee-hee'd a minute.

'Yes, sir,' said the official, unsympathetically. 'What happened when you knocked on his door?'

'He said he'd finished – sounded a bit scared, I thought. After about a minute I heard this chair go over, and I began to wonder if he was a bit – well – a bit blotto, but of course a man who's in that state can't generally type at a pretty even speed for the better part of an hour. I did just tap on the wall when I heard the noise to warn him that some people have to be up early and go to work and need their sleep, but I didn't want any unpleasantness if I could help it. And the next thing that happened was this lady screaming the place down.'

'Can't blame her for that,' said the official stolidly. 'Not a pretty sight.'

'I might have gone in myself when I heard him groaning and uttering the way he was,' said Mr Rush a shade uneasily, 'but I don't believe in sticking your nose into other chaps' affairs . . . '

'Quite,' said the official. There wasn't anything more to be learnt from Mr Rush.

The doctor Hunter had called in wasn't the police surgeon, who was laid by the heels with influenza. This man was abrupt, young middle-age, couldn't see any sense wasting a lot of time on a chap who was past help, and he wanted to get some sleep before his next call which would probably be about four a.m. He was very brief with the police, said cause of death was strangulation, and what the devil did you expect with hooks sticking out of the ceiling asking for half-wits to drape themselves on them, and off he went. He'd have to attend the inquest anyhow, and there was more time wasted. Miss Mittens detained him by asking tremulously whether there was anything she could have done if she'd been quicker, and he said no, nothing, it wasn't her fault, and if the chap was that sort no one was much worse off for his loss. He offered to give her something to make her sleep, but she said she'd take an aspirin. It had the most wonderful effect. She thought it was because she was very temperate about drugs.

'So are most people,' snapped the doctor who, like Mr Dick's aunt, hated a fool, and off he went. Later still there was a discreet sound of wheels and then feet on the stairs, and not long afterwards the same feet going down, more slowly, more carefully, more heavily than before, because they were carrying something now, and even a small man makes an absurdly heavy corpse.

Chapter 9

AFTER he had parted from Bletsoe James Goodier did not go straight home. He didn't think much of his hotel, which was the best he could afford, and all the men there seemed close-fisted chaps who'd pass out sooner than ask you what's yours? As for the girls, it was a long time since they could hope to pass even in a crowd. What with one thing and another he was worried to death, and he didn't attempt to disguise the truth from himself. He hadn't even the spirit necessary for self-deception. Ever since the murder he had felt anxious, because Bletsoe was such a weak little chap, the sort of fellow you could get the truth out of by twisting his arm or threatening him with a gun – practically. This evening's conversation had done nothing to reassure Goodier. True, Bletsoe had been prevented from visiting Crook, but you couldn't count on a fellow like that. By to-morrow his weak obstinacy might have reasserted itself and off he'd pad, hot-foot, to put his neck in a noose, and, if possible, imperil someone else's neck, too.

Goodier made the familiar journey from anxiety to dismay and from dismay to anger. He went into the Grey Swan and ordered a double whisky and slammed out and dropped in the Lovely Bully and had another double there. They wouldn't give him more than one, said the stuff was short, and he said so was life, and crossed the road to the Bag of Nails and managed to get a couple before the barman, an ex-Service chap with a voice like a bull of Bashan, began to shout 'Time, Gentlemen, Time'. By this time he felt better able to manage his fate and, eluding a lovely lady who tried to stop him, he paid one or two more calls, and, still feeling disinclined for his solitary uninviting rooms, he succumbed to the blandishments of a blonde by the grace of Shaftesbury Avenue, and it was two o'clock when he slunk in. It was nearly nine o'clock when he opened his morning paper and saw the story of Mr Bletsoe splashed right across the front page.

At first he simply couldn't believe it. He rubbed his eyes, which were bleary, with a hand that was shaking and read through the column again and it made exactly as much or as little sense as it had done before. Whatever he'd anticipated it hadn't been reading this story before he had so much as a cup of tea inside him. The press wasn't giving much away, presumably because it hadn't got much. It made the most of Miss Mittens and Mr Rush and said the deceased had left a letter for the Coroner. It was very guarded, indeed, as newspapers have to be about the manner of death, since no one would know for certain how Bletsoe died until they had been instructed by a coroner's jury, though the Man-in-the-Street might, with justice, think his guess as good as the next man's. Goodier frowned. He didn't know much about police procedure in England, and he wondered if there were anything significant in the fact that the press gave no hint of the contents of the letter. Perhaps that had to wait till the inquest.

'If my name's mentioned in the letter I shall have the police round here,' reflected Mr Goodier, laboriously getting out of bed, and seeing himself (with a pardonable shudder) in the long wall mirror that hung opposite. He didn't look his best in pyjamas, with tousled hair and something of a pot-belly, and the curly moustache was definitely ragged after the frolics of the night. He staggered over to the built-in washbasin and turned on the cold tap.

The more he thought about the case the less he liked it. He felt like someone walking along a board in the dark. He might fall off any minute and crash to a horrible death. Crook had complicated matters abominably. He wasn't like the police,

steady, reliable, going right through the alphabet, A to B,
B to C. Crook jumped from A to Z and back to N or M, with
no sense of not playing fair. By the time he was dressed he had
decided it was his duty to get in touch with the police, and he
set out, after a sketchy sort of breakfast, to assist justice. If
they found the taxi-driver who took Bletsoe home last night,
the fellow would be certain to remember that he had a friend
with him, and Goodier didn't care for the idea of seeing himself in the press as 'the man the police are anxious to interview.' So when he had finished shaving he put on his hat and
coat and went out. He was a bit shocked to find that the police
displayed no special enthusiasm at the sight of him. He had
to explain more than once who he was and what he'd come
about. He said he was the last chap to see Bletsoe alive, if you
excepted the taxi-driver, and if there was anything he could
do, well, here he was.

The first policeman he saw asked him to wait and went and
fetched a red-haired sergeant whose mother might have been
the original Lady into Fox. Mr Goodier explained that he
was a stranger to England, having spent most of his life sleeping under the stars in Patagonia, etc., etc., but he thought
that as he had known the deceased and as he'd never heard
him mention any relation he might be a chap the police
would like to contact. The police sergeant warmed a little and
asked a few questions, which Goodier answered readily
enough, saying that Bletsoe had seemed badly upset the night
before, though he had had no reason to suppose that he intended violence. He had spoken quite wildly about the arrest
of Anne Vereker for a murder that, he swore, she had not
committed, and had even tried to concoct some cock-and-
bull story that he proposed to take to the defence.

'But he didn't get there?' suggested the foxy sergeant.

'I had to warn him he was simply calling attention to himself,' said Mr Goodier. 'He was one of those chaps who don't
know how to take care of themselves. He saw my point after a
minute and a taxi came by and he went off.'

Questioned, he said he supposed this would be about half
past nine.

'You didn't hear from him again?'

'Well, there wasn't much time.' He stopped, struck by a new thought. 'You mean, he might have tried to ring me? But he hadn't got a telephone in his room, he told me that, and in any case I wasn't in.'

He completed his statement, said he'd had a drink or two and then met a friend. He was indignant when the police asked for the friend's name.

'I must say I quite see why people aren't anxious to help the force,' he exclaimed. 'What's all this got to do with Bletsoe committing suicide?'

'Just routine,' said the sergeant.

'Well, I don't know her name – or her address,' Goodier had to confess. 'I got in about two. The night porter could confirm that.'

He signed the formal statement in his usual flourishing hand, and was told that the inquest would be held at two o'clock and he would be wanted. He tried to find out if the police had read the letter referred to in the press, meaning to lead on (if he got any encouragement) to a further question as to whether he was mentioned in it. But receiving no encouragement at all he held his peace and went out looking rather as though he expected the authorities to stop him. It was a relief to think that by to-night it would all be over.

*

Crook also saw the news – Witness in Bishop Murder Case found hanged – rubbed his big nose, picked up the telephone and got in touch with Aubrey Bruce.

'This is right up your street,' he said. 'Fishy. See?'

Bruce, sounding as restrained as a strait-waistcoat, thought Crook, said yes, he saw.

'Too damn convenient, followin' the telephone call and all that,' elaborated Crook.

'I see he left a letter for the Coroner,' murmured Bruce.

'I don't like these death-bed confessions, supposing that's what it is, and what's more, the police don't like 'em either. Mean to say, there's no proof, and if a chap's going to put

123

himself out he may as well take responsibility – and if he didn't do it, Bruce, that means justice is defeated.'

'Bit new for you to worry about justice,' suggested Bruce.

'I've a pretty good idea who killed Lewis Bishop, and I'm pretty sure it wasn't Henry Bletsoe.' Crook sounded as indignant as a man who had been promised a peerage and suddenly has all his anticipations defeated by some backstairs intrigue.

'Still, a chap doesn't hang himself for fun,' objected Bruce.

'I don't think Bletsoe had much fun.' Crook's voice sounded grim. 'He was bein' blackmailed – that we do know – and he was feelin' a bit desperate. If he couldn't keep up the payments when he was in a job things were likely to be a whole lot worse when he was on the unemployed list. Oh, I daresay life didn't look too good to him. Besides, there was that chap he was talking to on the Embankment, the one who put the fear of Arthur Crook into him, so that he didn't dare keep his date with me last night. He may be the blackmailer. Y'know, we'll never get true justice in this country till they hang for blackmail. It's the most insidious form of murder there is.'

'We don't yet know that he has confessed to Bishop's murder,' said Bruce in his mildest voice.

'Don't seem much sense in him swinging from a doornail if he hasn't,' said Crook, sounding a bit contemptuous. 'Anyway, I don't mind betting that's what he has done. He's probably a romantic little cuss at heart. These rabbity little chaps usually are. Here's a chance, he thinks. I'll take the blame. And some sentimental fool may say that one about nothing so became his life as the leaving of it. As a matter of fact,' he added thoughtfully, 'the police are pretty fly. They may not take his confession – assumin' he left one – at its face value.'

And as it happened the inquest held surprises for them all.

*

It began tamely enough. Goodier identified the body, the manager not being able to go further than say that it was the body of the man who had registered as Henry Bletsoe. Goodier, however, cleared up any doubt that might have existed on that head, and repeated his story of his last night's meeting with that ill-fated little man. The taxi-driver had been traced and he confirmed Goodier's evidence. It was a little after half past nine when he picked up his fare and about a quarter to ten when he deposited him at the door of the Hunterscombe House Hotel. He had thought at the time that the gentleman was queer.

'What exactly do you mean by queer?' asked the coroner.

'Well, funny-like. To tell you the truth,' he added expansively, 'I thought 'e'd 'ad one or two. Sort of dazed 'e was. I 'ad 'arf a mind to say I 'adn't got the petrol – well, I can't afford to 'ave gents being sick in my cab – but I couldn't smell nothing on 'is breath and I thought it might be just the fog and the cold ... '

'And you got this impression during the few seconds he was speaking to you?'

'I'm telling you, ain't I?' said the taxi-driver indignantly. 'It wasn't only 'im, it was 'is friend. Seemed too blooming anxious to me, and I didn't want 'im dying in my cab either. Mind you, I don't say there was anything wrong, but I got the feeling 'e wasn't 'imself at all.'

The coroner said he supposed witness meant that deceased had been in a state of considerable distress.

'And what the 'ell does the old so-and-so expect?' muttered one juryman wrathfully to another. 'If you was thinking of dousing your glim, would you be as merry as a sandboy? I ask you.'

The taxi-driver having been dismissed, Miss Mittens was called. She, like Bletsoe the previous night, was clearly suffering from nervous strain, but she told her story fairly clearly. She thought it was about ten, possibly a few minutes earlier, when Bletsoe returned. She hadn't noticed that he was particularly upset, but then she had had no conversation with him. She had heard the typewriter going overhead for a considerable time, but it did not bother her. She supposed he was a writer and had to work when inspiration visited him. She had first suspected something was wrong when she heard a crash – yes, the typewriting had ceased a few minutes earlier – and she had hesitated, etc., etc. But – oh she didn't think more than five minutes had elapsed, and the doctor had assured her that it hadn't made the smallest difference. She couldn't bear to think . . .

The Coroner, a plump cushiony little man, said 'Quite, Miss Mittens. We sympathize with you very much and we admire the kindness of heart that prompted you to go so quickly to the aid of a fellow-creature. Now I wonder if you can tell us approximately what time it was that you heard the crash.'

'I should think about a quarter past eleven. They were reading poetry on the wireless, and they had just begun that beautiful poem *Trees* . . . '

The coroner said that helped them to establish the time of the crash almost exactly and thanked her for the clear way in which she had given her evidence. Mr Rush then took her place.

He said that he had heard Mr Bletsoe come upstairs at about ten o'clock. He himself usually went to bed shortly before ten. He had noticed that deceased seemed very restless, opening and shutting doors and once he had heard a sort of groaning sound and had contemplated asking whether there was anything he could do. Since the sounds ceased very quickly, however, he abandoned that idea. Shortly afterwards the typing had begun and had continued pretty steadily for almost an hour. He had borne it as long as he could, but bearing in mind the clause in the average lease prohibiting the use of wireless, musical instruments, sewing machines, and typewriters after 11 p.m., he had presently ventured to knock on the door.

'And this was, you say, about eleven o'clock?'

'It was about ten past. I remember particularly telling Mr Bletsoe that it was after eleven – and I must say he had the grace to sound guilty. He said he had just finished, and I admit I heard no further sound until the chair was overturned. Again, I thought of going in but I contented myself

126

with rapping mildly on the wall. Nothing happened – and then I heard Miss Mittens knocking and calling and before I had time to do anything else she began to scream and the entire house was disturbed.'

The Coroner said he thought the jury fully understood the position and the doctor who had examined the body came into court. He should, of course, have been at the inquest from the moment it opened, but he wasn't the police doctor and he had obstinately preferred to remain at a danger-point until he felt he could be spared. He was a dark abrupt man in the late thirties and his name was Symons. He said impatiently that he had been summoned to see the body at about 11.20 and had no hesitation in saying that the man had died of strangulation, death taking place between an hour and an hour and a half earlier, that is to say between 9.50 and 10.20. Having said this he glared at the jury and prepared to leave the witness-box, apparently quite unaware of the complete havoc he had wrought.

The Coroner's reaction to this piece of intelligence must have satisfied the most critical. He was, as they say, struck all of a heap. He made goloptious noises, he stared at the witness, he stared at the jury (who stared patiently back), he looked at the people assembled for the hearing of the inquest and noted sub-consciously a large, rather common-looking man in a bright brown suit who was looking, not shocked, not dazed, but positively entranced by this development. And indeed, for Mr Crook, misplaced cogs were falling into place like (he would have said) water falling out of a punctured bucket.

The Coroner, Mr Jenkin, after that first spasm of incredulity that had rendered him momentarily speechless, made a commendable recovery.

He recalled Dr Symons as he was about to barge out of the witness-box. 'One moment, if you please. I take it you are absolutely sure of your facts?'

Dr Symons turned turkey-cock red and snapped furiously, 'Damme, I ought to be. If I can't tell the difference between a man who's been dead over an hour and a chap who's only just conked out I've no right even to the slum practice I do hold.' It was obvious that he was very angry indeed. Crook liked him at once. That's the stuff – cut-and-come-again – to give the troops, he thought.

The Coroner, however, was not without a certain courage of his own.

'You have not, of course, overlooked the coincidence of the open window and the fireless state of the room, combined with the low temperature . . . ?'

'Low temperature my foot,' said Dr Symons contemptuously. 'The room was as warm as anyone could want. And if you're thinking that an open window can reduce the temperature of a dead man within five minutes of his death to the state this chap was in when I saw him . . . '

Before anyone could prevent him Mr Rush had bobbed up again. 'The doctor's right,' he said. 'There was a fire. I heard him light it. There's air in the pipes, and it makes a curious whistling sound that's quite unmistakable.'

During this speech the proper people tried to make him shut up, but the spirit of defiance, let loose by Dr Symons, was abroad, and Mr Rush stuck gallantly to his guns.

'Mind you, I see your difficulty,' acknowledged the doctor. 'You've got a pack of witnesses who say they talked to this chap and heard him writing letters an hour after he must have died. Well, that's nothing to do with me. All I'm here for is to give you the medical evidence, and I've given it to you.'

Even the dull minds of the jury were beginning to be a little receptive now. They seemed to be given the choice of two equally appalling alternatives. Either all the previous witnesses were mistaken, a coincidence that the most wooden-headed of them was not prepared to accept or else the work and the voice belonged to a dead man. It was a few minutes before it occurred to the brightest of them that there was a third possibility, though as horrible as either of the others. For, since it was established (a) that Mr Bletsoe had returned shortly before 10 o'clock, (b) that at approximately 10 o'clock he had died and (c) that between 10 and 11 the typewriter in his room had been driven at a regular pace to produce a document now in the Coroner's possession, it followed that, assuming the document aforesaid had been written by machine through the agency of a living hand, whoever was responsible for it had produced it with the unfortunate deceased gentleman dangling from his hook not more than a dozen feet away. This solution they all found perfectly horrid and at first, in fact, refused to accept it.

Not so Mr Crook. This kind of thing was absolutely up his street. As he had already observed to Aubrey Bruce, he didn't believe life was quite so tidy as this case would make it appear. It was, he meant, altogether too convenient for Henry Bletsoe to die at this particular moment, leaving a signed confession of his guilt in the Bishop case. Because that, the coroner divulged, was the gist of the long manuscript before him. And even the jury were able to put two and two together sufficiently accurately to assume that (1) if Mr Bletsoe wasn't the author of the letter then he must have been murdered by the man who was, (2) that the writer had very accurate knowledge of his (Bletsoe's) movements that night and ergo, (3) that it was long odds on the writer of the letter being at one and the same time the murderer and the man whom Bletsoe had met on the Embankment. Some of them went further still and deduced that the man who murdered Mr Bletsoe was, by inference, also the murderer of Lewis Bishop.

The coroner, of course, was not permitted to assume this, and in fact he maintained a vast indifference to Mr Bishop and the manner in which his fate had overtaken him. All I am here for, proclaimed Mr Jenkin's manner, is to decide how Mr Bletsoe met his death, and to this end he recalled Mr Goodier, and asked him to go over in his mind the conversation that had taken place between him and the deceased.

Mr Goodier complied, though, he said, the court would appreciate that in these very trying circumstances it was difficult to be sure of every word. He added that he was aware that Bletsoe was being blackmailed, but he was sharply pulled up there. If Bletsoe hadn't, in fact, written the spurious confession, then he hadn't committed suicide, and they

129

were no longer seeking a motive why he should take his own life. Mr Goodier enlarged a little and said Bletsoe had spoken of being followed perpetually, but had not offered any explanation of why this should be. He, Goodier, had assumed it was in connexion with this blackmailing job.

'Did he give the impression that he was expecting a visitor?' inquired the Coroner.

Mr Goodier would obviously have liked to say yes, but replied honestly, no. All the same, he said, he'd wanted to see Mr Crook because he was afraid.

This, in fact, got them very little further. The jury by now had realized that the signature to the confession was a forgery, and were thankful that it wasn't for them to discover or identify the forger. That was a job for the police, and after some prompting they brought in a verdict of murder by some person or persons unknown and left it to the authorities to give him a name.

The journalists had a field-day, only marred by the fact that Dr Symons was a busy man, with insufficient enterprise and/or ambition to be interviewed. He slipped away from the court as soon as he was allowed to do so, and didn't display even the normal man's curiosity as to the outcome of this extraordinary inquest.

Mr Crook, claiming preferential treatment as acting for the defence in the Bishop case, was given an opportunity of seeing the famous letter. The police were furious about the whole thing. This, they inferred, was what happened when your own side were laid by with influenza. It was infamous of Symons not to have mentioned the time of death, which must have been obvious to him at once. Dr Peters would never have let them down like this. Symons was quite impenitent. He said he hadn't known all the rigmarole they were going to produce in court, and maintained that he had never given the impression that the man had been at his last kick when medical aid was summoned. He added that he wasn't the authority, and seeing the sizable grant a docile House of Commons gave to the Home Secretary for his Department you might expect a competent police force. Having thus delivered himself he retired to deliver Mrs Brown's twins; his expression said he wished every policeman in the metropolitan force could have twins within the next hour without medical assistance. It was obvious to Crook that they would have slapped him down, too, if they dared, but his reputation was a formidable one and his motto that of Zacchaeus – If I owe any man anything behold I pay him fourfold. Crook looked at the letter with such a desultory eye he clearly couldn't have taken in more than half of it (and half, in Crook's opinion, was a damned sight too long) and then asked if he could look at Goodier's statement. This favour also was granted him, and he accorded this second manuscript no more detailed attention than the first. Handing both back he crammed his horrible hat lower over his eyes and went off to Hunterscombe House. He travelled by bus. He said only fools took taxis, by which they could instantly be traced, while even the most astute conductor or conductorette would hesitate to identify a casual passenger seen for the space of a couple of seconds while he paid his fare. At the hotel a slatternly maid, with a face moulded from solid vinegar, said Mr Hunter wasn't seeing anyone. Mr Crook said wasn't he just? unless he wanted to find himself in jug for obstructing the proper course of the law, and a minute later the two men met.

'I,' announced Crook instantly, 'represent the defence.'

'The defence?' repeated Mr Hunter, both too ignorant and too innocent to know anything of Crook's reputation.

'The suspected murderer,' replied Crook briskly, and without giving the dazed Mr Hunter any opportunity of asking inconvenient questions, he continued, 'Don't want to keep you long. I just want to see Bletsoe's room for a moment. I daresay it hasn't been touched.'

Hunter agreed that this was so. He added mournfully that it reduced the value of a room to have a death take place in it. Crook told him robustly that at the present time he could let a room at top prices if he had the body stored in a trunk in the corner, and they went up together. The room was mean and small; there was a little gas fire just far enough from the cheap black iron bedstead to ensure that you couldn't switch it off without getting out of bed. The curtains were poor and hadn't been very successfully washed. There was a table in the window with a typewriter standing on it, the machine, no doubt, on which the letter had been written. The hook was still in the wall, but to-day it was naked and innocent.

Mr Crook stood by the table, just where the doomed man must have stood when he signed the emotional confession that was now in the hands of the police. The pink blotting-paper he had used had not been touched since. The signature 'Henry Bletsoe' was perfectly clearly to be read in reverse. Putting out his great freckled paw Crook took a pen from the fluted glass tray, dipped it in the ink-pot that, for once, was freshly filled (it was Crook's experience that no hotel of this type ever refilled an ink-pot, chiefly because the proprietor and his assistants were practically illiterate), and wrote a signature on the back of an envelope he took out of his pocket. Henry Bletsoe. Henry Bletsoe. Henry Bletsoe. The bold black letters stared back at him.

'See me do that?' said Crook to the puzzled Mr Hunter.

'Yes,' conceded Mr Hunter.

'Well, just you remember. That's all.' He threw down the pen and carefully abstracted the sheet of pink blotting-paper, putting it in the little cracked shiny black Gladstone bag he carried everywhere. On account of that bag he was sometimes rapturously hailed by complete strangers as a job-bing plumber, but more often he was taken for one of those lucky blighters who have successfully bested the black market in spirits.

'Be seeing you,' said Crook with an air of one bestowing a favour, and departed. His next visit was to Aubrey Bruce's chambers.

'You ought to have come with me,' he said earnestly. 'More your cup of tea than mine really. Local colour and all that. All the walls and doors the colour of weak gravy and nearly as greasy. On the upper floors bead curtains coyly concealing what Americans call the toilet, and bits of yellow string curtain over the windows. And every door a flat stone behind which lurked its peculiar creature . . . '

132

'You sound like one of the Old Testament prophets,' Bruce told him admiringly.

Crook dropped the artistic element and went on in a brisker voice, 'Funny thing, Bruce, how every criminal slips up on some minor point. The chap who killed Bletsoe thought of so much, even opening the window and putting out the fire to induce rigor more quickly. He didn't make the old mistake of switching out the light as he left the room – did you ever hear of a man who hanged himself in the dark? – it wasn't his fault the body was found too soon – he couldn't conceivably have guarded against that. But he overlooked a simple detail like signing the confession with the dead man's own pen. If you remember, Bletsoe was one of those chaps who couldn't use a fountain-pen; anything of that nature went back on him; wrist-watches, automatic lighters, once they passed into his possession they were no damned good at all. The most reliable pen on the market only had to recognize him to leak all over his pocket, cross its nib and smash its protector. That's why the ink-pot in his room was full of fresh ink. Not because the hotel had filled it up; hotels like Huntercombe House don't go in for the niceties. But Bletsoe kept it filled in his own interest. And that ink was good hard black-drying ink. Look at this.' He produced the sheet of blotting-paper. 'That's where I wrote his name. And that,' and he indicated the bright blue Henry Bletsoe in reverse higher up the sheet, 'is where the chap blotted the signature to the confession?'

'And you know who wrote that signature?'

'I asked to see Goodier's statement, the one he signed. It's got his name written in bright blue ink, just the same colour as that.' He tapped the blotting-paper afresh. 'Funny, ain't it, Bruce, the little things that hang a man.'

Chapter 10

I⊤ seemed to a good many people, though not, of course, to the police or Arthur Crook, that the discovery of the real killer of Mr Bletsoe signed Finis to the Bishop case also. It

was obvious, said the man-in-the-street, that Goodier had committed a second crime to cover his first.

'And so he did,' agreed Crook, 'only the first crime wasn't the murder of Lewis Bishop. Of course I'm certain.'

'And you are certain that he killed Bletsoe?'

'Ain't you?' inquired Crook simply. 'Who else could have written that letter? Who else knew where Bletsoe was staying or who else he'd met that night? Besides, they found finger-prints . . . I daresay Goodier was as careful as he knew how, but when he turned off the gas-tap he forgot that a metal surface retains finger-prints. No, he's as guilty as hell. But he's got some nerve. He must have slipped in soon after Bletsoe – say when *they* closed, which is ten o'clock. He'd had a good few by then and I daresay he'd had one or two before the meeting on the Embankment. He must have felt he couldn't risk Bletsoe spillin' the beans to me – and possibly to the police – and it seemed to him he'd hit on a very pretty scheme to fool everybody.'

Bruce said, 'It's a pretty horrible story. Think of that fat chap sitting at the typewriter with Bletsoe hanging – he strangled him, I suppose?'

'They'll tell us when they've made up their minds, but – yes, I should say that's the way it was. Mind you, I don't know that he intended to kill him when he got there. That chap, Rush, said he heard noises and doors opening and shut-ting. The second door must have been Goodier coming in.'

'Rush didn't say he heard voices,' was Bruce's slow comment.

'Which makes it look as though everything had been fixed. That groaning – that ain't a nice thought, Bruce. He must have slung him up there and then sat down and pegged out that confession, thinking that 'ud be the end of everything. He always said he didn't know much about English law, remember. Then he turned out the fire, opened the window, knocked over the chair and vamoosed. If that old hen in the room below hadn't stopped to be so damn modest she'd probably have cannoned into Goodier comin' hell-for-leather down the stairs. Of course he didn't mean the body to be found till next day, when even a chap like Symons, who'd back himself against God Almighty, wouldn't be able to swear whether death took place before or after eleven. It ought to have worked out very well, but it's what I've always said, Bruce, you can't reckon without your luck. That's the mistake Goodier made. Well, it's the little covered shed for him all right, and no one tryin' to get up a reprieve.'

Bruce nodded soberly. 'Bletsoe must have known something pretty damaging,' he suggested.

'Guilty conscience,' said Crook. 'Oh, Bletsoe knew something all right, but I don't think that something was that Goodier had killed Bishop. But I fancy Goodier was afraid that if Bletsoe told all he knew the police would drop on him for the murder and might get away with it.'

'And what do you suppose that was?'

'I think Bletsoe knew why Goodier was in the library that night, and Goodier was afraid he was comin' along to tell me.'

'The reason being?'

'That Goodier came down to pinch the diamonds. That he did, in fact, pinch 'em. And that Bletsoe knew it.'

'Serious,' agreed Bruce, 'but not quite a hanging offence.'

'You want to be like that poet who saw things steadily and saw 'em whole. You want to remember the end of the story. Supposing the police knew Goodier was down in the library to get the diamonds, and that all the time Bishop was behind the curtains watchin' him get them, and then the family intervenes and there's talk about searching pockets, and Bishop says "No, I'll tell you who's got 'em," and then the lights go out and when they come on Bishop's shot, even past speech, well, who's the average bobby going to pick on for the crime?'

'A good case,' agreed Bruce. 'Obviously the chap with the most to lose.'

'Besides, we've got a bit more proof. Where were the diamonds found? In Bishop's pocket. Right. But – who found 'em? Goodier. And why?'

'You're like the young lady who went faster than light,'

was Bruce's dry comment. 'Meaning he shoved the diamonds into Bishop's pocket, while he was pretending to look for a handkerchief.'

'Don't it seem like that to you?'

'Did he know then they were fakes?'

'I doubt it. They were a first-class imitation, Goodier was in no end of a hurry and he'd hardly got his hands on the diamonds before he was interrupted. The interesting point is – who put the fake string into the safe and why?'

'Bishop was the only chap, besides Goodier, who knew enough about jewels to know the difference,' murmured Bruce.

'And Bishop – so young Vereker tells me – said something once about having a fake string. Y'know, I was never happy about those diamonds in Bishop's pocket. If he'd been behind the curtain all the time he knew what was brewin' – and if he had the diamonds in his pocket, would he, could he have been such an all-fired fool as to come out and offer to empty his pockets, knowing what was in them? He was behind the curtains, he could have hidden the stones somewhere, under a cushion, dropped 'em out of the window, anything. The one thing you can be sure he wouldn't do is walk into the lion's den with a string of diamonds in his mouth, so to speak.'

Bruce drew a lightning sketch of a shark wearing a diamond necklace. 'Then, you assume he'd changed the real diamonds for faked ones, put the faked ones in the safe, and the real ones – where?'

'That's one of the things we've got to find out. Did you notice that though the police combed the place from heel to crown they didn't find those diamonds? And yet Mrs Goodier was wearing them that very night. She gave 'em to Bishop to put away. That was his chance. He must have done his quick-change act then. For the minute we'll have to stay in the dark as to where he put 'em.'

'He might have packed them up disguised as a pair of spectacles or a set of false teeth, meaning to post them next morning,' suggested Bruce.

'If he did that,' objected Crook, who seemed to have gone into the situation pretty thoroughly, 'where are they now? "Pale hands I loved beside the Shalimar, where are you now? Where are you now?" I've had Bill keeping his eyes on the ends of sticks for the real Goodier diamonds ever since *the* night, but he swears they haven't turned up, and not much gets by Bill. The only possibility is that Bishop disposed of 'em somehow before he was put out of the way, and who-ever's got them would have to lie pretty damn low if he didn't want the flatties kickin' at his front door. On the other hand, it could be that Bishop hid 'em somewhere where they haven't so far been uncovered.'

'And where does Bletsoe come in? Does he know Goodier's got the diamonds?'

'Oh, I think so. I never did cotton to Goodier's story of wanting to see Bishop. For one thing he must have seen more than enough of him, and for another if you want to talk to a chap who's under the same roof as yourself you don't wait till an hour when he and everybody else in the house has generally gone to bed, and then go slinking down like a tom-cat to look for him. No, my notion is that Goodier was in a jam, couldn't get hold of any of his brother's money, couldn't stay put and thought of the diamonds. He's been in the trade, he'd know how to get rid of them, how to disguise them – you'd have to disguise anything as well known as the Goodier diamonds, though it goes against the grain to think of that piece being broken up. Well, there he is, got the safe open, got the diamonds, and then, like the Demon King on a small scale, down comes our Mr Bletsoe. Curtain!'

'Why doesn't he give the alarm at once?'

'Our Mr Goodier's too fly for that. You say a word, he says, and I'll swear I've just come in and found you here, burgling the safe. Neither of them knew Bishop was behind the curtain, remember. And everyone would believe Goodier's story. To begin with, he'd tell it a lot more convincingly than Bletsoe would, and for another it was much more likely that Bletsoe would know where the safe was and where the key was kept. Mind you, Goodier did know. I'm certain of that. He used his eyes to some purpose. But no one could prove he knew, and everyone knew Bletsoe did.'

'But what use would the diamonds be to Bletsoe?'

'There I'm with you. I doubt if he'd have the first idea where to dispose of 'em, and he's such a mug he'd probably be caught with them in his pocket. Goodier was far too shrewd. When he saw the way the wind was blowing he shoved the diamonds into Bishop's pocket and let everyone draw their own conclusions. Significant, don't you think, that they were in Goodier's possession, accordin' to such evidence as we have which admittedly is biased, and it was Goodier who took 'em out of Bishop's pocket, after he was dead and couldn't do any contradicting.'

'Oh, I see you could be right,' Bruce acknowledged. 'You usually contrive that.'

'And it provides Goodier, and nobody else, with a motive for puttin' Bletsoe out of the way. Goodier's terrified Bletsoe's going to talk, and though he's a poor little worm and can't do much on his own, once he's turned and seen me coming down the garden path, things might begin to happen. So there's Goodier in a worse jam than ever tryin' to fix things so they'll be safe for himself. Y'know, Bruce,' he went off at a characteristic tangent, 'I suppose I'm one of these chaps that roll rocks in the path of progress. All this chat about security, social and otherwise. Why don't they ask the chaps that know? We could tell 'em. What's got Goodier into his present jam? Desire for security. If he'd left Bletsoe alone things might have been uncomfortable for a while, but nothing would have happened, because Bletsoe couldn't prove a word of any story he chose to tell. But no, Goodier isn't satisfied. Security's in the air. Those chaps at the headquarters of the Gas Company (which was Mr Crook's rude way of describing the House of Commons) can't talk of anything else, and some poor devil like Goodier who, for all his sleeping out under the stars and so forth, don't know enough to come in out of the rain, gets caught.'

'Which still brings us back to the question – where are the real diamonds?'

'Either Bishop had an accomplice in the garden, which is improbable, or they were still on the premises at the time of his death, which is my fancy. He's not the sort to let 'em out of his sight, not till he saw the cash down for 'em. Besides, I don't think he wanted to put his life in jeopardy, as the apostle has it, and it's a mite dangerous sending stuff like that through the post when it can be traced. Bishop knows as much about blackmail as anyone, I'd say. No, he put those diamonds somewhere in the house, and the answer to our question must be here.' He slapped the papers on the desk in front of him. These papers contained copies of the testimony of the various members of the household. 'I'll have to apply for relief under the Beveridge Plan at this rate,' he said. 'I'm losin' my touch and that's a fact.'

'No one but yourself has noticed it,' said Bruce encouragingly.

'Let's get down to it,' said Crook. 'Bishop and the old girl were going to be hitched up within forty-eight hours. He'd already told her her necklace wanted some attention. When it came back it's all Lombard Street to a china orange that she'd not notice any difference, and if some time later it was pointed out to her, why then Bishop would start inquiries, when did she wear it last, who was with her, etc., etc. She wouldn't tumble. She's got hot air in her brain-pan and her memory's what old nannies call chronic. She's the only woman I've ever met who could commit bigamy and swear she'd forgotten about the first husband's existence and I'd believe her.'

'So you think Bishop meant to bring both strings up to London on his honeymoon?'

'I do. Which means that they were both on the premises on the night he was killed. Now the police went round with a tooth-comb and didn't find anything, which means either he'd put 'em somewhere so damn sly even the police couldn't find 'em, or someone else found 'em before the police did. It don't give us much margin, but it's just enough because it's got to be enough. What I've got to find in this stodge of evidence is somethin' a bit out of the ordinary, somethin' no one's tried to explain. And if it's there, Bruce, I'll find it or go sign up at the Labour Exchange for a job as night-watchman.'

'You seem pretty sure you'll find the evidence,' demurred Bruce.

'I'm like that chap who said there should never be one lost good, meaning that everything's part of a pattern and fits in somehow, even if it looks out of place. Well, we've got to find the odd bit and stick it where it belongs. Perfectly simple, my dear Watson.'

He nodded and lighted yet another cigar.

Bruce, genuinely envying so simple and confident a faith, said nothing, but lighted a fresh Turkish cigarette, while Crook fell to on the evidence as starving men are said to fall to on a square meal. For a time there was no sound in the room but the grunt of Crook's breathing, which meant he was desperately in earnest, and it wasn't any use the truth trying to conceal itself, because he meant to haul it out of its hole and expose it like a pound of sausages on a fishmonger's slab (at least, that was where they used to be found). And his patience was rewarded. For after a while Crook looked up to say in a puzzled tone, 'Now why did I miss that one? Of all the blithering asses.'

'It it's the hiding-place of the real diamonds the police haven't got there yet either,' said Bruce, meaning to be consoling.

'When I get to police level I'm sunk,' was Crook's grim comment. 'They have the book of rules to support them; I've only got my big flat feet. Look here. After they left the library they went into the morning-room, parlour, whatever you nobs call it, and Goodier wanted to go upstairs and get a cigarette. Someone suggested he might look in the cigarette-box on the table, and someone else said what was the use, there were never any cigarettes there and if there were they were musty. But – mark this! – when Goodier opened the box it was full of cigarettes – and not just cigarettes, but Bishop's specials, the sort he never handed round if he could help it. Now, what does that suggest to you?'

140

'That he and no one else had filled the box,' returned Bruce, playing up nobly.

'Right. Then why?'

'Because he wanted to hide something,' said Bruce in the same voice.

'It could be,' said Crook, 'it could be. Only – the diamonds ain't there now, Bruce. And if it wasn't the diamonds Bishop was hidin', what was it?'

'And who do you imagine has got them now?'

'We'll have to work it out,' said Crook. 'Now most of those wallahs were so nice-minded they wouldn't care about smokin' a dead chap's cigarettes. Vereker wouldn't and I don't suppose the girl would. Bletsoe didn't, as we happen to know, but Goodier did. Now we know Goodier's sort. Not above liftin' anything. The kind of chap that would let a kid drop a threepenny bit and then pocket it when the kid had gone bawling home. He wouldn't mind how many of Bishop's cigarettes he pinched. And here's another thing. He was the last of the party to give evidence, which means that he was alone in that room for at least five minutes, possibly more. The chaps who'd told their story were shunted off to bed to prevent collusion. Goodier must know the game's practically up. He came down to raise money; he hasn't raised it. He meant to pinch the necklace and he's been done in the eye by Bletsoe. Actually, of course, it wasn't Bletsoe but Bishop himself who did him in the eye. He was like that chap in Shakespeare who picked up everything in sight, sort of human jackdaw . . . '

'Autolycus,' said Bruce.

'I knew you'd know. Well, he'd say, I haven't got much, but no harm filling my case out of this box. I should say Goodier was the kind of chap who always filled up his case from other people's boxes – and for once it's a winning move.'

'Because, when he'd near-emptied the box, he saw something he hadn't anticipated.'

'I think so, Bruce, I think so. I examined that box myself. It was a fair-sized box, and it wasn't half-full. I supposed Goodier had lifted the other half – I'd got evidence that it

141

ANTHONY GILBERT

was full on the night he was shot – but it didn't occur to me then that he might have taken, not the cigarettes, but what the cigarettes concealed. He had a chance, and by that time they weren't looking for the real diamonds, or if they were they'd only look in the chaps' pockets, and I don't think Goodier would be such a jay as to shove it in his pocket.'

'Wear it round his neck like a lady, I suppose?' said Bruce, to which Crook replied seriously, 'It wouldn't surprise me at all.'

'And now?' said Bruce.

'That's the point. Goodier don't seem to be worrying quite the way he was. It could be that he's managed to raise a bit of money. Of course, the diamonds haven't been seen anywhere. Even a fence thinks twice before he handles stuff that's mixed up with a murder. But that don't mean they're not lying quietly in some fence's safe. These chaps are careful, as a rule; they have to be. And they learn to take the long view. They can afford to wait a bit. No murder's more than a nine days' wonder, not even the Brides in the Bath Case, and I don't remember any crime that attracted more attention than that. After a bit you'll be able to go into any pub and mention the name of Lewis Bishop and no one'll take his nose out of his pint pot, and when that time comes X. will start disposin' of the diamonds. No, I don't think Goodier's got 'em now. There aren't above five or six men in London who could handle a job like that. All you've got to do is keep your eyes on sticks and sooner or later one of the chaps will turn the diamonds in. It don't interest me personally,' wound up Crook, putting on a rather million-dollar manner. 'Murder's my pigeon, not petty larceny. But the police ain't such fools as all that. They could probably make a good guess where the diamonds are, and when the time comes they'll pounce.'

Bruce nodded. 'I see.' He was accustomed to letting Crook do most of the talking. 'And – do you think Goodier killed Bishop?'

'Speaking for myself,' said Crook, 'I don't. I've got ideas of my own.'

'Putting any cards on the table?' suggested Bruce.

Crook told him what he thought.

Bruce stared. 'Anything to back up that idea?'

'A bit.' He elaborated some more.

Bruce frowned. 'Not going to get a conviction on that,' he said.

'You bet we're not,' agreed Crook, heartily. 'We've got a lot more work ahead. I shall have to be as wily as a serpent and cooing as a dove and persuade my young lady to help me a bit, but it ain't going to be an easy job. I have an idea she'd just as soon I wasn't in the case.'

Bruce didn't say anything.

'All right,' said Crook, 'I can take it. Too feahfully common, deah! But remember, it's the common man that clothes the gentleman and the common Crook who saves the lady.'

But if Mr Crook in his lordly way was prepared to by-pass Goodier, as it were, the police were less considerate. Goodier had heard the verdict with a sinking heart, and had sat in his room anticipating the inevitable visit from authority ever since the rising of the court. Over and over again he called himself a fool for being so apprehensive. They might come to see him, they might think of fresh questions to ask him, but that they should suggest he was in any way responsible for Bletsoe's death – why it was unthinkable. They had no evidence.

He was not left very long in suspense. He was sitting by his window pretending to read an evening paper when a car drew up at the door of the dingy little hotel and two men got out. There was nothing about them to cause his heart to beat like a kettle-drum, so he told himself, but after they had disappeared from sight he sat stiff, tight, ears strained for the inevitable footstep in the passage. He was surprised all the same when the door opened and the two men came in. He had assumed that a messenger would come up for him, and this unexpected move threw him off his balance. The men were not menacing or threatening in any way. They asked him if he were James Goodier, and since it was impossible to deny it he said yes, he was. They said he was under no obligation to answer any of the questions they were going to put to him until he had consulted a lawyer, but if he chose to make a voluntary statement it might be used in subsequent proceedings in connexion with Bletsoe's death.

'I thought that was what you'd come about,' he said roughly. 'But I've told you everything I know.'

'There's one thing you haven't told us,' pointed out the senior of his two visitors, 'and that is why we've found your fingerprints in Mr Bletsoe's room.'

They cautioned him again after that – a pretty piece of tyranny, he thought it, and hypocritical into the bargain, since they knew they had him in a cleft stick – and he said he'd tell them, and if he'd been less of an amateur he'd have told them straight away. The fact was he had been in Bletsoe's room that night, but he had had nothing to do with his death. That had been accomplished before his arrival.

It took even the hardened policemen a moment to get acclimatized to that.

'You mean, he was dead when you arrived?'

'Yes. It was the most terrible shock, and yet in a way I wasn't surprised. I suppose that's really why I turned out again, because I was so anxious about the poor devil. After he drove off in his taxi I couldn't get him out of my head. He'd seemed so odd, so excited. And he'd harped so on how he must save this girl, Miss Vereker. "I know she didn't do it," he kept on saying, "I tell you, I know she didn't do it." Well, there was only one way of proving she didn't, and that was by producing the chap who did.'

'I thought you said he wanted to go and see Mr Crook and tell him all this and it was you who stopped him. Why was that?'

'It was quixotic perhaps,' Goodier shrugged his massive shoulders, 'but I had the feeling he hardly knew what he was saying. Crook's got a reputation. Not much gets past him. He'd have got any story there was out of the fellow before he knew he was being examined. And in the state he was in I – oh, I felt it wasn't fair. He didn't seem to me really responsible, and he might have been jockeyed into admitting anything. Besides, I only had his word that he was really going to see Crook. I saw him coming up from the Embankment, late in the evening, looking as mad as a hatter, telling this improbable yarn. And it occurred to me the Embankment's a damned odd place to go if you want to telephone. What was wrong with the instrument in his own hotel?'

'Are you trying to tell us, sir, you think he was contemplating suicide even then?'

'In the light of what happened later, I'm certain of it. And you remember the taxi-driver didn't want to take him at first, thought he was so queer. Well, I went off and had a drink, and thought about going back. But half-way I turned. I had to.'

'There's another thing, sir. How was it you happened to be on the Embankment that evening?'

'It just chanced. You know how things do. I was going past the House of Commons when I saw someone who looked a bit familiar crossing the road. I said to myself, "Who the devil's that? I seem to know him," and being curious and not having anything particular to do I crossed the street and went down after him on to the Embankment. When he came back, either from telephoning or contemplating the river, I saw it was Bletsoe and spoke to him. He was obviously startled, and then opened up with this story about Crook and the girl and how he'd got to save her, and some ridiculous yarn he'd thought up, that wouldn't have held water for an instant and so I told him.'

'And presently you went round to his hotel just to make sure he was all right?'

'That's it.'

'What time would this be?'

'Well.' Goodier considered. 'The locals all shut at ten. And I went round right away, say 10.15. I didn't notice particularly. Well, I couldn't know it was going to be important. I knew Bletsoe had a room on the top floor, because he told me so, and the front door wasn't locked. I just walked right in and up the stairs.'

'You didn't think of ringing or anything?'

'I waited a minute in the hall, but there was no one about.

They didn't seem to run to a night porter. So I went up to look for him.'

'You knew the number of his room?'

'There were only three on the top floor. I happened to see a tallish, thinnish chap – Rush he turned out to be – whisking out of the bathroom into one of the bedrooms as I came up the stairs, so I knew that wasn't Bletsoe's. The first door was locked and there wasn't a light under it, so if it was his, that meant he wasn't back yet. I went along and tried the third door. There was a light there all right. I knocked, but nothing happened, so I just turned the handle. As I say, the light was on and I got a full view of him. My God, it was pretty shocking, even for a chap who's knocked about in his time . . .'

'Quite,' said the official woodenly. 'How was he?'

'He was hanging from a hook in the corner of the room. Poor little so-and-so. Couldn't face the music, I suppose.'

'And he was dead?'

'Lord, yes.'

The policeman frowned. 'I must admit, Mr Goodier, I don't understand why you didn't call someone immediately.'

'That was my original intention, and then I saw it might be a bit awkward for me to explain what I was doing there. Meant involving Bletsoe and all that. Matter of fact, I decided his conscience must have been too much for him, and I went round looking for a letter.'

'He hadn't had much time,' suggested the official stolidly.

'That's true. But he could have been brief. "I'm taking this way because I killed Lewis Bishop and I can't see innocence suffer for my crime." Something like that.'

'Romantic sort of gentleman,' reflected the second of the policemen, who hadn't spoken yet. The other said, 'And there wasn't anything?'

'Nothing at all.'

'And all this time you didn't think of cutting the gentleman down or getting a doctor?'

'It was too late to be any good. I could see that. I've seen dead men before.'

'According to the doctor, he must have died about the time you got there. It could have been he wasn't dead . . . '

'He must have gone straight back and strung himself up. Couldn't take it, poor little devil.'

The officer looked harshly incredulous. 'Are you trying to tell me, sir, that you sat down to the typewriter and wrote that letter with him hanging there?'

Goodier squared his shoulders. 'Shocks you, does it? But then you chaps haven't had the sort of raw experiences that come the way of rolling stones like myself. And I felt sure I knew why he'd done what he had, and it seemed a rotten shame no one should profit from it.'

'Taking a lot on yourself, weren't you, branding a dead man as a murderer without a ha'porth of proof? I don't think a jury's going to like that story much, Mr Goodier. Besides, manufacturing evidence is an offence in itself.'

'There was no other conceivable explanation for what he'd done,' explained Goodier, desperately. 'And now he was out of it who could possibly exonerate the girl?'

'I thought you said the story he was going to tell couldn't hold water, anyhow.'

'Ah, but if he'd told the truth, not trying to spare himself, that would have got her off all right.'

'Meaning you knew what the truth was?'

Goodier doubled and twisted like a hare sore beset, but the authorities were too much for him.

'After all,' he protested, 'Bletsoe had tried to steal the diamonds . . . '

'They weren't found on him,' the policeman reminded him.

'No. I daresay not. But I saw him with them before the others arrived.'

'Yes, sir?' said the policeman.

Goodier began to lose his head and his temper with it. 'Do you mean to say you don't believe me?'

'All I'm saying, sir, is I'm surprised. I'm very surprised indeed that a gentleman like you couldn't think up a better story than that. And what made you turn off the fire? We know you must have done that because we've got one of your fingerprints marked clearly on the tap.'

'I – it's second nature to me to put out fires when they're no longer wanted.'

'And then, having signed the letter with his name, you left him hanging there, never gave the alarm or anything?'

'By that time it was too late for me to do anything.'

'No one had seen you come, you said?'

'No one. And if they had I daresay in that bad light they'd have thought me one of the residents.'

'You didn't forget much, did you, sir?'

'I suppose I was crazy to think I could pull it off, but – well, Bletsoe wasn't the only one who was haunted by that girl, and it seemed a fighting chance . . . '

It wasn't any good, of course. He must have known that from the first. But he stuck to his story just the same.

'It's a bit like the Thorne case,' said Crook when he heard the news, referring to a famous murder of the nineteen-twenties. 'He swore he didn't kill his girl – what was her name? Elsie Cameron – just found her hanging in his shack, lost his head and carved her up. The general public, bless its muddled heart, considered that what he had done on his own admission was worse than what the police said he had done. Norman Thorne was hanged, by public opinion, for cutting up a corpse. That genuinely shocked the masses. Anyone might commit a murder, they said, but cutting up a girl you'd been in love with – well! Though, come to that,' added Crook whose romantic sense could have gone under a pre-war threepenny-bit, 'a lot of husbands would like to do the same if they hadn't got the sense to know no dame's worth it. As a matter of fact, Bletsoe's the type who would have left a confession. Got a tidy sort of mind in that way.'

'It's not a very nice story,' said Bruce unemphatically. 'One supposes he crept in, strangled the poor devil before he'd time to raise the alarm – no one heard any conversation, I suppose you noticed – and then slung him up. You know, he had a nerve of a kind.'

But Crook only said in unsympathetic tonès, 'He's goin' to need it. Anyway, he ain't our pigeon. It's nothing to us who killed Bletsoe. I don't believe, for the reasons I've given you, that Bletsoe killed Bishop, and I don't believe the Vereker girl did.'

'But Goodier might have done, or that's what a lot of people think.'

'That may be good enough for them, but it don't affect the Metropolitan police, who ain't interested in Bishop, only in Bletsoe, and it won't satisfy the local force who've taken Anne Vereker for Bishop's murder. Oh, I know how convenient it would be if it could be proved that the same chap was responsible for both crimes, but it ain't so simple. I think,' he added, 'I'll go pay a little visit to Four Acres, and see if anything new has turned up.'

Chapter 11

ALISTAIR had seen the news of Bletsoe's death, and had indeed made a point of attending the inquest. But since Goodier had been called in to identify the body and he had no desire to make himself more conspicuous than necessary, he had remained in the background and listened to the evidence. When he first heard the news he had thought, with a sudden hopeful leap of his heart, 'If he's really hanged himself he may have – must have – left a confession behind. There's no sense in it otherwise. That lets Anne out.'

He had held loyally to his bargain with Crook and made no attempt to hustle or harry that master among men, but he was secretly in great fear as to the result of the inquiries. He knew little of the workings of the law, but the questions put by the local police and the systematic way in which they had ferreted out relevant information and pieced it together had alarmed him. Crook's confidence was not, of course, without effect, but when he went to London it was in the hope that he

149

would hear what, in fact, the spurious confession did contain. The bombshell exploded by Dr Symons swept him for the moment off his feet; unlike Crook, he did not at once grasp the implications. He only realized that here was another hope dispersed.

Crook had a word with him before he left. 'Keep your pecker up,' said Crook. 'Must give the police a run for their money. Your young lady's all right. That Bishop writing his piece in the paper last Sunday hit the nail on the head. What's wanted in this generation is faith. You cultivate faith in me and get the young lady to do the same, and you can both sleep like infants.' And off he bustled, as cheerful and apparently unconcerned as before.

Since Bishop's death Alistair had avoided Four Acres. Tessa Goodier, so both Dutchy and Alicia wrote him, had had a sort of breakdown which had apparently quite changed her former easy-going nature. Now she was sullen, temperamental, and suspicious. 'Sometimes,' wrote Alicia, 'I feel it's more than I can bear. She seems to think I have an underlying motive for everything I do. I would come up to London and begin to make a career for myself, but I don't feel I can leave her just now when she has no other member of the family in the house, and though Dutchy is wonderful it's not fair to leave the whole burden on her.'

She said as much when she met Alistair a day or two after the inquest. Tessa had inquired what had happened and why Alistair never came down, and Alicia had passed the information on. Alistair, therefore, answered the summons and was met at the station by Alicia, driving Tessa Goodier's big, old-fashioned car.

'You'll have to get one of your own,' she warned him, abandoning the wheel and slipping into the seat next the driver. 'This monstrosity eats petrol.'

'Not much chance of getting a car yet. They're on priority, except the second-hand ones, like most other things. Besides, at present I don't need a car.'

'What are you doing in London?' Alicia wanted to know.

'Marking time. I can't do much about the future till this affair's settled.'

'I did think Bletsoe's death would end that,' exclaimed Alicia. 'After all, if Goodier killed him, and I suppose he did, doesn't it follow that he shot Bishop, too? Anyhow, couldn't it be made to look that way?'

'I agree it would be very convenient,' acknowledged Alistair dryly, 'But I'm afraid that sort of argument doesn't cut any ice with the police.'

'It seems a pity not to kill two birds with one stone,' sighed Alicia.

Alistair experienced the familiar male exasperation at this typical female illogicality.

'It might seem a pity to you, but the job of the police in the main is to preserve justice, and if Goodier were to die branded as the murderer of Lewis Bishop when, in fact, he was nothing of the kind, justice wouldn't have been done.'

'Anne would be all right, though.'

This sort of conversation infuriated Alistair. It was like any woman, he thought, and Alicia in particular, to waste time on the past when it was the present and the future that mattered now.

'Anne will be all right anyway. Crook will see to that.' Then he asked after his aunt.

Alicia looked troubled. 'I'm not a bit happy about her, Alistair. As I wrote to you, she seems absolutely changed. She's got so – ferocious – about Anne, I mean.'

'She doesn't believe she's guilty,' said Alistair quickly.

'I don't know whether she believes it or not, but she wants to believe it. She goes out of her way to talk of Anne as a murderer, and I'm certain she feels that she is, in a symbolic sense . . . '

Alistair made an impatient movement. 'You can't be a murderer in a symbolic sense in a court of law,' he said. 'I suppose what you're trying to say is that she feels Anne murdered her chances of happiness, though what those chances were is pretty problematical, and what Anne did beyond telling the truth about Bishop's previous alliances –

legal or the reverse – I don't understand. The fact is, Aunt Tessa hates Anne, if she does hate her, because she knew the truth. It's quite a common reason for feuds.'

'You'd back Anne through thick and thin, wouldn't you?' said Alicia, softly.

'I don't think she did it. I don't think any of us believe she did it.'

Alicia said nothing. 'Or perhaps you do?' Alistair continued. 'Well, I suppose I've no right to ask.'

Alicia turned in sudden warmth. 'Alistair, I'd give anything to believe absolutely, as you do, that she didn't. It's difficult for anyone like me to be fair to Anne, she had so much by divine right, and I had so much less and had to fight so hard, first to get it and then to keep it. I know what girls feel like who save and save to buy an imitation leopard-skin coat for ten pounds, and then see someone wearing the real thing, costing a hundred, and wearing it without a thought, taking for granted that they should have it . . . '

All this was wasted on Alistair, who didn't possess that peculiar brand of sympathy that makes one person sensitive to the disappointments and distresses experienced by another. Take it by and large, Alicia had done pretty well out of her uncle and aunt, and even now she was at large and free to choose what she'd do during the day, while Anne, who had faced one appalling disillusion and accepted a decision with which you could disagree but for which it was difficult to feel anything but compassion, was awaiting trial in prison, with the probability of all the ugly past being eventually uncovered. Having money, such as it was, hadn't done much for Anne. Alicia, with her passion for economic security, her intense absorption in herself, irritated him.

'I do want to be fair to her,' Alicia was continuing. 'It's much harder for women to be fair to one another than men understand. So much of the power in the world generally still belongs to men that women are inclined to want to hold on to any little share they can grab, and they don't want to share, because they feel there isn't enough to go round. I would give anything to be able to believe, as I can see you

do, that Anne couldn't have shot Bishop, but it seems to me
no one had a better opportunity.'

'If it comes to that, we all had an equal opportunity. So
far as I know, no one saw me put the revolver down, unless
it was Bishop himself. You'd have o be hiding behind the
curtains, really, to see it properly. And when I lighted the
match and held it up, then everyone had an equal chance.'

'I know.' Alicia wrinkled her forehead. 'But say what you
like, Alistair, she did have motive.'

'No more than the rest of us. Bletsoe had some chap
blackmailing him, and he was in trouble with his accounts.
Goodier was in a jam, needed money and, but for Bishop,
would probably have raised it out of Aunt Tessa. He's got
no reason to love him. Speaking from a purely impersonal
viewpoint, Dutchy stood to lose a good deal if the marriage
went through – a job and a legacy and a decent home – and
she's not as young as she was. Aunt Tessa had just been told
she'd been led up the garden by a man not worth the flashy
watch he wore, and I stood to lose everything I thought I was
fighting for when I was overseas. Oh, I fancy the police
picked Anne simply because she happened to have the revolver in her hand when the lights went up.'

'The person I'm glad I'm not, is your Mr Crook,' said
Alicia frankly, as Alistair turned the car through the big
gates. 'He's got his work cut out if you ask me.'

Dutchy was waiting in the hall when they arrived. 'There's
been a telephone call,' she said. 'Someone called Crook –
such an unfortunate name for a solicitor. He's coming
down.'

'Something new?' asked Alistair, quickly.

'He didn't say. Alistair, do you think James Goodier shot
Mr Bishop?'

'I don't know,' said Alistair with commendable patience.

And then a door upstairs opened and a voice called out?
'Is that Alistair? Alistair, why are you hanging about in the
hall? I want you up here.'

He went up the stairs at once, Alicia at his side. He was
shocked at the sight of his aunt, in spite of the warnings he

had received. Her plump rather gentle features had sharpened and at the same time had seemed to become heavier; her eyes were suspicious, her mouth hard and thin.

'How long have you been here? Why didn't you come up straight away?' She shot the words at Alistair, paying no attention at all to Alicia.

'I've only just arrived,' he defended himself. 'How are you, Aunt Tessa?'

'How do you expect me to be? I hope you're not going to ask me a lot of absurd questions. I'm worn out answering them as it is. Dutchy and Alicia treat me as though I were an invalid. I may have been a fool – Theo used to say only fools put their cards on the table – but I'm not out of my mind. I suppose you've brought nothing new.'

'About Bletsoe or James Goodier? I'm afraid not. The police aren't satisfied that Bletsoe shot Bishop, if that's what you mean?'

Tessa greeted this statement with frank approval. 'Quite right. If they said he was guilty I'd know a great injustice was being done. Bletsoe could never have handled firearms.'

'If it comes to that, I was the one person who was really familiar with them.'

'You don't need to be familiar with firearms to shoot a man at point-blank range. Anyone could have done it, given the right temperament. Bletsoe hadn't the right temperament. Now Anne knew about firearms. She'd often handled them. She told me that when she went out on those lonely roads in Central Europe she was always armed. Very un-English, I call it, but then she was with a rather irregular brigade or society or whatever it was.'

'Aunt Tessa, you know you don't really believe Anne did it.'

'Of course she did it. Lewis knew something disgraceful about her past.'

'One doesn't risk murder . . . '

'You do, if there's a chance of hanging the responsibility on someone else. Everyone, except perhaps you, knows Anne's guilty. I can't imagine why you can none of you be honest about it. Say you want to save her, if you like, but don't pretend she didn't do it. As for motive, well, I always realized she was in love with Lewis, though I didn't think till that night there had been anything between them, and when she found he was in love with me she went temporarily out of her mind. I suppose she thought she could cut out a middle-aged woman without too much difficulty, particularly as she didn't mind stooping to blackmail.'

'Blackmail! Aunt Tessa . . . '

'How else do you explain the fact that my diamonds were found in Lewis's pocket? Of course, she had demanded them, knowing she had the whip-hand. Oh, Anne was up to no good.'

'What on earth could she have done with diamonds as famous as yours, if she had had them? The police would have been out after them, you can't smuggle them abroad these days. She'd have been arrested the moment she tried to sell them.'

'Oh, I daresay she met some very shady people when she was abroad. She hated Lewis when she realized he wasn't coming back to her. Did you see her face that night? I did. Besides, there's something else.'

'What?' asked Alistair, wondering if this appalling change in a woman who had always been kind was permanent.

'You think you knew Anne well, don't you? You were wrong. You thought she was one of us, a little cold-hearted perhaps, but still one of the family, loyal, honourable. But she was nothing of the sort. She was absolutely unscrupulous. I tell you, I've found letters – parts of letters, rather – that she wrote to him. They make everything absolutely clear.'

'Where on earth did you find those? I thought the police had combed the place.'

'I found them where the police didn't think of looking for them, where Anne counted on no one ever looking for them. Otherwise, she'd have been more careful and destroyed them. Don't they say criminals always forget one detail? She used to spend a lot of time up in the big loft that Theo made into a sort of workshop. He had bookshelves built there, and a writing-table and chairs ... He said people wouldn't trouble to climb all that way, he could be sure of privacy there. In fact, he treated it as a kind of study. I was going to be his secretary,' she added with a pride half gloomy, half wistful. 'He bought a typewriter and I was to learn to type. But I could never hit the right keys. Then he suggested that Alicia – he was very business-like, you know, he said all women should be able to earn a living, not depend on getting married, and anyway it isn't every husband who can support his wife these days – he thought she should try. But though she was cleverer with the machine than I was she wasn't very good at spelling, and she didn't really like the idea, so gradually it was dropped. Theo was very impatient. I think clever people are. Things are so easy for them they don't realize they're difficult for other people. Of course Anne ought to have taken it on. She was quick and clever, too, but she was too restless. She couldn't settle to anything. Theo said she needed a man to control her, but he couldn't do anything. You see, she wasn't like Alicia. Money and a big place meant nothing to her. She wanted to get about, see things and people. She hated being kept in the same place.'

'That's true,' Alistair acknowledged. He thought of Anne, who hated to be cribbed, cabined, and confined, who always wanted to be on the move, making fresh contacts, trying new experiences, shut up now in a cell with no rights, no power to make her own decisions, no liberty, perhaps not even very much hope.

'She used to spend hours after she came back sitting up there,' Tessa went on. 'I asked her once if she was writing a book and she said no, she was only writing letters, her writing was so bad and it was a good thing to keep the machine running. Otherwise, it would rust.'

'It was a good machine,' agreed Alistair absently. 'I've often used it.'

'As a matter of fact, I used to think it was an excuse to get away from us. She found us so dull after the excitement she was used to. But it wasn't even that. She used to go up there

like a thief, writing letters to Lewis, threatening letters . . . '
She shivered. 'Alistair, I don't mean to stay on here when all
this is over. I shall sell the house. I should always feel it was –
haunted.'

The corners of Alistair's long mouth drew down in an expression of involuntary disdain at the notion that a cut-and-
thruster like Bishop could have any permanent effect on the
atmosphere of a house so soaked in tradition. That poor ghost
would have a pretty chilly time of it if it tried to take up
residence at Four Acres. But for the moment he let that
go.

'Are you trying to tell me that you found letters in the
attic?' he asked patiently.

'Yes. Drafts of the ones she didn't send. Oh, she was a
wicked creature, Alistair. She'd no pity, no sense of decency.
I put the bits of paper together and pasted them up. Well, I
had to find out what it all meant. She speaks of meeting him
in the Middle East, and once – once she says something about
his being her lover.'

'How many of these letters are there?' inquired Alistair.

'They're all scraps. I found them in the waste-paper
basket, and I caught sight of Lewis's name. I had a right to
know what was in them.' She threw up her head defiantly.
Both of them had forgotten Alicia, who stood looking from
one to another with an expression both perplexed and
thoughtful.

'If you think they're evidence you should hand them over,'
said Alistair.

'I won't have it said that I did anything to get my own
niece hanged,' cried Mrs Goodier, excitedly.

'Then let Crook see them. He's coming down.'

Mrs Goodier scowled. 'What for?'

'I don't know exactly. He's acting for Anne, you know.'

'I don't believe you care in the least if she did kill him,'
Aunt Tessa accused her nephew. She opened a big cretonne
work-bag that hung on the back of a chair, and pulled out
some sheets of paper on to which pieces of torn letters had
been pasted a little unevenly so that the letters were some-

times incomplete. Alistair took the sheets and glanced through them. To him they seemed absurdly melodramatic, but then the whole situation bristled with melodrama. It might be that Aunt Tessa was right, he warned himself, yet what could the steadfast resolute Anne see to admire in the shoddy polished rascal who had swept poor addlepated Tessa Goodier off her uncertain feet? He was still looking at the letters when Dutchy came in to announce unceremoniously that Mr Crook had arrived in his puffing Billy.

'I told him I didn't know if you were disengaged and that you'd only just come yourself,' she said. 'You can see he's no good the noise he makes. Like one of those rocket bombs we used to have. I wouldn't go out in that car of his if you paid me. I should know it would blow up any minute.'

'He wouldn't pay you,' said Alicia with a little gurgle of laughter, and Dutchy looked more offended than before.

'I'm always disengaged when Mr Crook calls,' said Alistair, going off with the letters in his hand. Alicia hesitated, then followed him. Dutchy stayed with Tessa.

'They're all for that girl,' said Mrs Goodier. 'I suppose they think right and wrong don't matter any more than an old woman like me. I suppose they think . . . '

'You know quite well you don't want to see Anne hanged any more than anyone else does,' Dutchy told her robustly. 'What were those papers Alistair had in his hand?' Tessa began to explain. 'Well, I don't see what good you think they'll be unless they were in her handwriting. However, I daresay Mr Crook will think of that, too. You'd have to be clever to make up for looking like that,' she added dryly.

*

Crook, however, was like the Ancient Mariner or someone of that kind, who knew that you shouldn't despise anything great or small. Anyway, he didn't get on to the papers for some time. First of all, he said, he'd like to see the cigarette-box in the parlour, and when it was shown him, about half-full of cigarettes, he asked, 'Who smokes these, now Bishop's gone

where better men have gone before him? A very nifty cigarette, if you ask me,' he added. 'Proper lounge lizard I'd
call it.'

'I don't smoke them,' said Alistair. 'Not that kind. Bishop
never handed his case round, and after he was dead – well,
there's something about smoking a visitor's cigarettes when
he's died suddenly by violence . . . '

'So there is something to be said for tradition,' approved
Crook. 'If you'd been a lot of hooligans you'd all have gone
helter-skelter for that box when it became clear that owner
had no further use for same.'

Even Alistair, who thought of himself as a man who'd got
free from the deplorable caste system in the course of the war,
winced sometimes at Crook's blatant vulgarity. He thought
it a pity brains and breeding couldn't go together more often
than they did. He had once said so to Aunt Tessa, who had
replied instantly, 'But, darling, it wouldn't be fair. Like one
person having two buns and someone else having none.
Nobody can have everything.'

Crook, reading Alistair's mind perfectly, and quite unmoved by what he found there, went on, 'Well, perhaps the
young lady likes this sort of cigarette.'

'I'd hardly be smoking Mr Bishop's in the circumstances,'
returned Alicia, dryly.

'Well, but Mr Crook's right. Someone must have smoked
them,' argued Alistair in his thoughtful way. 'That box was
practically full the night Bishop died. Bletsoe was offered a
cigarette and refused, you didn't have one, I had Anne's, she
didn't smoke.'

'James Goodier did. I remember his taking one.'

'He must have smoked like hell to get through all those
cigarettes,' suggested Crook.

'He could have filled his case, I suppose,' Alicia murmured, but Alistair said no, he didn't think so, because
Goodier had offered him a cigarette the same night, saying
he was afraid they weren't up to Bishop's standard.

'As a matter of fact,' he added, 'I do remember now seeing
the box standing open the same evening, and then it was less

159

than half-full. I wondered who'd helped himself to such a number, certainly more than a cigarette-case would hold.'

'And if he put 'em in his pocket, quite apart from ruinin' 'em, there was the chance the police 'ud ask you to turn your pockets out, and just think what an ass you'd look with your pockets weighted down by another fellow's fags. Why, in a country like this one, it's almost enough to hang you out of hand. What you want, when you're looking for diamonds,' he added forcibly, 'is a strip to the buff policy, ladies and gents. And then an X-ray to make sure no one's doin' a swallowing act. If you ask me, I think there's a better explanation about the box bein' full that day when it had been heck-empty all the other days than just that Bishop was feelin' generous. I think those cigarettes were put there to hide something else.'

'You mean – the diamonds?' That was Alistair.

'It could be, Major, it could be.'

'But the police . . . '

'Well, I suppose someone was left alone here for five minutes, and the only member of the household who didn't mind smoking a dead chap's cigarettes was Goodier. Mind you, I don't say that's the way it happened, it's just that I have a hunch it is. Anyway, Bill's on the trail, and wherever those diamonds are he'll smell 'em out.'

'If you're right,' said Alistair, 'it would give the lie to Aunt Tessa's idea that my cousin was in league with Bishop to rob her of the diamonds.'

'The bees that old lady keeps in her bonnet!' exclaimed Crook, admiringly. 'You know, the way women have it in for one another is one of the things science has never been able to explain. Scratch each other's eyes out for twopence, and they don't know what to do with the eyes when they've got 'em.'

Alistair looked more sober, if possible, than before. 'I don't know about them all being bees,' he said. 'She's given me some typescript she found upstairs, something for which she thinks my cousin is responsible. I haven't read it all yet, just glanced over it. But it looks like the draft of a letter.'

'All dames are dotty,' said Crook in his sweeping way. 'Who tore these pages?'

'According to my aunt, Miss Vereker wrote them and then destroyed them.'

'And left them nicely about for somebody to find?'

'That's her story. Well, they were torn in pieces and nobody goes up to the attic much.'

'Not very small bits,' Crook pointed out. 'And don't they ever empty the waste baskets in the attic?'

'Things are a bit at sixes and sevens,' Alicia murmured. 'It's surprising how much a – a sudden death of this kind can disorganize a house.'

Crook was reading the patched manuscript. 'The old lady isn't the only one who's goofy,' he observed after a moment. 'Might as well leave a box of matches around in an arsenal full of dynamite as leave this where anyone could pick it up. Listen to this: "I need money. You know why, and you know, too, where to get it . . . It's absurd at this stage of our relations to pretend to be too scrupulous to rob Peter to pay Paul. It's what you are proposing to do in any case. I will be in the library on Tuesday night when everyone has gone to bed. You can bring them then. It will be easy for you to lay hands on them. You will appreciate the need for secrecy. I don't think it would suit your book very well if I were to tell Aunt Tessa all I know." '

'Might have been written for the films,' said Crook approvingly to Alistair, who was looking over his shoulder and letting his eyes race along the lines. 'All the same, this don't make sense to me.'

'No,' agreed Alicia gently. 'Nor me either.'

Crook looked at her with sharpened interest. 'It was the first time he had even noticed I was there,' she said afterwards. 'I do detest men who treat women as if they were something to be had for half-price.' The girl, Crook was thinking, had some wits after all.

'Seems phoney to you, too, does it?' he suggested.

'I don't see why she should have written that, if she wasn't going to send it, I mean.'

161

'Maybe she did.'

'Then why do it as a draft? You don't need to draft letters of that kind. And where's the original? I'm sure Bishop would have kept it, if he'd had a signed letter of hers, blackmailing him. And she made the appointment that evening by word of mouth. I heard her. I told Alistair.'

'Yes, I remember you did. Still, she may have meant to write and . . . '

'Left these about for someone to find? Y'know, it don't hang together. If she didn't write this letter she could slam her cards down as easy as easy, and never mind what Bishop knew about her, she wasn't aiming to marry money and he was. And if she said her piece his plans were all shot to hell. No denyin' that.'

'You mean, the letter's a fake? That Aunt Tessa – oh, but that's absurd.'

'I've told you all dames are daft. And a lady past her first youth bein' fooled by a chap like Bishop gets very odd ideas into her cranium. I tell you, if I broke a wish-bone with your aunt and she got the half that counts, she'd pray for a noose for your cousin, and if she told me otherwise may she drop dead in her tracks.'

'It's the way it looks to me,' acknowledged Alicia. 'You see, Alistair, she has got a sort of complex about Anne, and – what was she doing up in the attic? She never does go up there.'

'She went up to fetch the pieces, of course,' said Crook sensibly.

'Having first put them there?'

'Well, you don't really think the young lady put them there, do you? I mean, I'm not a fussy man and I take on cases that other chaps would tell you stink, but I don't like working for complete maniacs, and if your cousin really wrote this stuff and then pushed it into the basket, she deserves to swing.'

'She didn't.' said Alicia in a small voice she had used before. 'Oh, I don't say she didn't shoot Bishop. I don't know. But when I went up to the attics after Anne had gone those pieces of paper weren't in the basket then. So you see what that means.'

'That someone put them there since.' That was Alistair.

'Or walked out of the attic and said they'd found 'em there. Bite on the bullet, chaps, because that's the way it is.'

'I wondered what she was doing there when I saw her coming out. As a matter of fact, I think it was just curiosity again. She was always asking Anne what she was doing up there, and when I went up she asked me what I wanted. I told her the truth. Lewis Bishop's death changed everything for me. I didn't know what Aunt Tessa's plans would be, but I realized I wouldn't play any part in them. So I thought I might as well be prepared for something. That's how I know the papers weren't there. I took the cover off the typewriter, and there were no pages lying about anywhere, no paper, no nothing. I practised for a bit, but I shall never really like typewriting, and anyhow typing's no good without short-hand, and I don't want to spend all the best years of my life sitting on the edge of a chair in some fusty old gentleman's club or else some hideous up-to-date office . . . ' Her voice shook. For a moment the disgusted Mr Crook thought she was going to burst into tears. But she recovered herself.

'Well, well,' said Mr Crook soothingly, when it was obvious that there was not going to be a scene, 'there's no end to the things ladies can do nowadays. Now, you're sure about the papers not being there when you went up after my client had been carted off to gaol?'

'Absolutely sure,' said Alicia emphatically, looking side-ways at Alistair to see if he was wincing. But Alistair looked as expressionless as a bread-board. He picked up the paper Crook had put down and began to look at it more carefully, saying, 'Whoever did this was in a precious hurry. Several of the letters have slipped or got left out.'

'Needn't have been in a hurry,' murmured Crook. 'Some of the slowest typists come to grief that way.'

'What do you make of it?' inquired Alistair bluntly.

Crook looked at him in some surprise. 'Pretty clear, ain't it?' he said.

'I – suppose so. But where's the sense?'

'Just the lady backing up her case.' The lawyer drew a deep breath. 'Poor old lady!' he said.

'In any case there's no signature. It's not evidence.'

'Not against my client – no.'

'You mean – you think . . . ?

'Little drops of poison, Little bits of clues, Pass 'em up to Arthur Crook, And he will see you through,' chanted the irrepressible Mr Crook. 'You know what they say. Straws show the way the wind blows. See here, I think I better stick around a bit. Will the old lady let me sleep in one of her attics?'

'Of course we can arrange accommodation,' returned Alistair, stiffly. 'I'll see about it at once.'

Alicia, left alone with Crook, seemed nervous of saying anything for a moment. He, however, had no such inhibitions. 'Funny case,' he said.

'What enrages me is that Mr Bishop wasn't worth it,' she exploded.

'No man is, sugar. Just you remember that while you've the chance. There's lots of times when it 'ud be a relief to take a meat-axe and do a bit of chopping, but – don't you do it. It's messy and what's more, it's dangerous.'

'When you said you were going to stay here,' pursued Alicia, 'did you mean because you expected to find out something else? I mean, are you on the track of anything?'

'I mean, if I'm here things may happen,' explained Crook, 'and if I'm not they won't.'

'What sort of things?'

'Where a dame's concerned it might be anything. And this case isn't fixed yet, don't you think it is.'

'They say that people who are – unbalanced – become very cunning, don't they?'

'Lots of folk can be cunning without being unbalanced, and lots of folk never are balanced anyway, so where's the odds? Look here, don't you say anything to the old lady about all this.'

'Of course not.' Alicia sounded outraged, but Crook only

said, heartily, 'There's a good girl,' and turned to greet the re-entering Alistair with a cheerful, 'All set? That's fine. What do you do about dinner here? Soup-and-fish or just a clean collar?'

Chapter 12

DINNER was a difficult meal. Mr Crook's notions of evening dress affronted Dutchy, who quite clearly resented his presence in the house in any case. Mrs Goodier made the mistake of asking him whether he had ever defended a man or woman and achieved an acquittal only to discover afterwards that his client had been guilty.

Crook didn't actually lay his finger against his big nose, but his expression was so subtly vulgar that it amounted to the same thing.

'Never!' he said emphatically. 'Discretion's my middle name. When a case is finished, I don't even remember my client's names. That's the way they like it, too.'

'But did you never find yourself mistaken half-way through a case?' Tessa persisted.

'Of course not,' said Crook. 'It's part of my job to get all the facts first.'

Dutchy intervened with a sort of cold venom that made Alistair feel hot and wonder why women seemed born without the social skin that is natural to all men. 'Then you've been more fortunate than a number of very famous counsel, Mr Crook. They've had to admit on occasions that their clients were, unhappily, guilty, and throw up the case.'

'Damned dishonest of them, if that's true,' returned Crook, scowling so that his thick red brows met above his formidable nose. 'Their job isn't to satisfy their own conscience but get their client off. Besides, it was up to them to find out in advance whether the chap was guilty or not. And don't tell me it can't be done,' he added forbiddingly to Miss Dutchley to whom he had taken an instant dislike, 'any chap worth his

165

salt knows exactly if he's working for the chap that did it or not.'

'But Mr Crook!' Tessa sounded horrified. 'You wouldn't work for anyone you thought was guilty!'

'That don't make sense to me,' returned Crook. 'Someone's got to do his best for them. Seein' they ain't sustained by a clear conscience,' he added in explanatory tones.

'But – it's wrong.' Mrs Goodier looked staggered.

'Only if the jury see through you, and most of the time they don't. Besides, right's what you can make other people believe, and if I and my counsel can make a jury believe that A didn't kill B even though we all know he did, then A's innocent. It's quite simple really.'

Tessa laid down her knife. Alistair had a sudden premonition of what was coming and tried to speak, but he was too late.

'Mr Crook,' said Tessa with appalling clearness, 'do you know, as we all do, that my niece, Anne, killed Mr Bishop?'

There was a little flurry and clamour, Dutchy, Alicia, and Alistair all making sounds that fell a little short of words. Only Crook remained unmoved.

'I don't know it,' he said, 'but then I wasn't there. But if I did, it wouldn't make any difference. Y'see when you're on a job the way I am you get the facts and then you make the best pattern you can. Like playing cards or needlework, though I can't say I'm much good at either.'

'And if you had evidence?' breathed Tessa.

'You don't know much about the law, do you, lady?' suggested Crook, but his voice was quite kind. 'I haven't got any evidence the other side hasn't got. It's like a game of skittles. I try to knock down their skittles, and they try to knock down mine. Take these notes you found in the waste-paper-basket, for instance. You say, and the prosecution will back you, there's proof Miss Vereker was in a plot with Bishop and had good reason for murdering him when it looked as though he was going to spill the beans. I say, "There's no proof she ever wrote the letter. Someone else did thinkin' it made a better case against her." See what I mean?

It's like a penny; it has two sides. Unless it's a fake penny, those two sides are different. It's just luck if it comes down heads or tails.'

'I quite understand,' flashed Mrs Goodier. 'You'd rather suspect anyone than my niece. Me – or Alicia – or my nephew here – or – Dutchy, can you typewrite?'

'No,' said Dutchy bluntly, 'I can't.'

'It's very useful,' said Mrs Goodier. 'Theo always said so.' Her mind seemed to have wandered away suddenly. 'Alicia, you should practise more. If you want a job . . . '

'Oh, I don't want that sort of job,' said Alicia airily. 'It doesn't lead anywhere. I shall probably go on the stage.'

The suddenness of this decision took them all by surprise. 'But I thought you had to go on in your teens,' exclaimed Alistair.

'People don't always.'

'I didn't know you could act,' added Mrs Goodier tactlessly.

'I daresay I shouldn't be any worse at that than at typing, and at least I might get some fun. Besides, I've done a lot of amateur acting and I could do impersonations like that Pollock woman. She's frightfully successful. And I could stage-manage, I know. Uncle Theo's ideas about women were absolutely archaic. Marry and be a domestic drudge; work and be an office one. He thought there was something wrong about having fun.'

'He didn't think it was a very good aim to have in life,' said Mrs Goodier loftily. Anyone to hear her, Alicia observed in stormy tones to her cousin later on, would think she'd worked her fingers to the bone ever since she was a girl, instead of having quite an easy time of it and marrying a rich man. 'I loathe rich people; they always think their money is a sort of virtue that gives them the right to dictate.'

Crook said, 'One man's fun is another chap's chokey,' and no one quite knew how to take that, so the subject got itself changed, and conversation remained fairly amicable until the end of the meal. Crook eased the situation by disappearing pretty early in the evening. Alistair had found an opportunity to say to him, 'You mustn't pay too much attention to my aunt, Crook. This affair's shaken her up badly – well, you can see that for yourself – and she's really not quite capable of getting things into perspective.'

'It's when they see things crooked they're generally the most dangerous,' returned Crook, dryly. 'I think I'd be wise to keep an eye on your lady aunt, and you might keep an eye on that old battle-axe you call Dutchy. She'd put out my light without any hesitation, if it suited her book. Women like that don't have consciences, they have intuitions, and her intuition at the minute is tell her to shoot straight up my street.'

It was soon after this he said he'd call it a day. Mrs Goodier had put him in a room a little way away from everyone else – she was sure he'd like to be quiet and not interrupted by the rest of the household was her way of putting it – in a little wing up a flight of stairs. Then he could sit up all night if he wanted to, figuring things out, she explained. Crook said the bogies never bothered him; if one came to do a frightening stunt he always got there first, and he didn't need to look in a mirror to see why. He was capable, too, of a directness of speech that left even Dutchy at the post. When Mrs Goodier was explaining about the isolation of his room he nodded comprehendingly and without apparent rancour.

'Don't think I'm going to make a speech,' he said. 'I leave that to the johnnies in Parliament who haven't anything better to do – but don't think I don't know you don't want a fellow you regard as a private dick roaming round your premises. You won't be pleased enough when it's time for us to part; well, I've got some other jobs on hand too, but I explained to Major Vereker, I had to come down here to hammer in the screws.'

'You mean you have a theory?' suggested Dutchy, taking the lead as she was accustomed to do when men came to the door trying to sell writing-paper or soap or patent stocking menders and someone with sense had to head them off.

'Lady!' Crook looked hurt. 'I've more than a theory. I know who shot Lewis Bishop.'

Even Mrs Goodier, who had done her best to ignore Crook since his arrival, stiffened with excitement.

'You know?' she repeated.

'Yes, lady. Only, knowing a thing ain't enough. You got to be able to prove it. And I won't be able to prove it for, say, twenty-four hours.'

'Do you think you're going to find something down here that will help you?' asked Alicia, looking perplexed and instantly glancing at Alistair to see what effect the announcement had on him.

'I figure something's going to happen. Things mostly happen when I'm around.'

'And when it has happened – whatever it is?'

'Then it'll be time to stage the last act and show you who did the job. As I say, I give the situation twenty-four hours to develop but it might take a bit longer. The result'll be the same, though.'

'When you say something will happen – what does that mean?'

'I mean, I think the murderer will show his hand and I'll step right in and shake it.'

Then he offered the party a bluff good-night and went off to bed.

He left behind him a very puzzled quartette, looking sideways at one another, each wondering what the others suspected, what would be their reactions to Crook's confidence.

'I wish I could make up my mind if he really knows what he's talking about or if it's all bluff,' said Dutchy frankly.

'From all accounts, he doesn't go in for bluffing – much,' Alistair told her. 'I've been going through the facts we have and wondering what we've missed. We were all on the spot at the time, we've been in and out of the house ever since. He's only just come in on the case and yet he can see through the dark, and we're still blinded.'

'All of us but one.'

'One?'

'The one who did it, of course.'

'Oh yes.' They all looked uncomfortable at that, and Mrs Goodier increased the tension by saying suddenly in a loud, emphatic voice, 'Alistair, I don't want that man here in my house. I don't like him. I'm sure Theo wouldn't have wanted him to be here. He may be very clever, but he's so common, like a tradesman. I don't like to think of him wandering about as if the place belonged to him, peering into all the rooms. I don't feel safe.'

'I don't think you've anything to be afraid of,' said Alistair gently. 'And it won't be for long. But I can't turn him out neck and crop. He's Anne's one hope.'

'I don't believe he's honest,' exclaimed Tessa vehemently. 'He hasn't got an honest face. He's the sort of man who'd do anything for money. If anyone offered him more to prove that Anne did do it, he'd throw you over at once.'

'That isn't his reputation,' murmured Alistair. 'He thinks a lot of his reputation.'

'He's as bold as brass, I'll say that for him,' contributed Dutchy grimly. 'Telling us all to our faces that he knows which of us did it. Too clever for the police, I suppose.'

'Personally I was backing James Goodier as the murderer,' Alistair acknowledged. 'And in fact it may turn out that way even now. It never seems possible that a member of one's own family could be guilty of murder.'

'Going round and laying traps,' whispered Tessa. 'Asking us questions and trying to make us betray ourselves. I didn't think you'd have a man like that in the house, Alistair.'

'No innocent person has anything to fear,' Alistair began, without much conviction, but Tessa interrupted him with a loud laugh.

'You heard what he said, that all he wanted was a number of facts and then he could arrange them as suited him best. He's like Judas Iscariot . . . '

'Well, the more we help him the sooner he'll go,' prophesied Dutchy sensibly, foreseeing an emotional collapse. 'Maybe he's going to prove that Mr Bishop shot himself. Anyhow, nothing we can do will make any difference now. Mrs Goodier, it's high time you came to bed.'

But Tessa shook her head dreamily. 'I can't go yet. I shouldn't feel safe with that creature about. You go, dear, and Alicia. I'll come up presently.'

Dutchy looked despairingly at Alistair, picked up her large useful knitting-bag and marched out.

'I've got my accounts to finish,' she said. 'Don't forget about turning off the lights.'

Alistair went off to his room, wondering where on earth all this was going to end. Every member of the household was keeping his or her counsel, and that seemed to him a bad thing. It seemed to suggest that no two of them were prepared to trust each other. It had another consequence also; it meant that there was no likelihood of picking up any hints or the smallest scrap of information. They were all afraid, that was the truth, afraid of self-betrayal. Even the innocent ones couldn't be sure that their simplest words would not be twisted and used against them. They were like an armed garrison, each man watching not for an enemy beyond the gate, but his neighbour and one-time friend.

Alistair found himself wishing desperately that it was all over. The strain would tell on the most steadfast mind. Let the whole affair be cleared up and life return to something like normality. And to him normality meant Four Acres. He began to wonder if perhaps he had gone a little crazy, lost his sense of proportion where the estate was concerned. Anyhow – he shrugged furiously – there was nothing to be done now but keep an eye on Crook. He'd look in on him before he went to bed, make sure nothing had been left undone.

Presently there was a light tap on his door and Alicia appeared on the threshold.

'Am I interrupting you, Alistair? It's Aunt Tessa. I can't do a thing with her. She won't go to bed or listen to anything I say. She's just sitting with her hands folded on her knee, staring into the fire, and when I spoke to her just now she looked at me as though she had no idea who I was.'

'I'll come down,' said Alistair. 'Though I daresay I shan't be able to do much. You ought to be asleep, Alicia.'

'I can't sleep. I never felt so wide-awake in my life. I think

171

it's having Mr Crook here, though he's sleeping all right.
I should think you could hear him in Piccadilly Circus.'

'I know he's a rough diamond, but in an emergency
like this we can't afford to pick and choose, and he's
much more likely to be helpful to us than any Piccadilly
Percy.'

'I'm like Aunt Tessa. I shall be glad when it's all over. He's
got some plan in his head and he won't care who suffers so
long as he wins his case. You can say that even Crook can't
make out some one is guilty who isn't, but according to you
that's exactly what the police have done.'

'I suppose that's true,' Alistair agreed. They had reached
the first floor where the drawing-room was situated. Alistair
put out his hand to open the door. Alicia, who had been
hesitating, turned suddenly.

'Alistair, if there's anything I can do to help you, about
Anne or anyone, you know I will. Never mind about me being jealous of her, I can't help that. But there's nothing I
wouldn't do for you. You know that, don't you?' Her voice
was gentle and steadfast, but Alistair immediately felt panic-
stricken. She waited a moment and then, when he did not
speak, she went on, 'At least you'll let me help. Won't you?
Won't you?'

'Of course, if you can. The trouble is there's nothing any
of us can do.' To his relief Dutchy suddenly appeared on the
staircase.

'Isn't anyone going to bed to-night?' she demanded
crossly. 'That Crook creature is trumpeting like an elephant,
and everyone else is gossiping – there won't be a chance of
getting to sleep . . . '

'I don't feel like going to sleep,' declared Alicia.

'You will if I bring you some hot milk. And you can take
one of your sleeping-tablets.'

'Oh, but . . . I wonder if it would be a good idea.'

'You can't do anything this hour of the night,' said Dutchy
impatiently. 'Alistair, I wish you'd persuade Mrs Goodier to
go to bed. We shall be a mass of neurotics before your Mr
Crook leaves us, and I daresay that's what he wants. Thinks

172

if he can get us all raw enough we shall tell him everything we know.'

'Well,' said Alistair, thinking it wasn't going to be much fun if Dutchy collapsed, 'I daresay that wouldn't take most of us long.' He smiled at both women and went into the drawing-room. Dutchy said crossly, 'Now then, Alicia, get to bed and I'll bring your milk. We don't want to have you catching your death of cold,' and went off. Alicia watched her go and then moved on to her own room. When you've dreamed a dream for years you don't abandon it because the circumstances aren't propitious. She knew what she wanted, meant to have it, if she could. It might mean taking a chance, putting cards on the table, but some risks you have to run. Like Mrs Goodier, she wished Mr Crook anywhere but at Four Acres.

Alistair went into the drawing-room and found Tessa sitting as Alicia had described her. Quiet, rigid, her hands folded on her knee, her eyes fixed on the falling flames. Yet for all her posture of resignation life burned in her. He felt it like something physical as he came close.

'Aunt Tessa!'

She turned sharply, her face changing into credulous pleasure as though some miracle had taken place and she could not yet believe it; but after an instant her face resumed its stiff impersonal lines.

'Oh, Alistair, it's you. I told you not to bother about me. I wish you'd all leave me alone. You and Alicia and Dutchy . . . Oh, I know you mean well, but there's nothing any of you can do and all I ask is a little peace.'

'We want you to go to bed,' said Alistair patiently. 'I'm going to turn off the lights.' For that was Tessa's latest fad – she knew the house would be burnt down while they were all in their beds. A similar catastrophe had occurred to someone whom she knew in the neighbouring county a few days ago and a faulty electric wire had been blamed.

'If it could happen there it could happen here,' she insisted. 'I'd feel happier if all the lights were turned off.'

So now Dutchy went round putting candles in all the bed-

173

rooms and grumbling at the unnecessary work. It was much more dangerous having candles, she said, because candles were a naked light and there were so many old-fashioned curtains and covers at Four Acres it would be a miracle really if the place wasn't burnt down.

'Well, turn them off,' said Mrs Goodier impatiently this evening as Alistair made his ineffectual efforts to coax her to move, 'I have the fire. I can see quite well by that.'

'But when you go to your room . . . ' he urged.

'I'm not going to my room. It's no good, Alistair. I can't sleep there. It's haunted. You can look as sceptical as you please, but it's true.'

'By – Bishop?' He couldn't believe she really meant that.

'You thought he was second-rate, didn't you?' The calmness of her voice startled him. 'But you don't marry a man because he's first-rate. Any woman would understand. Even Alicia . . . Alicia's been very good. She talks of going to London, getting work. I must see she has some money just to tide her over. Yes, as I say, she's been very good, but I was never one of those women who're satisfied just to have women all round them. Theo was such a man, that's why I miss him so. It really isn't worth all the trouble it takes to keep life going just for yourself or another woman. That's why I first thought about marrying Lewis. It put some meaning into my days. And now he's gone and the meaning's gone, too.'

Alistair tried to say, 'There are other men,' but the words stuck in his throat. She seemed to-night so old, so wild, a creature of legend and witch-lore. He saw that she had lost flesh since the night of the tragedy. Her hair, that was so abundant and in which she formerly took so much pride, looked draggled and dull.

'Do you believe in ghosts?' she demanded. 'Theo didn't, but then he didn't need to.'

Alistair hesitated. Any man of imagination and spirit who had his experience might well hesitate before giving a good round 'No' to that question. 'I don't think Bishop is haunting this house, if that's what you mean,' he said at last.

'Perhaps not. But someone is. And I don't think it's Theo. I'm sure I'd recognize Theo's ghost.' He looked at her in increased apprehension. At this rate she would surely soon be certifiable. But he saw that she did not seem to appreciate that there was anything strange in what she said.

'When you say haunt, Aunt Tessa, what exactly do you mean?'

'Footsteps – outside my door – and if I open it there's no one there. Hands at the door, invisible hands. I hear it open, the door, I mean, and then I lie waiting, waiting, for the hands to touch my throat.'

'You know, you've let all this get on top of you,' said Alistair sensibly. 'You'd do much better to go into an hotel for a while.'

'And be pointed at by everyone as the woman who meant to marry Lewis Bishop and was fooled by her own niece staying under the same roof?'

It was hopeless. He couldn't get anywhere.

'Besides, you don't escape things by running away from them. Alistair, you don't think I'm going mad, do you?'

This was so completely what Alistair did think that once again he had to hedge. 'You're overwrought and no wonder,' he said. 'But it's important we should all be as clear-minded as we can just now. You don't want Crook to get the idea that any of us are unreliable witnesses.'

She exclaimed in a sort of proud fury, 'It's nothing to me what that creature thinks. I don't want to have anything to do with him. I don't want to answer his questions or have to speak to him at all. I don't know why you couldn't have got a gentleman. But I suppose none of them would take it on. Has Dutchy said anything?'

'About Crook?' Her changes of mood were bewildering.

'No, no. About me. She thinks I'm deranged. I realize that. I believe she and Alicia are in a plot together. Perhaps it's they who creep about at night just to frighten me, though what good they think I shall be to them in a lunatic asylum I can't imagine.' Suddenly her eyes brightened; her hands

175

twitched at his coat. 'Alistair, will you do something for me? Something to help me to prove what I suspect? Will you sleep in my room to-night and let me have the spare-room? I wouldn't let Dutchy put Mr Crook in it. I'm not going to have that creature sleeping practically next to me, I told her. Alistair, will you?'

'Of course, if you wish it, but . . . '

Her grip tightened. 'Don't you see, no one will know. If there's a plot you'll be able to uncover it. Have the others all gone to bed?'

'I think so. I certainly hope so.'

'Then there's no need for them to guess. Don't keep your candle burning, Alistair, and don't go to sleep. Then you'll probably find out I'm not such a fool as you think.' She stood up, standing so close to him he could have encircled her with his arm, yet, in spirit, he felt so remote that a county might have separated them. She put out a hand in one of her customary vague gestures, and he took it and led her to the door in a manner which he felt to be ridiculous. As they reached it she turned to him and said with extraordinary emphasis, 'Wait till the morning, Alistair, everything will be different in the morning.'

Dutchy had heated the milk and taken it along to Alicia's room. This was kind of her, since she had never really come to regard the girl as one of the privileged members of the family and generally held that if she wanted fal-lals she could look after them herself. Alicia was sitting up in bed, her cheeks smeared with the thick cream she always put on at night, her hair in two dark plaits tied with ribbon framing her pale face. She was carefully rubbing cream into her hands.

'How long does it generally take you to go to bed?' asked Dutchy dryly.

'About twenty minutes. How kind you are. I really think I will take a sleeping-draught. I agree with Aunt Tessa. Things will be much more comfortable when Mr Crook's gone.'

She opened a bottle of sleeping-tablets and shook one into her palm.

'May as well take two while you're about it,' advised Dutchy. 'Make certain of a good night.'

'Do you think so? Oh, all right. I could certainly do with some sleep.'

She took a second and put the two into her mouth. 'That's right. Now drink the milk. Good girl. You won't let the rest of it get cold, will you?' Alicia shook her head. 'Got your candle and all that? Alistair's going to turn off the light before he goes to bed.'

She went out of the room and shut the door. She stood for a moment on the mat outside, thinking.

Alistair, meanwhile, had gone round the house performing the round of small jobs he had set himself before retiring for the night. He had decided not to warn Crook that the electric light would be switched off at the source. It wasn't, he decided, necessary. It did not take him very long to complete his duties, and then he went cautiously along to Mrs Goodier's room. By this time the house was in complete silence, a silence that afterwards seemed to him too deep to be natural. It is in the depths of silence that sound begins to stir.

Lying awake in the big bed Aunt Tessa had once shared with Theo Goodier, Alistair considered the position from the day of his return to Four Acres until the present stage. He had refrained from questioning Crook, having made a gentleman's agreement with him to this effect, but he had not been able to resist an occasional indirect suggestion. Crook, however, was not easily caught out.

'It could be, Major, it could be,' he would say in his robust way. 'But what we want is facts, honest-to-Bow-Street facts.'

'And if you can't get them?' Alistair had once asked.

'I'm here to get 'em,' had been Crook's terse reply. 'The chap that can't get the facts he needs is no use, and don't you believe anyone who tells you different. If they ain't on the surface you dig; and if you dig and they ain't there, then you manufacture them, don't ask me how. That's your job. The only thing you can't do is not produce the facts when they're wanted. I'm here to show that your lady cousin couldn't be a murderess – at least, that she didn't kill Bishop, and you can be sure I shall do it.'

How much, reflected Alistair, turning restlessly in the big bed, did he see? Of his own personal danger, and he must surely appreciate this factor, he did not appear to think at all. And yet in what peril he really stood! After a while Alistair found his attention wandering; his body became rigid, his ears strained. He knew that he was waiting for something to break the unearthly stillness of the house. He looked at the luminous watch on his wrist – it was a little after two.

It was almost half-an-hour later, thirty minutes during which he lay unnaturally tense, before the sound he had somehow known would destroy the night's peace actually materialized. It was heralded by the stealthy movement of feet over a carpeted surface, then the door of the room in which Alistair lay opened inch by inch. While this happened Alistair himself held his breath. A minute later the cry rang out – 'Fire! Fire!'

Alistair's voice, strong and clear, followed it. 'Coming!' He felt in the dark for his candle and succeeded in knocking it on to the floor.

'Damn!' he muttered.

The cry sounded again, very near at hand. Then he heard Dutchy's voice from the end of the corridor.

'What's the matter?'

'I'm coming,' he called again, tying the rope of his dressing-gown. 'Wasn't that Aunt Tessa's voice?'

Then they heard Tessa herself. 'Fire!' she shouted and came hurrying down the passage. 'Where is it? What is it?'

'That's what we want to know,' returned Dutchy, sounding cross.

'I always knew this would happen,' exclaimed Tessa. 'We should be burnt in our beds.'

'Is there really a fire?' demanded Alistair. 'Dutchy, can't you . . . ?'

'There is a fire,' said Tessa wildly. 'Of course there is. I warned you . . . '

'You've warned the whole house. I never heard such a shriek. If there had been a ghost you'd have waked it. Was it your idea of a practical joke?' She looked appealingly at Alistair.

'Were you having nightmares?' demanded Alistair. 'You shouted fire all right. I heard you and so did Dutchy. It was as obvious as – as . . . '

'An air-raid warning,' said Dutchy. Then she stiffened. 'Where's Mr Crook? He can't be sleeping through all this. Anyone would think an army had arrived at the door.'

'Where's Alicia?' demanded Tessa querulously.

'Sleeping, I hope. She took a double draught. We don't want the whole house peopled with neurotics,' added Dutchy under her breath. 'Alistair, had you better go along to Mr Crook's room?'

Alistair looked at her curiously. Did she suspect that when he got there he'd find only another corpse? Things go in threes, said the old legend. They'd had two bodies already – Bishop and Bletsoe. And perhaps Crook would complete the trio.

'I'll go along,' he said. 'If he's really sleeping through this half a dozen murders could take place under his nose.'

'He's probably drunk. I thought his manner most peculiar after dinner. And I meant to tell you, Alistair, good stuff's wasted on a man like that. Anything's good enough for him.'

When Alistair reached the head of the little staircase where Crook's room was situated he found the subject of Tessa's objurgations standing there in pyjamas as crude in their effect as the brown suit he wore by day – bright red with a blue collar was what he thought suitable for the nobs – looking as unperturbed as ever.

'Here's a thing and a very pretty thing. What's the meaning of this pretty thing?' he greeted Alistair.

Alistair came up to stand beside him. He could hear movements from other parts of the house, as the servants came agitatedly on to the scene.

'Nice sense of theatre!' suggested Mr Crook. He wore bright red leather slippers and there was a red monogram

179

that looked as though it had been designed for Medusa embroidered on the pocket of his pyjama coat. Alistair couldn't keep his eyes off it.

'No need to worry about the fire,' said Mr Crook amiably. 'You'd smell it if there was one. Or if you wouldn't I would. Why, I can smell a fire as easily as I can smell a corpse and that's saying something.'

'Then what . . . ?' began Alistair, but Mr Crook, who was as fresh as a daisy in spite of the hour, interrupted him.

'Ain't I telling you what? Look at this.' Alistair looked. It was a very simple contrivance, one of those old-fashioned traps that are as efficacious in 1945 as they were a century earlier. Someone had stretched a piece of coiled wire at the height of a man's knee, across the head of the stairway. It was attached at either end to a nail that someone had knocked into the wainscot on one side and one of the bannister rods on the other. The nails had clearly only been put there recently; there was a chip in the wood where the hammer had missed its mark.

'Very neat,' said Crook, approvingly. 'It's the simple things that win every time. The chap who slugs you over the head with a club and leaves you in a ditch gets off as often as not, while the one who works out some plan by Euclid and trigonometry flops at the first fence. Shame it didn't come off, isn't it?'

Alistair bent his lean six feet to examine the trick. 'I suppose the idea was that in the dark you'd trip over this . . . '

'Through ticket to Kingdom Come.' Crook nodded his red head vigorously. 'Now you see why I'm so sure there's no fire.'

'You mean, it was a trap to bring you out at the double?'

'That's how I see it.'

'And – what prevented you from obliging the plotter?'

(Damn it, thought Alistair in alarm, I'm beginning to talk like one of those bogus chaps on the films.)

'We-ell.' Crook was shamelessly theatrical, smothering a cavernous yarn when it was perfectly obvious that he'd never

180

been wider awake in his life. 'Tell you the truth, Major, I was rather expecting something of the kind.'

'What, to-night?' The words escaped from Alistair before he could stop them.

'Some time during my visit, and I thought if I was to drop a hint that I'd be goin' back in twenty-four hours X might get a move on.'

'And that cry of fire – that was to make you come dashing out? Did you hear the cry?'

'I wouldn't be surprised to hear Bill Parsons heard it in Marylebone High Street,' returned Crook in his twopence-coloured way. 'Sounded like your auntie's voice.'

'Yes,' Alistair agreed. 'She seems absolutely confused though.' His eyes fell on the wire again. 'Oh no,' he said quickly. 'That's not possible.'

'I didn't say it was.' Crook stooped and released the wire; it was actually a coiled curtain runner. 'Look, Major, let you and me keep this to ourselves. You know what women are when you start telling 'em things, and we're likely to have plenty of high-strikes without makin' any extra trouble for ourselves. Besides, they'll only ask a lot of questions.'

'I feel inclined to ask one myself,' acknowledged Alistair. 'Does this help you to identify the chap you're after?'

'You don't think I'm going to let anyone try to put my light out and just do nothing about it, do you?' Crook sounded staggered as well as incensed. 'Sure I'm going to use this. I'm afraid,' and here he recovered his normal urbanity, 'I'm goin' to be a big disappointment to somebody. But the truth is you don't catch an old bird like me first go off. The advantage I have over the rest of you is that I'm a professional and you're all amateurs, and while an amateur may make a lucky shot in the dark and pull off what's nowadays called a coo once in a while, mostly they're like the seed in the parable that withered away because it didn't have any root. I mean, they ain't got the stayin' power. Now me, I'm like that river or whatever it was the poet wrote about, I go on for ever. That's what X don't allow for. Pride, that's his trouble. Thinks he can put one over on Arthur Crook. Ah well, he'll learn. You can win a game of bridge by a fluke, but you can't fluke your way right through a rubber.'

Alistair had bent and was examining the wire that lay like a long silver worm on the shabby carpet.

'I know what that is,' he said. 'It was used during the war for blackout curtains.'

'Thus pointin' to a woman's hand,' agreed Mr Crook dramatically. 'Now, you tell the ladies they won't have to be bothered with me much longer. Me and the Scourge will be off by eight o'clock, and we'll be back about eight o'clock in the evening.'

'You mean, you're going to go back to London?'

'That's right. You must remember this may be a life and death matter to you, but it's just another job to me.'

'I still don't understand – I suppose you're going to London to round off some clue or other.'

'No need,' said Crook. 'Everything I want I've got here already.' He tapped his forehead. 'I look for a bit of home help, of course, but I shan't want that till I get back.'

'Why wait so long?' urged Alistair. 'Can't you finish the case now?'

'Well, hell.' Crook looked hurt. 'I haven't been here long, have I? Not long enough to wear out your hospitality. And you're going to get shot of me the whole of the day and I'll only trespass on your sheets for one night more, and then we're through.'

'I suppose you won't tell me . . . '

Crook shook his head. 'Lead and the ocean. Oh!' as Alistair goggled at him. 'I suppose that one was before your time. Wait and see. Got it? And I can't finish now because it ain't the right time. The witching hour may be all right for poets, but it's all wrong for chaps with an honest living to get. If ever you tried an experiment at two a.m. you'd know that for yourself. What I want is a party full of a good dinner and feeling right sides with themselves. No one feels that way at two o'clock in the morning. No, I'll be down to dinner on the dot, and after dinner we'll just run over the facts and then you won't need me to tell you who really shot Lewis Bishop.'

Chapter 13

CROOK went off cheerfully enough, but the household he left behind him was the reverse of gay. Alistair had passed on the message and repeated several times that he couldn't say what it meant, that he couldn't insist on Crook pursuing a certain line of conduct and that, having put the job in his hands, they could now only sit back and await developments. Alicia pestered him with questions as to what had happened that had made Crook suddenly depart.

'It's no good saying nothing,' she said with sudden anger, 'because everyone's wearing the most mysterious expressions. And it's no answer to say that Aunt Tessa had nightmares. And it's very odd to me that whatever it is should take place the one night Dutchy insisted on my having a sleeping-draught.'

'You couldn't have done anything,' said Alistair. 'There wasn't anything to do.'

Alicia said it sounded like a conspiracy. The fact was the tension of the atmosphere was affecting them all. No one knew what Crook had in mind, and their ignorance seemed to have bred a mutual mistrust. Which perhaps was what Crook had intended. It was Alicia who put the thought into words.

'I've been thinking,' said Alicia. 'Do you think he could be at the bottom of it? I mean, do you think he's gone away and left us on purpose because he knows that suspense will begin to wear us down, that we'll start thinking "I wonder if he . . . " "Could she possibly . . . ?" '

'Don't be so morbid,' said Tessa, sharply. 'I don't suppose he's thinking of us at all. I call it most remiss of him to go away before he's finished his job. No better than a plumber really. Just tears up all your pipes and then goes away for a week and leaves you without any water. Anyway, I can't think why he's making such a mystery about it. I'm certain who shot Lewis and I've said so all along.'

Even Dutchy looked almost at the end of her tether at this,

but Alistair stopped further altercation by saying in a slow voice, 'I wonder what it is one of us has been trying to hide and he's found out. Because Alicia's right. He's quite unscrupulous in one way. He wouldn't in the least mind destroying our faith in one another, if he thought it would help him.'

As the day went on the position, as military correspondents write, continued to deteriorate. Mrs Goodier bit Dutchy's head off, saying that the fact that she'd been treated like one of the family for twenty years didn't make her the head of the house. Dutchy responded tartly that living with a mad woman would try anyone's nerves. Alicia, asked by her aunt for the twentieth time what she thought Mr Crook had in mind, was goaded into saying in an hysterical voice, 'Well, I wasn't there when Lewis Bishop was shot, so perhaps he'll be able to prove I did it.'

Only Alistair contrived a surface control, and even he was aware of fears and panics moving under the surface of his mind. More imaginative than any of them, he could visualize Crook like a great lobster sitting in his office, drawing into his ruthless claws every titbit within reach, unhurried, unflustered, contemplating the evening's diversion as part of the day's work, possibly even forgetting that Four Acres existed until the time came to get back into the Scourge and come snorting and plunging back to the country.

All through the day the suspicion grew, until at six o'clock the atmosphere was as electric as though a real storm gathered and growled in the distance. Tessa, Alicia, even Dutchy stole to the windows when they thought themselves unobserved and watched for the sight of the car. They sat about, avoiding one another's company, recalling this and that, wondering about the nature of the experiment, their individual share in it. Each suspected a trap into which the unwary might fall. Crook's big, grim, unemotional face seemed to hang on the air at these moments, like the face of the Cheshire Cat appearing and disappearing from the Wonderland tree. When he came it was at a moment when no one was watching for him. And his hearty presence seemed to shatter all ghosts and lurking devils in the house. He came striding up to the front door, and he had brought what Alicia thought of as a posse of men with him. He introduced them without apology, standing in the panelled hall with its worm-eaten chest where an earlier Vereker had concealed the body of a foe not slain in honourable fight and watched by the cynical derisive features of an earlier generation, now hanging upon the wall.

'This is Bill Parsons,' said Crook, indicating a tall man with a handsome ruined face and a limp he couldn't altogether conceal. 'He was a recruit to the angels about ten years ago. That's when he came in with me. You must get him to tell you about it some time. This is Fred Foster and this is Henry Ward. Bill can tell you all about the diamonds. He's as good at finding stones as I am at finding stiffs, and an angel can say no more.'

'And – your other friends?' That was Tessa, barely restrained from outright rudeness by Dutchy and Alistair.

'I've just told you. They're down here to help with the experiment. We're a man or so short, y'see,' he added, as though that explained everything.

'What is this experiment?' asked Alistair on behalf of his side, all of whom were goggling with amazement or apprehension or indignation, he wasn't sure which, at the immediate prospect.

'I got the idea that if we staged a reconstruction of what happened that night we might get pretty near the truth,' Crook suggested. 'I have a notion how it was done, but then I'm not the chap who needs convincing.'

There was a sort of combined intake of breath at his brisk yet casual words. It seemed so obvious this was just a job to him, though it might easily turn out to be death for someone else.

'What are we expected to do?' demanded Tessa.

'I suppose he's going to tell us when he's ready,' replied Dutchy.

'I'm ready now,' said Crook. 'What I say is that, after dinner, we just go through what happened the night Lewis Bishop was killed. Anyone who was there that night can play the same part, and the rest of us will double for the absentees. We don't want to give you a lot of bother. Bill and me can put the library ship-shape.'

'There's nothing to be done there,' said Tessa uneasily.

'Nothing been moved? Chair, tables, curtains, everything the way it was? Well then, that's fine, isn't it, boys?'

'The curtains had to be sent to the cleaners, of course. They were in a terrible state. He was standing with his back to them, you see . . . '

'I get you,' said Crook. 'But you've got something you can put up in their place, I daresay.'

'I don't think we have,' returned Tessa coldly.

'Oh come, what about all that blackout you used to have hanging up here? You haven't cut all that down for petticoats for the heathen.'

'Surely we can imagine the curtains are there,' interposed Dutchy, seeing that Tessa looked like throwing a fit at any minute.

'Wouldn't be the same thing,' returned Crook. 'Mean to say, I'm goin' to be Bishop, standin' behind those curtains with my ear glued to the crack. If you could see me there you'd lose the spirit of the thing. No – no spontaneity – that's the word. No, don't you worry. Give us the tools and we will finish the job. We'll get it all ready before dinner and we can go into session immediately afterwards.'

It was Dutchy who reluctantly found the necessary yards of utility blackout that was all Theo would consent to buy. A lot of nonsense he had called it. Some chap in the Home Office has probably got a brother-in-law who's got the monopoly of this type of thing, and doesn't see why he shouldn't sting the country. 'Well, he won't sting me for much.' That was the kind of thing Theo always did say, and there were plenty of Theos up and down the country right through the war.

'He may not have been right in this instance,' said Crook. 'I wouldn't know. But there's plenty of graft going on all over the map all the time. Still, I ain't complaining. If there were no bad people there'd be no good lawyers.'

He trundled off, short and bright and determined, to join his three colleagues in the library. After a bit he shouted for Alistair.

'Now you were there most of the time, weren't you?' he said. 'Just draw me a plan, as near as you can make it, of how the party was standing that night. Put in the curtains, the place where Lewis Bishop came through, make it as watertight as you can. Fred and Henry,' he added chattily, watching the two men hanging the long blackout curtain over the window recess, 'are going to do Goodier and Bletsoe for us, I'll be the victim and Bill shall be props man, do the lights and so on. Oh, and I've brought a property gun.' He put his hand into the pocket of his monstrous ulster and lugged out a pretty handy-looking weapon. 'It's not loaded,' he said, 'though I daresay you could do quite a lot of damage if you hit someone on the head with it. Now, you'll want that presently. Or wait a minute. Don't the old lady produce it in the first place? I suppose she's not likely to run amok or anything? She looks a bit daft to me.'

'Oh, I don't think you need be afraid of that,' said Alistair a little stiffly. 'She's been rather shaken by all this.'

'It could be,' allowed Crook generously. 'She's no chicken either, is she? Anyway, there's no sense giving it to her too soon. Now, got that plan?'

'I'm doing it now. This is how we all stood as near as I can remember.'

'You'd better come and have a look, too,' Crook invited his colleagues. 'Forward, the backroom boys. Henry, you can be Bletsoe – same name, see. Fred plays Goodier.'

He pored over the plan and they pored with him. It was simple enough. It didn't take long to memorize it.

'Now be sure you get it right,' Crook implored them. 'Everything depends on inches here. Where's the table where you put the gun?'

'Down by the curtains here. Dutchy put the lamp on it, too, or at least I did, when I took it from her. Of course, the gun had gone by that time.'

'And Bishop comes through this gap in the curtain.'

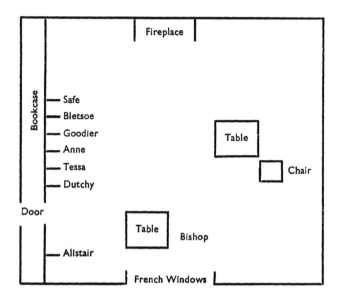

'Well, he makes the gap and doesn't quite close it behind him.'

'And he's not so far from the little table.'

'Meaning he could have put out his hand and got the gun before making his spectacular appearance? Well, he could, of course, but . . . '

'Look here,' said Crook, 'this is a life and death matter. We can't afford to do guess-work. What we've got to do is prove something. Got those curtains fixed, Fred? That's fine.' He vanished into the recess. 'By gum, it's dark in here. The reading-lamp don't throw much light. Like a little room it is, ain't it?'

There was no storm to-night, but it was black beyond the window-pane, a sky like ebony with no stars, only a little wind sighing among the trees. Crook came back again.

'Of course, he could peek through the curtains, and that's what he did do. That's why he was dangerous perhaps. Or not, as the case may be. Now we're all set. Give me that plan, Fred. I've made out a sort of dialogue I'll hand you boys presently just to guide you. I'll get Miss Turner to take Miss Vereker's place. Didn't you say she knew something about acting?'

'Amateur,' said Alistair vaguely. 'Talks about doing stage-managing or something. I daresay there's not much in it.'

'She doesn't like me, that girl,' observed Crook in reflective tones. 'Thinks I'm too bossy, I shouldn't wonder. Maybe if I knuckle down a bit and ask her advice – stage-setting, say – she'll be a bit more helpful. After all, she's goin' to be important and I don't want her to muck things up for me. Well, well. That'll do. Now we'll wash our celluloid collars and we're ready to eat.'

At dinner, Bill Parsons, looking, thought Dutchy disdainfully, like something out of an Egyptian collection, told them about the diamonds.

'Goodier had 'em all right,' he said. 'That could be what Bletsoe knew about him. Tryin' to do a bit of blackmailin' on his own account, poor little devil. But if it's true there are some fellows born to be martyrs, so there are others born never to succeed. I guess Bletsoe was one of that crowd.'

'Success didn't help Mr Goodier much,' said Dutchy hardly. 'Perhaps he was born to be unlucky, too.'

'Take the tip of a pro.' said Bill in earnest tones. 'Work on your own. It's the only way to be safe. If a job needs two pairs of hands, don't touch it. It'll be too expensive in the end. I tell you,' his face assumed the concentrated intelligence of a Minister laying down the law of his Department in the House of Commons, 'working with anyone else, you're about as safe as a fellow on an ice-floe during a heat-wave. Our prisons are packed with chaps who took partners or joined gangs and sooner or later they were sold up the river.'

'Bill's speaking from first-hand experience,' contributed Crook. 'No one knows more about that side of life than he does. He must have been a perpetual headache to the police force for about fifteen years, before he turned his coat and came over to me.'

189

Tessa, it was obvious, had not taken in the implications of this. Dutchy, who had, looked disgusted. Alicia, freed of the inhibitions of an older generation, asked frankly, 'Do you mean you've been associated with thieves?'

'I was telling you,' said Bill, suddenly looking bored, 'I was never associated with anyone.'

'Bill's coming along a treat,' continued Crook admiringly, this time to Alistair. 'He's one of the nobs really. You know what I mean. Adapts himself to his company. In a bang-up setting like this he knows he's expected to sing for his supper – and is he a nightingale?'

*

The meal seemed endless. Crook chirped away like a London sparrow, and ate in a manner that made Dutchy scowl. Even if the food position wasn't quite as stringent as it had been, most people were careful as to how much they ate in strange houses, particularly in the country where you couldn't eke out your rations by meals in hotels and restaurants. But Crook ate steadily through everything that was set before him. The household, however, scarcely touched their food, even Alistair making the veriest pretence of eating. Dutchy, who was angry with Crook for his excellent appetite, was also illogically angry with Alistair because he left his food practically untouched. She refused to admit that this attitude was the result of a deep inward fear; and when she looked, not openly and frankly as was her wont, but with quick side-ways glances, at her companions, she was convinced that she saw a reflection of that fear on each face. Alicia was right. Whether it had been his intention or whether the result was purely fortuitous, Crook had succeeded in filling them all with – not precisely fear perhaps, but mistrust of one another. He himself was so horribly cocksure, so certain that in the course of the next hour he would have pinned down the criminal. It might be bluff, but was ever bluff so assured as this? And, argue with themselves as they might, not one could escape a sense of profound unease at the thought that someone round that table in all probability knew what exactly had happened on the night of Lewis Bishop's death.

At last Crook said, if everyone was finished, he thought they might as well get started. He didn't want to hurry anyone, he added politely, but the experiment might take a bit of time . . .

'I don't yet understand what Mr Crook proposes to do or what value he thinks any action of his is going to have,' remarked Tessa. She didn't address Crook directly, just spoke to the table at large.

'I understand we are going to have a – a re-enactment of what happened on the night in question, and that will show us just what took place.' That was Alistair, cool and polite as ever, but looking a good deal less than happy all the same.

'Since Mr Crook wasn't there I fail to see how he can hope to convince us,' cried Tessa, impatiently.

'I take it that's what he intends to do just the same.'

'And whatever he proves or thinks he proves I, for one, shan't be convinced,' continued Tessa scornfully. 'I'm sure the police are right, and I'm almost sure we're disloyal trying to obstruct them.'

'So you'd never put up a fight, Mrs Goodier? You might make life simpler if you had your way, but you'd make it infernally dull.'

Alistair had the thought, Theo would have liked this chap. He liked the penny-plain method and the twopence-coloured suiting.

'Well, if we must go through with this,' said Tessa, 'we may as well begin now. It's going to be very embarrassing, though I suppose I could hardly expect Mr Crook to appreciate that.'

'Oh, it'll be embarrassing all right,' Crook agreed, 'Still, it's goin' to be illuminatin' too, which is more than you can say of the night.'

Alistair thought, 'If Aunt Tessa were a Borgia she'd have prevented all this very simply by seeing to it that henbane was put in Crook's goblet. Why does she feel so strongly about it?'

He supposed that in his heart he knew the answer to that. But he couldn't pretend to like the situation. It was too dangerous altogether. As they got to their feet he heard Bill Parsons heave a sigh of relief. He had been trying to sustain a conversation with Dutchy, but had been unable to find a subject of mutual interest. Dutchy realized that he came out of a different drawer from Mr Crook, but when she tried to find out anything about him he shut up like a hedgehog shrinking from an exploring finger. Like his employer he defied sympathy just as he defied curiosity.

The library struck extraordinary chill, although a sulky fire had been lighted there. The blackout curtains, hanging limply from their high rod, were a poor substitute for the rich gaiety of those that had hung there on the night Lewis Bishop died, and behind which he had concealed himself.

'An arras!' exclaimed Alicia suddenly, and they all turned to stare.

'What on earth?' began Dutchy and Alicia explained, 'It was the setting. It reminded me – I don't know why – we did *Hamlet* once with our Society – I was Ophelia . . . It's always the same with amateur productions,' she went on. 'You read the instructions, you know exactly what you want, probably marble pillars and cloth of gold, and you have to do the best you can with a couple of broomsticks and some blackout curtains.'

Crook, who acted all the time, secretly thought pretty small beer of amateurs, people who played at work and gave themselves airs because they weren't paid for it. But he remembered his intentions regarding Alicia, and, putting on his best alligator smile, he said, 'I was thinking, Miss Turner, you might help a lot, seeing you know about acting and so on. I'm not much of a hand at that sort of thing myself. Now, the Major's written out a plan of the way everyone was that night, and seeing we're short of a man or two Fred and Henry are going to read off their parts from some notes Bill and me have made out, and maybe you could vamp for Miss Vereker and just keep an eye on things generally.'

'Are we supposed to remember what we said that night?'
demanded Tessa.

'Well, the general idea would be enough. Stands to reason
we're bound to gag, but if we get the sense we can't go far
wrong. Now here's the table – so. That's right, Major? Okey-
doke. And you must be standing pretty near it, right up
against it, in fact, with your lady aunt against the bookcase.'

'That's right,' said Alicia briskly, who had no intention of
being overlooked. 'Then – let me see – I'm here. And Mr
Bletsoe and Mr Goodier just beyond.' She spoke as though
she were opening a charade. Her tiny taste of power delighted her. Yes, thought Crook shrewdly, and it'll prove her
ruin too. I've seen it happen before. These bossy females! He
looked from her to Alistair, but the young man was wearing
his wooden expression again. You might get more information out of the kitchen door.

'I know where I stand, thank you,' said Tessa, deliberately
moving a few inches out of her own place. 'Dutchy, you were
close beside me. I do hope, Mr Crook, this won't take very
long.'

'No longer than I can help,' said Crook. 'We'll have to do
it twice, y'know. Once to show that Miss Vereker didn't do it,
and once to show who did.'

Even Alistair was startled by that. He threw Crook a sharp
glance, but Crook was busy with window-dressing and appeared not to notice.

'Now!' he said, looking rather like one of those people who
conduct entertainments on our less spectacular seaside piers,
'all set? That's where everybody was when the light went
off. But we'll start earlier than that.'

'How much earlier?' inquired Tessa.

'Begin at the beginning, don't you think?' said Crook.
'I'll play Bishop. I'm sitting in a chair by the reading lamp?'
He took up his position. 'What next? Cigarette case, isn't
it? Bill, lend me yours. That's open, isn't it, because Goodier
says that's the way they knew he hadn't gone to bed. Right.
The rest better wait in the hall for their cues. I'll leave all that
to you, Miss Turner. Vamping don't matter so long as you

keep it short. It was deeds not words killed Lewis Bishop.'

'Surely that's only indirectly true,' objected Dutchy, who could not resist trying to score off this odious little upstart on every conceivable occasion.

'Oh, I don't think so,' said Crook, who would never be popular with ladies, he always refused to rise, no matter how tempting the bait. 'I think he was for it, anyway. But, of course, it was convenient for X, that the tragedy, crime, call it what you like, should take place when as many of the family as possible were gathered together in one place. Now, who comes on first?'

'Goodier,' said Alicia in her most professional tone. 'Who plays him, by the way?'

'Fred. Good Lord, I didn't give you the scripts. I forgot.' He hauled them out of his pocket and handed them across. Alicia looked scandalized.

'Do you mean, they haven't even read them yet?'

'Have a heart, lady. This ain't Drury Lane. All they've got to do is read off what's written down there. We ain't going in for atmosphere or art for art's sake or anything of that kind. It's just to get the picture right.'

'Is it necessary to have them in at all?' asked Tessa.

'Well, they were there at the time, they can't be eliminated. And if they were there they had to come in somehow. Now, let's go. Make it as snappy as you can. No need, f'r instance, for the long scene between Miss Vereker and Bishop. That don't lead us anywhere. When I come in I'll say, "It's about time we had a bit of light on the scene," and then Bill can switch off the reading-lamp and the fun begins. Got your match-box, Major? Right. Curtain up.'

He sat down, opened the paper and settled himself comfortably. 'Don't forget to give me some warning you're coming, Fred,' he added over his shoulder.

'Surely James Goodier wouldn't have wanted to attract any more attention than he could help?' suggested Alicia, jealous of her rôle of mentor.

'Well, the way I figured it out is he couldn't be sure he'd find the library empty and if he should be seen coming down the stairs he had the sense to know he'd attract a lot more attention if he crept on all fours than if he came the usual way. Bletsoe can creep, if he likes. I daresay he did. He was the creeping sort. Besides, honest men don't carry torches around, not when they're indoors.'

He shook open the paper again. The rest of the company retreated, Alicia very much in command, Dutchy in almost open revolt, Tessa resentful and bewildered. Only Crook's two henchmen and Alistair walked through their parts according to schedule, and they made no attempt to create atmosphere. Alicia thought that no real amateur company would have used them.

You could have heard Fred Foster coming a quarter of a mile away, thought Crook, grinning a bit but serious enough underneath, because so much depended on this experiment. It was a wild shot and it was quite doubtful whether it would find its mark, but since it was the only shot he had in his locker he had to make use of it.

The door opened and the pseudo-Goodier came in. He must be wearing nailed boots or else those wooden-soled footgear an enterprising Board of Trade tried so hard to popularize during the second World War. By the time the fellow was inside the room it was, to all intents and purposes, empty. Following the lines of the script the actor crossed to the safe, removed the books, mucked about a bit with the lock, and then crossed the room to where the key hung on a nail with a number of others. Although the atmosphere fairly tingled with apprehension, and mutters could be heard from the group assembled in the hall he refused to be hurried. It had been arranged that he should drop a book as a signal to the next man to make his entry, but he timed his movements to perfection. He opened the safe, located the diamonds, replaced them with a string of beads a thoughtful Bill had provided, relocked the safe and was turning to replace the key when his elbow knocked one of the books on to the floor. Instantly the door opened again and Henry came in, his eyes glued to the manuscript. The play that followed was factually correct but for sheer lack of animation and display it drove Alicia half-frantic. Both men read stolidly from their scripts, pausing where necessary for any action indicated. It went like this:

Bletsoe: Oh hallo. Didn't expect to find you here. I was looking for Bishop. Good Lord, what are you doing with those diamonds?

Goodier: What do you suppose I'm doing with them? Taking their photograph.

Bletsoe (unemotionally): I always knew you were a wrong 'un.

Goodier: Had plenty of experience identifying 'em, I don't doubt.

Bletsoe: Wisecracking won't help you. Where's Bishop? Or have you knocked him out?

Goodier: I couldn't say. Gone to the gents' perhaps. Anyhow, you can be sure he'll be back in a minute. He's left his cigarette-case there. He wouldn't leave that for anyone else to find. What do you want with him anyway?

Bletsoe: What's that to do with you?

Goodier: Seems a funny sort of time to choose. Or were you interested in the diamonds, too?

Bletsoe: I'm not a thief.

Goodier: That's news, that is.

Bletsoe: I don't know what the devil you mean. If I'd wanted to lift the diamonds I could have done it long ago.

Goodier: Instead of which you've been lifting a bit of the ready.

Bletsoe: You're crazy.

Goodier: That's why you're carrying a torch, I suppose.

Bletsoe: I didn't want to disturb anyone.

Goodier: I'll say you didn't.

Bletsoe: As it happens, it's very fortunate I did come down.

Goodier: You've got your head screwed on all right, haven't you?

Bletsoe: I don't know what you mean by that. I'm going to rouse the house.

Goodier: I wouldn't be surprised if you'd done it already.

Bletsoe: And tell them the truth.

Goodier: That's a funny thing. That's just what I was thinking of doing.

Bletsoe: You wouldn't dare.

Goodier: Truth, my dear fellow, is what you can make the other chap believe.

Bletsoe: I don't understand you.

Goodier: I'm going to tell them I came in and found you with the diamonds in your hand.

Bletsoe: That's absurd. How about the key? You're holding that.

Goodier: That's easily remedied. (Moving towards nail he replaces safe key.) And they might think it a bit odd that a chap who hasn't been here long should know where the key was kept.

Bletsoe (sharply): How did you?

Goodier: I didn't. I didn't open the safe, you see.

Bletsoe: But . . .

Goodier: Aren't you going to rouse the house? Of course, it may look a bit odd, you coming down – with a torch, too – this time of night – especially when it becomes known that you need money.

Bletsoe: Who says so?

Goodier: Having a bit of trouble with the accounts, aren't you?

Bletsoe: What do you know of my affairs?

Goodier: And it wouldn't be the first time either. There was that woman – hallo, what's up?

Bletsoe: What do you suggest I should do, then?

Goodier: In your place I'd be inclined to go to bed and have a lapse of memory.

Bletsoe: You mean, I'm just to keep my mouth shut and let you get away with it?

Goodier: Well, why not? What do you suggest?

Bletsoe: It might be worth your while offering to go shares . . .

Goodier: Ever heard of blackmail?

Bletsoe: You can drop that, because I . . . Look out! Someone's coming.

Goodier (slipping diamonds into pocket): Remember, if we're asked, we came down to see Bishop.

Bletsoe: What about the books?

Goodier: We don't know anything about the books. (Enter Anne.) Why, Miss Vereker, were you looking for Bishop, too?

Anne: Yes. But I didn't expect an audience.

Goodier: Bishop's unusually popular to-night.

Anne: Who left the safe that way?

Goodier: Bishop presumably. Shall we tidy up a bit?

Anne: If he left them like that no doubt he had his reasons. Hallo, the rest of the house seems to be on the war-path, too.

Alistair (outside): I think this is our cue, Aunt Tessa.

Tessa: I think it's perfectly ridiculous, and most disrespectful to Lewis's memory.

Dutchy: It's for his sake, anyway. Now remember to wave the revolver and that gives Alistair his chance of taking it away from you. (Enter Tessa, Dutchy, and Alistair.)

Tessa: I suppose it doesn't matter if I don't use the exact words. What on earth's going on here? Is it a party or something? And why wasn't I invited?

Dutchy: If it's a party, it's a very queer one.

Tessa: If it isn't a party, I call it most inconsiderate, waking everyone up. Don't you know it's nearly midnight? Alistair was in bed.

Anne: Poor Alistair!

Tessa: And I'm sure I saw you go up some time ago.

Anne: Yes, I know.

Tessa: Did they wake you too?

Anne: I wasn't asleep.

Goodier: As a matter of fact, I wanted a word with Bishop, and I didn't get a chance all day. I gather Bletsoe's in the same boat.

Tessa: It all seems very odd to me. Did Anne come down to see Lewis, too?

Anne: Yes.

Tessa: I don't understand. What do you want to see him about?

Anne: A – private matter.

Tessa: You've no right to be having secrets with the man I'm going to marry.

Alistair: Perhaps Bishop's gone to bed.

Goodier: I shouldn't think so or he wouldn't have left his cigarette-case there. You know how he is about cigarettes. I wonder where on earth he can be.

Bishop (appearing like a Jack-in-the-box behind the curtains and looking exactly like Arthur Crook): I can tell you that anyhow. I'm where I've been for the last twenty minutes, picking up the pieces.

Tessa: Pieces?

Bishop: Of the conspiracy against you, my dear Tessa. Oh yes, there is one and they're all in it. They're all out to skin you if they get the chance, and it's up to me to see they don't.

Bletsoe: How long did you say you'd been there?

Bishop: Ever since the first arrival in the library this evening. I thought it might be interesting to find out why it was such a popular room at this hour of the night.

Goodier: Well, and what did you learn?

Bishop: Some very interesting facts.

Alistair: I think I come in again here. I suggest examining the safe. I say, can't we cut it a bit? I open the safe and find the diamonds are gone and some trumpery necklace substituted, and then we're all as rude to one another as we know how, and Aunt Tessa brings us back to the crucial point of why Anne is down here at midnight. I don't think we need go into the mutual accusations scene, need we?

Tessa: I'm sure we've had quite enough of this. If Mr Crook is satisfied . . .

(Mr Crook was understood to say that he wasn't, not altogether.)

Bishop: As a matter of fact, I think it's about time we had a light on the situation.

As he said that one of his gang – it was Bill Parsons – clicked off the light. 'Now then,' said Crook, 'get down to business. This is the bit that matters.' The dialogue broke out at once.

Dutchy: I'll get a lamp.

Tessa: Don't go away, Dutchy. I don't like the dark.

Alistair: Half a minute. I've got some matches.

Goodier: Bletsoe brought a torch with him.

Bletsoe: But I've dropped it on the floor. (Something like a book fell with a crash.) I'll feel for it.

Anne: I'll help you find it.

Bishop: What about those matches, Vereker?

Alistair: Coming.

A match flared up, a little point of light travelling from Alistair's breast to a spot just above his head, hung there for a minute like a toy candle, and went out. But as it flickered Alicia straightened and moved forward.

'Hey there!' said Crook. 'You've got to wait for the match to go out or everyone'll see you. Cut. We'll do that again.'

Alicia flushed furiously at her mistake. 'We'd better call Dutchy back.'

'Don't matter. She didn't murder him. She wasn't there. Now then. Hurry up with those damned matches, Vereker.'

'Here we come.' Once again they heard the scrape of a match against the box, the little light appeared, moved, flickered, hung suspended for an instant in the darkness and expired. There was a moment's silence. Somebody moved. Dutchy's voice said, 'Here's the light.'

'What about that shot?' asked Crook, as Dutchy appeared carrying a candle.

'I couldn't find the table in the dark,' explained Alicia.

'Lights, Bill,' said Crook. The light came on. 'Now then, how many people heard the Major put that gun down on the table?'

'I don't know how you expect us to hear,' said Tessa pettishly. 'With all that noise going on . . . '

'And now I come to think of it there was a newspaper on the table. Why should they hear?' That was Alistair.

'Right. Then if they didn't hear, they saw. Now, how many people saw that gun when the Major lit his match just now?'

'I wasn't in the room,' said Dutchy.

'Alistair was between me and the table,' said Tessa.

'I'd want what Sam Weller called a double pair of million power gas lamps to see it by matchlight from where I'm standing,' said Fred. 'That let's Goodier out.'

'And I was down on all fours combing the carpet, so that lets Bletsoe out.'

'And Miss Vereker was helpin'. That's right, ain't it? So that let's her out. Well, there we are. I told you I'd show she didn't do it. Anyway, it couldn't have been done in the time. Even if she'd seen the thing she had to plunge across the room, pick it up, shoot Bishop, throw it down, and *find it again, in the dark*, and that's not so easy.'

'I don't want to make out it was Anne,' said Alicia. 'Only – who could have done it?'

'Not much choice as I see it,' returned Crook in pleasant tones. His eyes fell on Alistair.

Tessa stiffened. 'What do you mean by that?' she cried, in a voice that was almost a shriek.

'Well, lady, I can see as much as most men, but even I don't see how anyone standing on the Major's further side could have got hold of that gun.'

Dutchy's mind worked more slowly than the others. 'But – we were all on the further side.'

'Q.E.D.' said Crook.

There was a silence that was first perplexity and then in-credulous horror. Dutchy and Alicia exclaimed simultane-ously, 'You can't mean – not Alistair! Oh, but that's absurd.' They both turned to see him watching them, an odd smile on his lips.

'Well, it was either him or someone who wasn't there,' said Crook agreeably.

'It's absurd, it's wicked. Alistair, tell them . . . '

This pale ghost of Alistair opened its mouth. 'This, I take it, is what is known as being hoist on one's own petard,' he said. 'I got Mr Crook in to prove Anne wasn't guilty and agreed not to cavil at any alternative solution.'

'There's the County for you,' approved Crook. 'Look, the

lady seems a mite upset. How say we show her how it was done?'

'Oh, you're capable of any trick,' stormed Alicia. 'I don't want to hear anything else you may have to say. But though you may think yourself a man of genius, Mr Clever Crook, you're not going to make a court of law believe that Alistair shot Lewis Bishop.'

'There's one point that seems to have escaped your notice,' acknowledged Alistair. 'How did I shoot Bishop at close range without getting saturated with blood?'

'I hadn't forgotten that,' Crook assured him. 'That's one of the things I'm going to show you.'

'If it couldn't have been anyone else,' said Alicia excitedly, 'why couldn't Bishop have shot himself?'

'You show me how a right-handed man – he was right-handed, wasn't he? – shoots himself behind the left ear with a weapon that size. Besides, if he'd been going to do it himself he wouldn't have wasted time doing gymnastics first. And another thing, when did anyone ever know Bishop to give a halfpenny away, let alone his precious life?'

'I suppose Mr Crook is prepared to prove all this,' intervened Dutchy, her voice full of cold hate.

'I don't understand,' said Tessa. 'What's going on?'

'Mr Crook's going to show us how Alistair shot Mr Bishop.'

'Remember what Sherlock Holmes used to say?' inquired Crook, mildly. 'Eliminate all the impossibles, and what remains, however improbable, is your answer. That's all I'm tryin' to do.'

'It was Anne,' said Tessa in a hard voice.

'No,' said Alistair. 'It wasn't Anne.'

'Don't tell 'em,' Crook besought him. 'They won't believe you. Let 'em see for themselves. Now, Major, you come and sit over here, and Fred'll sit with you. Henry, you do lights. Now, take your places everybody. Are we O.K., Miss Turner?'.

Alicia looked round. 'I think so.'

'Right. Now we shan't be long. Someone give me the words.'

'Where the hell is Bishop?' inquired Bill Parsons.

'Here he is, and I fancy it's time we had a little light on the situation. Lights, Henry.'

Out went the lights, the faint clamour started afresh. The torch was flung down by the resourceful Fred from his place at Alistair's side, a chair went over, the match was struck, lifted, expired. Fred was scrambling with the second match when there was a loud click, a thud and a heavy fall. And an instant later before anyone in the room could move they heard the noise of the french window swinging to as it had swung on the night that Lewis Bishop died.

'That'll do,' said Crook, his voice sounding remarkably near the carpet. 'Lights, Fred. Of course, on the night the girl picked up the gun, but that part don't matter now.'

Fred switched on the lamp to reveal Crook lying large and lumpish but in no way disconcerted on the floor.

'Well,' he challenged them, 'now do you understand?'

'It couldn't have been Alistair,' said Alicia warmly, 'because the match was still being struck when the shot sounded. A man can't fumble with a match-box and pick up a revolver at the same time.'

'No more he can,' agreed Crook. 'Well, that puts the Major out. Because somebody chucked that gun on the floor, and if it had been loaded would have put me with Lewis Bishop before he did it.'

'Miss Dutchley was holding my hand,' said Tessa. 'And she was the further side of Mr – Mr . . . ' She looked aloofly at Henry.

'Quite. Anyway on the night she wasn't there. And if she was holdin' your hand you couldn't have done it. And I didn't shoot myself.'

'Then – you've accounted for everyone? Or do you mean it was someone from outside? But . . . '

Crook shook his head. 'Too far-fetched, lady, even for me.'

'But – a ghost couldn't have shot Lewis Bishop.'

'No. It's what I told you before. It was the Major or the one who wasn't there. And it wasn't the Major . . . '

'Where's Mr Parsons?' cried Dutchy suddenly. 'He's disappeared. Where did he go?'

'Why, through the window, of course,' said Crook. 'Didn't you hear it close behind him?'

'The window?' They all stared. Like a lot of cows, thought Crook, rudely.

'Sure. The same way the murderer went the night that Bishop was shot.'

Chapter 14

INSTANTLY pandemonium broke out. The clash of voices drowned anything Crook might have been trying to say. Alistair stood up. The watchful Fred rose with him.

'I'm not sure I understand,' confessed Alistair. 'You are accusing one of us?'

'I ain't the police,' Crook pointed out. 'I'm just offerin' you the facts. As you saw just now, Bishop *could* have been shot by someone standin' *in this room* who afterwards made his getaway.'

'But there was no one short when the lights went on again,' persisted Alistair.

Crook cocked a sharp red eyebrow at him. 'Sure? What you mean is, when Miss Dutchley brought in the lamp you saw the same number of people as you'd seen when the lights went out.'

'And the same people,' Alistair insisted.

'That's right,' agreed Crook, affably.

'You mean,' Alistair stared, 'there was a kind of invisible man in the room?'

'It could be. Kind of. Look here, Major,' he condescended to explanations, 'you raised the important point just now when you asked how you could have shot Bishop at short' range without gettin' spattered with blood. Well, naturally, the same applied to your cousin. I was pretty sure from the start she wasn't guilty, because if she'd shot him the blood would have been all over her shoes, the uppers, I mean, but in fact it was only on the soles. That proves she stepped into a pool of blood, and our problem is – who's responsible for the pool? Who was stained with blood?'

'No one,' returned Alistair, looking more perplexed than ever.

Tessa said sharply, 'The curtains were ruined. I don't care what those cleaning people say. They'll never be the same.'

'There you are,' said Crook. 'That's the cue I was waitin' for. Now, suppose somebody had been wearin' those curtains, what would you say?'

Tessa observed, 'I don't know if he's taken leave of his senses or if he's – ' she paused. Drunk was what she meant, and she might just as well have said it.

Alistair, however, was quicker, 'I'd say that that person was guilty. I think I have got there at last.'

'I wish I had,' said Dutchy.

'Mr Crook's trying to tell us that whoever shot Bishop was hidden behind the curtains, shot him from that protection and escaped through the french window. That right, Mr Crook?'

'You're warm,' Crook agreed.

'But we were all here,' protested Dutchy. 'That is . . . ' she stopped, staring.

'Yes,' said Crook gravely. 'I see you're gettin' warm, too. Now, there's one effect we left out to-night. Had to. That was the fallin' glass. Can't go breakin' windows just for art's sake.'

'And anyway,' said Alicia impatiently, 'the broken window hasn't anything to do with the – murder. It was mine, as it happened.'

'The only person who wasn't here on the night Lewis was shot was Alicia,' remarked Tessa, who was always a field behind the hounds. 'And if you aren't there you can't be guilty.'

'Q.E.D.' agreed Crook. 'And where was she?'

'In bed, I suppose.'

'Of course,' said Alicia. 'And I came down when I heard the shot.'

'But not right away,' suggested Crook.

'As quickly as anyone could. I only stopped to put on a dressing-gown.'

'Quite sure it was the shot that waked you and not the breaking glass? It was your window, after all.'

Alicia moved impatiently. 'Quite sure. The shot came first. Anyway, I don't see that it matters.'

'It could,' said Crook.

'And I know it was the shot,' Alicia persisted.

'I don't know how you can be sure, seeing you were asleep,' Crook objected.

'Because I didn't find out about my window till after I'd seen the police and had gone back to my room.'

'That so?' asked Crook. 'Got a lot of windows in your room?'

'Only one. The lower pane was cracked anyway. That's why it broke the night of the storm.'

'And you didn't notice it when you got out of bed? Didn't feel the rain coming in?'

'There are thick curtains over my windows. I always keep them drawn at night. And I didn't feel any rain because the rain couldn't come through those curtains.'

'Well now, there's something I don't understand,' confessed Crook handsomely. 'I thought Miss Dutchley said when she brought you up some tea, you were drying off the little coat that had got wet through lying under the window. Still, leave that. Now you came straight downstairs? Didn't stop anywhere on the way?'

'Nowhere. I came along the corridor and down the stairs. Alistair was phoning in the hall.'

'I daresay it takes a lady longer to put on a dressing-gown than a go-getter like me,' acknowledged Crook. 'I mean to say, the chap had been shot, and that had wakened you, and they'd waited for a lamp and examined the body and found the diamonds and hooshed the rest of the family out of the way before they thought about telephoning.'

'It didn't take more than a minute or two, actually,' interposed Alistair. 'And it's quite true I saw Miss Turner come down the stairs, if that's of any importance.'

'It could be,' said Crook again, in that maddening way of his.

'Do you mean you don't believe me?' Alicia looked ready to scratch his eyes out.

'Sure I believe you,' said Crook, in what was intended to be a soothing voice. 'That's just the way I thought it was. So you came down and went into the parlour along of the rest. And then the police came?'

'Yes. It's perfectly simple.'

'Well, is it?' demanded Crook, looking honestly puzzled. 'I mean, what I don't understand is how you got your hair so wet just coming out of bed and down the stairs? It was dripping like one of these water nymphs – or somebody who's just come in out of the rain?'

Alicia threw back her head. 'That's just what it was. I looked out of the window and saw the rain, felt it rather. It must have been very heavy, because I got wet so quickly.'

'That won't wash,' Crook warned her. 'If you'd looked out of the window you were bound to see it was broken, and you didn't know that not till afterwards. You've just said so. More, if you'd really been in your room when the shot was fired and then the window broke, you must have known it was your window. And you'd have moved the little coat, wouldn't you. You'll have to think of a better one than that, Miss Turner.'

Alicia's face seemed to grow thinner and sharper under his pitiless gaze.

'What are you trying to say, Mr Crook?'

He leaned nearer. 'I'm waitin' for you to tell me what you were doin' behind the curtains the night Lewis Bishop was shot?'

Tessa let forth a desperate cry that chilled the blood. 'What's he mean? What's he saying? That Alicia did it? Alicia, who Theo took out of the gutter practically . . . '

'Aunt Tessa!' pleaded Alistair.

207

'She'd have gone into a shop if he hadn't brought her here. And that's how she repays me, the . . . '

Dutchy put her hand over Tessa's mouth. 'Mrs Goodier, you don't know what you're saying. And anyway, nothing's proved yet. Mr Crook has a theory . . . '

'Of course nothing's proved,' said Alicia scornfully, 'and nothing will be. How can it, when it's a pack of lies?' But the experienced Crook could detect panic in that flaring voice.

'Well, if you weren't there, how come you knew that Goodier was the first person to come into the library? In the letter he left the night he killed Bletsoe, he said Bletsoe came first.'

Alicia struggled for control of a situation that was already out of hand.

'I don't suppose anyone believed that. Naturally, it's what he would say. You wouldn't expect him to incriminate himself.'

'It's mostly what they do do.'

'You're very clever, Mr Crook,' cried Alicia, her eyes like head-lamps in that shadowy room. 'Very clever and quite, quite unscrupulous. I suppose in a minute you're going to prove that I put the curtain-wire in front of your door last night? Only if you can prove it, why didn't you do anything about it at the time?'

'Well, this is a surprise,' admitted Crook, handsomely. 'Who's been letting cats out of bags?' He turned to Alistair. 'I thought we agreed to preserve a security silence.'

'I've said nothing to anyone,' said Alistair flatly.

'Then how come the lady knows about the incident? There's only one person beside me and the Major who could know – till this minute, that is – and that's X himself.'

Tessa, struggling free from Dutchy's restraining hand, came forward, demanding, 'What's all this about a wire? And why wasn't I told? It's still my house, isn't it?'

'Someone,' explained Crook politely, 'put a wire across the top of the stairs in front of my door last night, just before the fire alarm was sounded.'

'How ridiculous!' said Tessa. 'And very dangerous. I don't like these stupid practical jokes.'

'Oh, I think it was more than a joke,' said Crook.

'And why should anyone want to do such a thing?'

'If there was someone who wanted me out of the way, well, it was quite a good idea. Y'see, there are no electric lights in this house after midnight, and if you wake up and hear some chap shouting "Fire!" well, the obvious thing to do is to dive out of bed and come hell-for-leather on to the landing and see what's what. And if there happens to be a bit of wire at the top of the stairs, stretched nice and taut, then, the odds are your impetuous chap comes down tip over arse and breaks his blooming neck doing amateur acrobatics. It's a good way of dousing a chap's glim, too, because there's nothing in-dividual about a bit of wire. Not like a revolver or poison, something that can be traced to any particular person. Probably the wire was lying about somewhere, or anyhow,' he caught sight of Dutchy's scaly eye, 'it was kept where anyone who knew the household could lay hands on it, and it don't retain finger-prints.'

'Then – do you suggest it wasn't my aunt who gave the alarm?'

'Be your age, Major. Of course it wasn't. Why should she, when there wasn't any fire?'

'It sounded like her voice. Miss Dutchley thought the same.'

'It's what you were meant to think,' explained Crook, impatiently. 'How near you did it sound?'

'Just outside my door.'

'And Miss Dutchley?'

'I was further off, but it certainly sounded as though it came from that direction.'

'From Mrs Goodier's room?'

'Yes.'

'But Mrs Goodier wasn't sleeping in her room that night.'

'No. But nobody knew . . . '

'Precisely. Nobody knew. So if you wanted to give the impression that it was Mrs Goodier who raised the house you'd stand just outside her door, wouldn't you, and let out a yell, and everyone would take it for granted that it was Mrs G. herself who called.'

'I told you all along I did nothing of the kind,' stormed Tessa. 'I'm not out of my mind yet.'

'Oh, I believe you,' Crook assured her. 'I've believed you all along. And at the moment I'm the chap that matters.'

She looked at him as though a rat had suddenly put its head through a hole in the floor.

'And seein' it wasn't you, there ain't such a wide field that it's hard to see who it must have been. You told us you wanted to go on the stage and do impersonations, didn't you, Miss Turner . . . ?'

'If you're trying to pin this on to me, you're out of your mind. Fortunately I can prove that I'd taken a sleeping-draught and slept through everything. Why, the lights hadn't been turned off when Miss Dutchley brought in the hot milk and saw me take two tablets. So, you see, that disposes of your absurd theory that I could have put the wire across the stairs or raised the call of "Fire!" '

'What the soldier said ain't evidence,' said Crook, not the least put out. 'You took the tablets yourself, didn't you? Well, what's to prove they weren't aspirin? or that you didn't put them out of your mouth the minute you were alone?'

Alicia's voice became shrill. 'Dutchy came in and shook me – hard – and I didn't wake. Isn't that proof?'

'It don't prove a thing except that you knew she came in and shook you, and if you were sleepin' so deep how do you know she did that? It's no good, Miss Turner. The game's up. You shot Lewis Bishop from behind that curtain – well, only you and the Major could have seen the gun by match-light – you went out of that window and round the garden to the garden-door, getting your hair and your coat wetted with the heavy rain, you went up to your room, you pulled off the coat and your dress and shoes, got into some night-things and came right down, not stoppin' even to put your things away. You had to know what was goin' on, see? Only – there was one important thing you forgot.'

'Yes?' prompted Alicia, in a voice that was meant to be haughty but was only terribly afraid.

'When a young lady like you goes to bed she takes all the muck off her face and puts another lot on, so as to be ready to start work all over again next mornin'. But you came down all painted and dolled up – and you're not tellin' me that you didn't have time to hang up your coat but you did have time to do your face and put on your earrings.'

And now Alicia was silent, looking from face to face. Everyone was very still, very quiet. Even Tessa had nothing to say. Alicia looked across to Alistair and he returned the glance with about as much feeling as a wooden dummy. Of course, she thought, he told them about my hair being wet – and – oh, it doesn't matter. But she didn't believe this was happening to her, because one never does. The men Crook had brought with him were utterly impersonal; to them she wasn't a creature of flesh and blood, but just the dame Crook had told them to watch.

Tessa said suddenly, 'Did you type those letters and put them on the machine?' but it was Crook who answered.

'I think so. I think anyone else would have improved the spellin'.'

Alistair remembered how she'd tried to thrust the blame on to her aunt. Dutchy watched her as the ancient Romans are said to have watched the Christian martyrs. Tessa looked like a delayed-action bomb. There wasn't an atom of sympathy anywhere.

'I suppose I had a motive,' suggested Alicia desperately.

'The same as all the rest. He was going to turn you out, wasn't he, get you disinherited? Didn't he say that? I daresay you didn't like the idea of goin' back to a world where girls go into shops, after livin' in a Manor House.'

Alicia's eyes blazed up. 'Sponges, that's what he called us – all of us. Alistair, James Goodier, me – standing there, warning us all that he could do what he liked, and we were helpless. That's what he thought.'

'That was about the last thing he said before the shot was

fired, wasn't it?' suggested Crook, but at that the man called
Henry intervened.

'I wouldn't answer anything else, if I were you, miss, I
wouldn't really. You can see a lawyer if you like. You see,' he
added explanatorily, 'you're liable to have it used against
you later.'

She swung round. 'Who are you? You can't arrest me, you
know you can't. You're not the police.'

Crook said dryly, 'A sideboard does sometimes contain a
hamadryad, same like Mr Chesterton used to say. And if you
want to cut a diamond you have to use another diamond to
do the job properly. Oh yes, Henry's got a uniform all right,
but he don't wear it if he don't want to be conspicuous.'

'I see!' she panted. 'How crooked. But, I suppose, how
characteristic. It's nothing to you, is it, who you get, so long
as you win your case.'

Henry spoke again. 'Perhaps the lady would help you put
some things into a bag, and we'll be getting along. It's kind
of late now . . . ' He looked hopefully at Dutchy.

*

'All the same,' said Alistair presently, when he and Crook
were alone in the library, 'I don't see they've really got the
evidence they need for a conviction.'

'Not yet perhaps,' said Crook, 'but anything they want
she'll give them. Amateurs always do.'

*

'If you ask me,' said Crook, as he and Bill drove thankfully
away from Four Acres, next morning, 'Providence has got
it in for women, givin' 'em tongues as long as their grand-
mother's hair used to be. Why do they have to talk so much?
If that girl had kept her head we'd never have got her. It goes
against the grain really to be mixed up in a case like that,
because it was a good murder. Not many criminals have the
wit to be invisible, and if she'd only stayed up in her room
and gone to bed right afterwards we'd never have got her.
She could have attended to her face and hung up her clothes,

212

and before anyone came to rouse her she'd have got her hair dry, and there wouldn't have been a scrap of evidence to show that she was ever in the room. But no, she has to come down, walk right into the limes, and then open her mouth and give tongue. She sold herself up the river half a dozen times to-night, telling us things she couldn't have known if she hadn't been there at the time. What did that French writing chap say about virtue not gettin' far without vanity? It wouldn't. It's vanity that leaves the finger-prints and virtue that picks 'em up.' He looked expectantly at Bill. It had been a trying case, ticklish in the extreme, and he could do with a bit of matey chit-chat and maybe a pat or so on the back. Bill, however, was out of small change. He drew up the Scourge outside the Four of Hearts on the Great West Road.

'It's nice they open so early in these parts, isn't it?' he said.

Crook flung him a glance of pure hate. 'Anyone,' he told him, 'could see you weren't a woman in disguise.'

And he slammed sourly out of the car.

››› If you've enjoyed this book and would like to discover more great vintage crime and thriller titles, as well as the most exciting crime and thriller authors writing today, visit: **›››**

The Murder Room
Where Criminal Minds Meet

themurderroom.com

www.ingramcontent.com/pod-product-compliance
Ingram Content Group UK Ltd.
Pitfield, Milton Keynes, MK11 3LW, UK
UKHW040435280225
455666UK00003B/81